FROM THE PAGES OF
THE RED BADGE OF COURAGE

As the landscape changed from brown to green, the army awakened, and began to tremble with eagerness at the noise of rumors. (page 3)

At nightfall the column broke into regimental pieces, and the fragments went into the fields to camp. Tents sprang up like strange plants. Camp fires, like red, peculiar blossoms, dotted the night. (page 18)

The youth had been taught that a man became another thing in a battle. He saw his salvation in such a change. (page 27)

Another, the commander of the brigade, was galloping about bawling. His hat was gone and his clothes were awry. He resembled a man who has come from bed to go to a fire. The hoofs of his horse often threatened the heads of the running men, but they scampered with singular fortune. (page 33)

The men dropped here and there like bundles. (page 38)

They were continually bending in coaxing postures over the guns. They seemed to be patting them on the back and encouraging them with words. The guns, stolid and undaunted, spoke with dogged valor. (page 44)

At times he regarded the wounded soldiers in an envious way. He conceived persons with torn bodies to be peculiarly happy. He wished that he, too, had a wound, a red badge of courage. (page 58)

The fight was lost. The dragons were coming with invincible strides. The army, helpless in the matted thickets and blinded by the overhanging night, was going to be swallowed. War, the red animal, war, the blood-swollen god, would have bloated fill. (page 73)

He believed for an instant that he was in the house of the dead, and he did not dare to move lest these corpses start up, squalling and squawking. In a second, however, he achieved his proper mind. He swore a complicated oath at himself. He saw that this somber picture was not a fact of the present, but a mere prophecy. (page 85)

It was not well to drive men into final corners; at those moments they could all develop teeth and claws. (page 100)

These incidents made the youth ponder. It was revealed to him that he had been a barbarian, a beast. He had fought like a pagan who defends his religion. Regarding it, he saw that it was fine, wild, and, in some ways, easy. He had been a tremendous figure, no doubt. By this struggle he had overcome obstacles which he had admitted to be mountains. They had fallen like paper peaks, and he was now what he called a hero. And he had not been aware of the process. He had slept and, awakening, found himself a knight. (page 103)

THE RED BADGE
OF COURAGE
AND SELECTED
SHORT FICTION

Stephen Crane

*With an Introduction and Notes
by Richard Fusco*

**George Stade
Consulting Editorial Director**

BARNES & NOBLE CLASSICS
NEW YORK

JB

BARNES & NOBLE CLASSICS

NEW YORK

Published by Barnes & Noble Books
122 Fifth Avenue
New York, NY 10011

www.barnesandnoble.com/classics

The Red Badge of Courage was serialized in 1894 and published in book
form in 1895. "The Open Boat" was first published in 1897. "The Veteran" was
first published in 1896. "The Men in the Storm" was first published in 1894.

Published in 2003 by Barnes & Noble Classics with new Introduction, Notes,
Biography, Chronology, Inspired By, Comments & Questions,
and For Further Reading.

Introduction, Notes, and For Further Reading
Copyright © 2003 by Richard Fusco.

Note on Stephen Crane, The World of Stephen Crane and The Red
Badge of Courage, Inspired by The Red Badge of Courage,
and Comments & Questions
Copyright © 2003 by Barnes & Noble, Inc.

The Red Badge of Courage and Selected Short Fiction
ISBN 978-1-59308-010-5
LC Control Number 2003100868

Produced and published in conjunction with:
Fine Creative Media, Inc.
322 Eighth Avenue
New York, NY 10001

Michael J. Fine, President and Publisher

Printed in the United States of America

OPM

16 18 20 22 24 23 21 19 17 15

STEPHEN CRANE

Stephen Crane was born on November 1, 1871, the fourteenth and last child of the Reverend Jonathan Townley Crane and Mary Helen Peck, a Methodist missionary. Stephen's interest in war and the military developed early, and he convinced his mother to enroll him in the Hudson River Institute, a semi-military school in upstate New York. On the advice of a professor who urged him to pursue a more practical career than the army, Stephen transferred to Lafayette College in Pennsylvania, to study mining engineering; however, he seldom attended class and failed a theme writing course because of poor attendance. His formal education ended after one semester at Syracuse University, where he was known on campus for his baseball skills. Despite his unimpressive academic performance, he wrote regularly while he was a student.

Stephen Crane became a prolific writer—of journalism and novels, short stories and poetry. By age twenty-three he had completed two major novels marked by an impressionism and a psychological realism that anticipated the "new fiction" of Ernest Hemingway, F. Scott Fitzgerald, and William Faulkner. His writing of fiction is informed by the keen, precise observation that also made him a journalist; for *Maggie: A Girl of the Streets* (1893), he shadowed a New York prostitute for weeks. Crane was born after the Civil War, and he relied on secondary sources and his own intuition and emotional insights in creating *The Red Badge of Courage* (1895), the story of a young recruit's experiences during one key battle. The book is often cited as the first modern novel.

While on assignment to cover the Cuban-Spanish conflict that preceded the Spanish-American War, Crane met his life-long companion, Cora Stewart, a well-read daughter of old money who owned a brothel in Jacksonville, Florida. Crane and Stewart later lived in England, where they socialized with Henry James, Joseph Conrad, and Ford Madox Ford, who admired Crane's unique writing style. The young American continued to publish novels, stories, and articles for journals, which solidified his reputation.

Illness cut Crane's life short. In 1899, in Badenweiler, Germany, he collapsed with severe hemorrhaging of the lungs brought on by tuberculosis and malaria. He died in a sanitarium on June 5, 1900, five months before his twenty-ninth birthday.

In his short but brilliant career, Stephen Crane produced six novels, two collections of poetry, and more than one hundred stories, which were compiled in a ten-volume edition published by the University Press of Virginia (1969–1976). He is remembered as a pioneering writer who anticipated the styles that modernized American literature in the 1920s.

TABLE OF CONTENTS

THE WORLD OF STEPHEN CRANE AND
THE RED BADGE OF COURAGE

1871 Stephen Crane is born on November 1 at 14 Mulberry Street, Newark, New Jersey, the last of his parents' fourteen children.

1878 Stephen enrolls in school. His father becomes pastor of the Drew Methodist Church in Port Jervis, in upstate New York.

1880 Stephen's father dies of heart failure.

1883 Stephen and his mother move to Asbury Park, a town on the New Jersey coast.

1885 Concerned about Stephen's digressions from Methodist teachings, his mother enrolls him at Pennington Seminary, a school where his father had once been the principal. He writes his first story, "Uncle Jake and the Bell-Handle." Stephen becomes intrigued by the battles of the Civil War and decides to pursue a career in the army.

1888 In January, Stephen enrolls at the Hudson River Institute, a semi-military school in upstate Claverack, New York. He works as a gossip reporter for his brother Townley's news agency; his vignettes appear in "On the Jersey Coast," a column in Townley's New York *Tribune*.

1890 In February, Stephen's first signed publication, an essay on the Christian virtues of Sir Henry Morton Stanley's African expedition, appears in the school magazine. In September, he enrolls at Lafayette College, in Pennsylvania, to pursue a more practical profession, mining engineering. He does poorly in his studies and fails a course in theme writing. After one semester, he withdraws from Lafayette. Rudyard Kipling's *The Light That Failed*, serialized in *Lippincott's* magazine, inspires Stephen to develop his own style of writing.

1891 Stephen's mother enrolls him as a "special student" in the Scientific Course at Syracuse University, where she hopes he will be influenced by the school's strict

Methodist codes. He joins the baseball team and transfers his Delta Upsilon fraternity membership from Lafayette. He continues to write for the New York Tribune and publishes a story, "The King's Favor," in the University Herald, the Syracuse literary magazine. In June, Stephen leaves Syracuse and joins the Tribune as a seasonal reporter. In August, he meets Hamlin Garland, a radical-minded young writer and critic from Boston, after he writes a review of Garland's lecture on William Dean Howells at Avon-by-the-Sea, New Jersey. Garland will have a profound influence on Stephen's development as a writer.

1892   In July, five of Stephen Crane's anecdotal stories about his camping and fishing trips in Sullivan County, New York, are published in the Tribune. He is dismissed from his job when his report of a parade of workers in Asbury Park embarrasses Whitelaw Reid, the Tribune's owner and a U.S. vice presidential candidate. In the fall, Crane moves to New York to work for the Herald. He begins to write Maggie: A Girl of the Streets, a novel about a prostitute in lower Manhattan.

1893   Maggie is published at Crane's expense, under the pseudonym Johnston Smith. The novel catches the eye of Garland and William Dean Howells, both literary realists, who befriend Crane. In April, Crane begins to write The Red Badge of Courage.

1894   In late February, Crane and a friend dress in rags, wait in a bread line, and spend the night in a flophouse—experiences that inspire the stories "An Experiment in Misery" and "The Men in the Storm"; the latter is published in an October issue of The Arena. In the spring, Crane begins another New York novel, George's Mother. An abridged version of The Red Badge of Courage is published in the Philadelphia Press and other newspapers in December.

1895   Stephen tours the American West and Mexico as a roving reporter for the Bacheller-Johnson Syndicate. He meets author Willa Cather in Lincoln, Nebraska. His experiences out West will inspire two of his best-known stories, "The Bride Comes to Yellow Sky" (1897) and "The Blue Hotel" (1898). Upon his return from Mexico, he settles in Hartwood, New York. Appleton publishes *The Red Badge of Courage* in October. Cuba, rebelling against rule by Spain, declares "Independence or death." The United States increases its involvement in resolving the Spanish-Cuban conflict. *The Black Riders*, Crane's first book of verse, is published.

1896   *The Red Badge of Courage* receives critical acclaim—Crane wins recognition from Joseph Conrad and H. G. Wells. "The Veteran," a short story that features the protagonist of *The Red Badge of Courage* as an old man, is published in *McClure's Magazine* in June and collected in *The Little Regiment and Other Episodes of the American Civil War*. In November, Crane travels to Jacksonville, Florida, as a newspaper correspondent covering the Cuban insurrection against Spain; he tries to book passage on a vessel that will run the blockade of the island. He checks into the St. James Hotel under the name Samuel Carleton and arranges passage to Cuba on the *Commodore*. He meets Cora Stewart, the well-mannered, literary-minded owner of the Hotel de Dream brothel, who will become his common-law wife. *George's Mother* is published.

1897   On January 1, Crane embarks on the *Commodore*, which sinks on January 2. Crane and three others escape in a dinghy and reach Florida's east coast on the morning of January 3. On January 7 Crane publishes a newspaper account of the sinking. While recuperating, he composes "The Open Boat," which recounts the thirty hours spent in the dinghy; the story is first published in the June issue of *Scribner's Magazine*. Crane serves as a correspondent during the brief Greco-Turkish War. He and Cora move to England; he is welcomed into the literary circle of Ford Madox Ford and Henry James, and meets Joseph Conrad, who becomes a close friend.

1898   The United States declares war on Spain. Crane returns to the United States to become a war correspondent for

the New York *World*. *The Open Boat and Other Stories* is published.

1899   In January, Crane returns to England and moves with
        Cora to Brede Place, an ancient manor in Sussex. The
        couple exchanges visits with Henry James, the Conrads,
        Ford, and the Wellses, often at Lamb House, James's cot-
        tage in Rye. While working on his novel *The O'Ruddy*,
        Crane falls ill with tuberculosis. In December, he is de-
        bilitated with severe hemorrhaging of the lungs. His
        second book of verse, *War Is Kind*, is published, as is *The
        Monster and Other Stories*.

1900   Despite his deteriorating health, Crane continues to
        work on *The O'Ruddy* and other short pieces. In the
        spring, while in Badenweiler, Germany, he collapses.
        Cora checks him into a sanitarium, where he dies on
        June 5. *Wounds in the Rain*, a collection of Cuban war sto-
        ries, is published after his death, as is *Whilomville Stories*, a
        childhood memoir.

1903   *The O'Ruddy*, an Irish romance completed after Crane's
        death by Robert Barr, is published.

1923–   A biography of Crane is published. Willa Cather and
1925   H. L. Mencken are among the writers who create intro-
        ductions to a new twelve-volume collection of Crane's
        work.

1950–   Author John Berryman's biography and R. W. Stallman's
1970   anthology of Crane's best work are published, as is a
        complete edition of his works by the University Press of
        Virginia. Crane is generally recognized as one of the
        major forces in modern American literature.

INTRODUCTION

STEPHEN CRANE SAID TO THE UNIVERSE

I

Sometimes, the most profound of awakenings come wrapped in the quietest of moments.

Early in April 1893, a struggling young writer embarked on a strange journey to tend to an uncomfortable task. He had been invited to an uptown party. He hoped to cultivate the patronage of its host, whose prominence in American letters was something he admired, envied, and feared. The young man's career thus far had been so unprofitable that it had brought him to the brink of starvation on several recent occasions. An endorsement could reopen many of the doors to publishing venues that had been slammed in his face.

The aspirant was a curious man to look at. Although he was barely twenty-one years old, his face and body were already showing signs of wear and abuse. He stood at 5 feet 6 inches, average for a man of his day. A few years previously, during two unsuccessful semesters at two different colleges, he weighed in at a taut 125 pounds, muscular and agile enough to stand out on a college baseball team. By 1893, however, his strapped diet and unrestrained smoking had taken their toll on the body and abilities that had once attracted the serious notice of a professional baseball club. His complexion had turned sallow. His shoulders on his emaciated frame had begun to droop. Several friends detected an increasing dullness in his blue-gray eyes. Cigarettes and cigars had stained his fingers and teeth with nicotine. He coughed deeply and regularly from the habit. That, plus his poor diet would beset him with a variety of dental problems for the rest of his life. His custom of writing late into the night frequently created dark circles under his eyes during the following day. To those around him, he often looked ill.

Although he preferred a more bohemian lifestyle, especially in the clothes he wore, the young writer did try to spruce up his appearance for the party. These people inhabited a very different social circle than the one he was accustomed to. His usually disheveled hair had been hastily groomed. He did not own a suit suitable for the occasion, so he borrowed a friend's best outfit. It obviously did not fit him very well, which reinforced his uncomfortable thought that he would be very out of place at such a gathering. On a subconscious level, he feared that this opportunity fitted him as poorly as his suit did. He wanted to be a writer on his own terms; he should control his public persona, not tailor it to acquiesce to the refined expectations of a social circumstance. As much as he admired his host and needed his help, the young man had misgivings about how playing the patronage game might compromise his art.

The journey to his host's home on the south side of Central Park was a study of the contrast between the haves and the have-nots in turn-of-the-century New York City. His starting point was fraught with failure. Ever since he had moved to the city to pursue his chosen vocation, he had lived in a succession of cheap boarding houses on the East Side. Such environs had provided the backdrop for his early fiction. He particularly liked to disguise himself as a derelict in order to mingle with the denizens of the infamous Bowery district. He had recently finished *Maggie: A Girl of the Streets*, a short novel about how poverty enslaves a woman to a prostitute's life. When no publisher would touch it (one had called it too "cruel"), he sold his last bit of patrimony—some stock his late father had bequeathed to him—and used the money to have the story privately printed. In 1893 few people took note of *Maggie*. Eventually, the young writer gave away a hundred copies and used the remainder as kindling. Friend and fellow writer Hamlin Garland brought the book to the host's notice. Thus, the aspirant's "calling card" had been presented.

In contrast, at the other end of his journey on that April day, his destination was distinguished by success. The home of his host was not outlandishly opulent but tasteful and understatedly elegant, befitting his status as America's most influential man of letters. Unlike the squalor omnipresent on the East Side, this house had a pleasant panorama of a lake situated at the south entrance to Central Park. Every item modestly bespoke eminence and success. The host's novels attracted immediate interest and financial reward. Only a few years ago, he had published to much acclaim *A Hazard of New Fortunes*, the most ambitious project of his career. His insights as a columnist in several stalwart literary magazines carried great weight in public opinion, which he used to promote his literary values and, with regal benevolence, to champion new writers who held similar beliefs. To the literati in America, he mattered. And the young writer wanted to matter too.

A twentieth-century biographer unearthed an interview with a New York newspaper that detailed the host's appearance around that time. Although approximately the same height as the young writer, the host was more "stout, round, and contented looking," but this excess weight visually enhanced his aura of confidence, refinement, and sagacity. His "iron-gray" hair and mustache were meticulously groomed. His pleasant voice hinted that he was "satisfied with his career and with the success he had made in life." The carefully tailored host greeting the awkwardly clad young guest would have made an interesting snapshot.

Despite the opportunity, despite the good wishes of his host, the young writer felt ill at ease for most of the dinner party. True, when a moment for a private conversation with his famous mentor arrived, it went well. The host later complimented the young man before his guests by pronouncing that *Maggie* accomplished "things that [Mark Twain] can't." But keeping his manners and language in check before polite company greatly taxed the young man's composure. He would not feel relaxed until long after the party when he kibitzed at a backroom poker game among black New Yorkers later that night.

During the course of this tedious rite of passage in the career of a young writer, however, a wonderful event occurred in a casual moment. The host had fetched a volume of poetry. He wanted to read selections from it to his guests. The author of this book had been dead for seven years. During her life, only a few of her poems saw the light of print. Few of them had been published with her consent. After her death, her family recovered among her possessions one of the great treasures of American literature—more than 1,700 brilliant poems, assorted and neatly sewn into many small bundles. Her family decided to do something that the poet could never bring herself to do—publish them.

A first selection was issued in 1890; a second in 1891. In 1893, both series had been combined into one volume. One of the editors was the host's professional friend, Thomas Wentworth Higginson, who was himself well respected for his publishing endeavors and for his command of a black regiment during the Civil War. Thirty years previously, the poet had sent him four poems, and he had not been very encouraging then. He found them "spasmodic," "uncontrolled," and, at times, incomprehensible. Thus, his assignment as her posthumous editor was not without the distaste of irony. Unable to fathom the true intent that underscored her genius, Higginson and his coeditor selected from among her safer poems for inclusion in the first volume. They manhandled many poems in their editing, replacing her idiosyncratic use of the dash with more conventional punctuation and ghost rewriting lines to create the traditional scansion and rhyme that a nineteenth-century audience expected. But despite all the ham-handedness of the editors, the publication of these poems propagated a revolution in American poetry.

The host had a pleasing voice and an ingratiating demeanor, which made him an excellent reciter. The poet had adapted the cadences of church hymns in her poetry, and so the host spoke at a rhythmic pace that his guests were very familiar with. With his devout Methodist upbringing, the young writer had heard such hymns all his life.

What poems were read that day are not known, but I think it

likely that the host performed the first poem of the 1890 volume:

> Success is counted sweetest
> By those who ne'er succeed.
> To comprehend a nectar
> Requires sorest need.
>
> Not one of all the purple host
> Who took the flag to-day
> Can tell the definition,
> So clear, of victory,
>
> As he, defeated, dying,
> On whose forbidden ear
> The distant strains of triumph
> Break, agonized and clear.

The aspiring writer was astounded. He had just experienced a revelatory moment equivalent to John Keats's first reading of George Chapman's translations of the Homeric epics or Charles Baudelaire's walking into a salon and first seeing a painting by Eugène Delacroix. Both the English and the French poets did not abandon what they believed in order to embrace something new; instead, they found artistic works that crystallized their own conceptions of art. This first contact permitted them to analyze what they already practiced in their own poetry and to speculate why they did so. During the 1890s in America, most good writers found such a muse by encountering the work of an earlier artist. In Saint Louis, for example, another writer also struggling to find her place and voice, Kate Chopin, used the fiction of Guy de Maupassant for such a purpose.

The recitation had multiple effects upon the young writer. He empathized with the pained failure described in the poem. More importantly, he saw aspects of his own emerging voice in the woman poet's surgical concision of language. In his recent novel about the "girl of the streets," for example, he had crafted intensely imagistic sentences: "The girl, Maggie, blossomed in a mud puddle." Inspired by the reading, the young writer soon began to compose poems of his own, rattling off a great many in a short space of time:

> Black riders came from the sea.
> There was clang and clang of spear and shield,
> And clash and clash of hoof and heel,
> Wild shouts and the wave of hair
> In the rush upon the wind:
> Thus the ride of sin.

Even in the heavily edited versions the host read that day, the young writer could hear the liberties the dead poet had taken with the hymnal form, and he would accelerate her assault against the conventions of poetry by abandoning rhyme and traditional cadences altogether. He called his efforts not poems but "lines." When he bragged that he usually had several poems configured in his mind ready to be put on paper, his friend Hamlin Garland challenged him to do so. The young writer immediately wrote out one without fumbling a word. His "lines" allowed him to distill his fatalistic notions, almost to the point of becoming epigrams regarding individual impotence:

> I saw a man pursuing the horizon;
> Round and round they sped.
> I was disturbed at this;
> I accosted the man.
> "It is futile," I said,
> "You can never—"
>
> "You lie," he cried,
> And ran on.

The poems the host read that April day excited another level of response in the young writer. The woman poet had composed much of her work in an intense spurt of inspiration during the American Civil War; consequently, many of her poems were populated with images and metaphors of battle. In his desperation to earn money, the young writer had been researching and writing a new manuscript that he hoped might exploit the curiosity by the American public during the 1890s about the Civil War. He first considered turning the novel into a romantic "potboiler" so as to ensure its financial success. But the embattled insights into the human heart contained in the poems he heard that day and his own evolving artistic ambitions turned the project into something finer. The host did not realize it then, but he had given his young guest the necessary ammunition to rebel against the literary values he had championed for a lifetime.

The host was William Dean Howells, the nexus of American Realism; the poet, Emily Dickinson, the private genius of Amherst; the aspiring writer, Stephen Crane, the self-consuming literary meteor of the 1890s; and the novel, *The Red Badge of Courage*, his most enduring and influential work. If you have made it thus far in this essay, I thank you for your patience and indulgence. In addition to recreating a brief but pregnant moment in Crane's emerging talent, I wanted to mimic (I hope not too poorly) his prose style and, in particular, one of his fictional devices. At a crucial stage in one of the drafts of *Red Badge*, Crane went through his manuscript and greatly reduced the number of times he employed character names, instead replacing them with epithets such as "the youth"; "the tall soldier," who becomes "the spectral soldier"; and "the loud soldier," who becomes "the friend." Later, in a newspaper account, Crane faithfully reported all facts regarding his near-death experience at sea in 1897, but he subsequently avoided naming his characters in the fictional story he composed based on the incident—"The Open Boat." Instead of names, he chose to emphasize occupations and their symbolic associations: "the captain," "the cook," "the oilman," and "the correspondent." (Only "Billy," the nickname of the oilman who was killed, was occasionally used in "The Open Boat.")

In these and in other stories, Crane emphasized the potential of all individual experiences to have universal implications. A "youth" struggling to find a physical, intellectual, and spiritual path through the horrors of war parallels the road every human must travel in coping with crisis. Four men in a flimsy boat on a storm-tossed ocean become metaphors for every individual scrambling to survive the whims of an uncaring universe. An aspiring writer first encountering the inspiring poetry of a misunderstood poet becomes the archetype for all artistic epiphanies.

Like most other consequential writers before him and since, young Stephen Crane was blessed with a good number of experiences and encounters that shaped and clarified his artistic path. While it is tempting for a modern reader to reduce these influences to just a manageable few, the truth of the matter is that the genius of Crane resides in his ability to blend so many different biographical experiences, philosophical and theological assumptions, previous and contemporary literary traditions and techniques, and political ideals in a deceptively simple prose style. In *Red Badge*, for instance, he has the wherewithal to juxtapose a stark account of a war incident drawn according to the precepts of Realism with a scene in which the protagonist, Henry Fleming, reverts to his animal instincts, as befits the tenets of literary Naturalism. Crane sews these two episodes with such a fine stitch that readers seldom see the seams. The possibility that both disparate aesthetic perspectives can appear simultaneously valid in close textual proximity begins to reveal how complex Crane's vision of the human experience was. Everything Crane was, everything he believed, every meaningful book that he read, every indelible memory from his life, every interesting idea he had ever heard went into the construction of the novel. In the rest of this introduction, I will touch upon a number of these shaping encounters, focusing especially upon those that manifested themselves in both open and disguised ways in *Red Badge*, taking great advantage in the process of insights by the many astute academic critics Crane's work has attracted during the past eighty years.

II

As one might suspect, Stephen Crane's family and childhood appear in *Red Badge* in covert and private ways. He was born in a parsonage in Newark, New Jersey, on November 1, 1871. He was his forty-five-year-old mother's fourteenth child, but none of her previous four babies had survived beyond their first year. Thus, among the Crane children who survived to adulthood, Stephen became the most indulged, a circumstance encouraged by the age gap between him and his nearest older sibling.

His father, the Reverend Jonathan Townley Crane, named his child after the first Crane to migrate to North America during the seventeenth century and also after a prominent New Jersey ancestor who had been active during the Revolutionary War. (Dr. Crane erroneously thought that the latter had signed the Declaration of Independence.) As biographer Edwin Cady has pointed out, young Stephen grew up as a "preacher's kid," a label that immediately defined his relationship with his schoolhouse peers and that definitely set up his subsequent rebellion against religious dogma. At the time of his son's birth, Dr. Crane served as the presiding elder for a group of Methodist churches in and surrounding Newark. Wanting to preach more, he gave up his administrative duties and moved his family to his new clerical position in Paterson, New Jersey, by 1876. When a dispute arose over his salary, he accepted another post in Port Jervis, New York, in 1878.

When Stephen was barely eight, his father died unexpectedly from heart complications arising from a viral attack. Stephen's most vivid memories of his father were likely of him at work in his profession, sermonizing before his flock. As a young man, Dr. Crane had embraced Methodism, in part as a rebellion against his own Presbyterian heritage. He had been studying for the Presbyterian ministry at the College of New Jersey (now Princeton University) when he began to question that faith's more strident doctrines, especially the notion of infant damnation, the belief that children who died unbaptized would be consigned to the fires of hell. While concepts such as damnation figured prominently in his sermons, Dr. Crane believed that God tempered His wrath with mercy and divinely discriminating judgment. He converted to Methodism because he saw it as a way to preach a more hopeful and nurturing view of God and salvation. At weekly prayer meetings his son undoubtedly heard his father stress his faith in a merciful God, one who lovingly embraced all. Damnation remained an omnipresent possibility, but Dr. Crane's God was more interested in saving than in condemning.

Stephen's mother came from a different religious tradition. Mary Helen Peck Crane was a woman capable of great kindnesses, such as the time she cared for an unwed mother despite the open misgivings of her neighbors. Nevertheless, she piously spouted the caustic Methodism long advocated by her family. The Pecks, according to Stephen Crane, produced Methodist clergymen "of the ambling-nag, saddle bag, exhorting kind." She passionately focused upon God's function as avenger of sins committed against His name. As an adult, Stephen fondly remembered his mother's intelligence, but he often winced at the memory of her religious fervor. Given the obvious difference between the conceptions of husband and wife, Sunday suppers in the Crane household must have produced interesting and, for young Stephen, confusing debates at the table.

These competing views of God appear throughout Crane's literary efforts, often at allegorical levels in his fiction but at more conspicuous ones in his poetry:

> The livid lightnings flashed in the clouds;
> The leaden thunders crashed.
> A worshipper raised his arm.
> "Hearken! Hearken! The voice of God!"
>
> "Not so," said a man.
> "The voice of God whispers in the heart
> So softly
> That the soul pauses,
> Making no noise,
> And strives for these melodies,

> Distant, sighing, like faintest breath,
> And all the being is still to hear."

I find it interesting that here Crane placed his father's gentle perspective at the dominant position by having it respond to his mother's "brimstone." In chapter XI of *Red Badge*, Henry Fleming fears derision by the rest of his regiment for his desertion in a manner that resembles how one may fear God's punishment for sin. Later, in chapter XIII, however, Fleming receives the tender ministrations of two comrades who tend to his wound. If his desertion represents a military sin, then Wilson's actions suggest symbolic forgiveness by a God who provides for atonement.

The complex dimensions of Crane's own religious beliefs ultimately had not two but three axes. By the time he was thirteen, Stephen began to rebel against his parents' values. The precipitating causes may have been the family dejection brought on by the death of his favorite sister, Agnes Elizabeth, in 1884 and the influence of his brother Will, who, like several of the older brothers, had functioned as a surrogate father figure for the boy since Dr. Crane's death. Will had himself experienced a rebellion, which was more a rejection of his parents' dogmatism than an embracing of any other creed in its place. Stephen's rebellion would need eight more years of intense reading and contemplation before he could articulate his personal philosophical position. Ultimately, he took the personality, the intentions, and even the presence of God out of the human equation. The principles of social Darwinism and of literary Naturalism (treated in the next section of this essay) suggested that man navigated his existence through a universe ruled by chance. Neither an avenging nor a nurturing deity intervened in daily human affairs. Man's ego is met only with nature's indifference, which Crane encapsulates in a brilliant poem:

> A man said to the universe:
> "Sir, I exist!"
> "However," replied the universe,
> "The fact has not created in me
> A sense of obligation."

This is the view that dominates Crane's oeuvre. In *Red Badge*, a defiant Henry Fleming valiantly and futilely struggles to assert his presence before an indifferent universe. In "The Open Boat," the heroic response of four men to their plight means nothing to nature, as represented by the billowing waves of the sea. The shipwrecked must carefully steer their dinghy into each ominous wave to avoid capsizing; their only reward for surviving one threat is another huge swell right behind it. For Crane, existence demanded the riding out of many such waves that threaten to annihilate us. In the final analysis, the only being who cares for an individual's life is the individual himself. In chapter XXIV of *Red Badge*, Fleming's summary self-assessment cannot redirect civilized destiny. He cannot even communicate it to Wilson, his "friend." It must remain private because all personal epiphanies are inexorably ineffable. Ironically, Fleming and his fellow soldiers cannot discuss among themselves their shared awakening to the realities of war. Thus, Crane attests to the isolation that each man, by his very nature, must endure. Just as Crane felt alone living amid millions of inhabitants of New York City during the 1890s, so too would Fleming dwell upon his spiritual solitude amid the 200,000 Union and Confederate soldiers who fought in the Battle of Chancellorsville.

By age twenty, Crane's rebellion against his family's values would manifest itself in a variety of large and small ways. His father had composed religious tracts and had given sermons that advocated abstinence. By the time he was fifteen, Stephen smoked regularly, and he would soon drink excessively. Dr. Crane believed that games like baseball distracted an individual from developing a religious life. During 1891 Stephen became a star shortstop in a brief stint with the Syracuse University baseball team. Only his desire to concentrate on his writing prevented him from accepting an offer to join a professional baseball team. His father abhorred novels; more than anything else, his son wanted to be a great novelist. Eventually settling in Asbury Park, New Jersey, after her husband's death Mary Crane began to fret over the bohemian manner of her son's behavior and dress throughout his teens. She recognized his extraordinary intelligence but worried that his lack of self-discipline would channel his energies in a wrong direction. She disapproved of his youthful desire to be a writer.

In 1888 she dispatched Stephen to a military boarding school in order to curb these tendencies, but she may have had another reason. Shortly after the death of her daughter Agnes Elizabeth, Mary Crane suffered a "temporary aberration of mind." The daily tension caused by her "critical condition," as it was called in one newspaper, likely strained young Stephen's still underdeveloped ability to cope. Consequently, he was sent first to Pennington Seminary in New Jersey (where his father once served as principal), which quickly proved to be ineffective, and then to the Hudson River Institute in Claverack, New York. Crane later remembered his days at the military school with fondness, even though he seemed to learn more through his own readings than through the curriculum itself. In the manner of the "blue demonstration" that Fleming complained about in *Red Badge*, Crane marched in military drills well enough to earn first a lieutenancy of a squad and later a student captaincy, but Claverack no longer maintained discipline to a degree that benefited its incorrigible students. At least Crane learned to play whist, a card game that he subsequently used to end an important chapter in his Civil War novel.

After departing Claverack, Crane spent one unsuccessful academic year at two colleges. In autumn 1890 he enrolled as a mining engineering student (obviously a concession to his mother's practicality) at Lafayette College on the eastern border of Pennsylvania. He played intramural baseball but could not make the varsity team. He joined a fraternity but then jeopardized his relationship with his frat brothers by brandishing a loaded revolver when they tried to haze him. He absented himself from class so often that three of his teachers did not report a grade for him in December. As one might expect, one of these three classes was on the Bible. Crane could quote many passages from scripture with accuracy, but he was too immersed in his own secular rebellion to revisit his religious past. By Christmas, Lafayette's administration advised Crane not to return for the spring semester. He therefore transferred to Syracuse University at the beginning of 1891. His acceptance was likely facilitated by the circumstance that his mother's uncle, the Reverend Jesse Peck, had founded the institution. Crane did make the varsity baseball team this time and became a very capable shortstop, but his performance in class proved to be even more lackluster than it had been at Lafayette. By the end of the semester, he passed only one course—he earned an A in English literature. Thus ended Stephen Crane's formal education.

He did learn much, however, during his one year in college. Taking advantage of both college libraries as well as the books owned by his fraternity, Delta Upsilon, he read eclectically but voraciously on his own, studying the works of writers such as Leo Tolstoy, Robert Louis Stevenson, Henry James, Edgar Allan Poe, and Rudyard Kipling. He worked as a stringer for the New York *Tribune*, contributing news items about the city of Syracuse and about the college itself. Several Crane scholars believe that after reporting about the poor in Syracuse, Crane probably composed the first draft of the story that painfully and eventually evolved into *Maggie: A Girl of the Streets* (1893). This early draft was doubtlessly plagued by a lack of sufficient convincing detail about the reality of poverty in America, so Crane returned to Asbury Park in 1891 in order to study firsthand tenement life in neighboring New York City.

For the next three years, while living in New Jersey and then in New York City itself, Crane pursued the strange existence of a writer trying to hone his talent amid squalor and a depressing lack of opportunities and encouragement. In the city, he occupied a succession of cheap quarters, sharing them with medical students, artists, and other aspirants at the impoverished end of ambitious careers. When his funds ran out, which happened often, he temporarily lived with and borrowed money from his older brothers. During this period, his ambivalent feelings about his mother intensified when she died in December 1891. Thus the anxious young man who visited W. D. Howells in April 1893 brought with him to the party all the confusion and hardship of his own frustrations as well as that of the Bowery in which he had immersed himself.

III

What still fascinates is how, amid such conditions, Crane was able to informally pursue his aesthetic education and produce a novel that is one of the better summations of American sensibilities in the 1890s. His mind was, in effect, a sponge, capable of absorbing the principles of past and current literary traditions, the insights of the leading writers of the day, the beliefs held by competing philosophical schools, the dogmas held by diverse Christian sects, and the trends of political and economic thought. His artistic genius resided in his ability to knit many dissimilar and, at times, conflicting perspectives so thoroughly in a text that we pay more attention to their similarities than their differences. He paints a grim but objective portrait of war's horror in one passage in *Red Badge*, yet when we turn the page we find ourselves immersed in Fleming's subjective reflection about that event.

Many critics have debated over the years whether Crane was essentially a Realist, a Naturalist, or an Impressionist. I and many others contend that he was all those things and much more. For Crane, the scene or the moment dictates the artistic device the writer should employ. Novels such as *Red Badge*, then, become compendia of many aesthetic possibilities. In a Crane text, this oscillation among so many ways of looking at the world reflects what all humans must contend with in life. The religious, political, philosophical, or artistic belief that seems best to explain one moment may prove inadequate for the next. Crane's novel about the Civil War offers a chain of partially successful attempts by Henry Fleming to comprehend his environment and purpose. *The Red Badge of Courage* thus not only chronicles Crane's own restless mind; it also embodies the multifaceted dilemmas with which all intellects curious about man's relationship with the universe must cope.

The dominant literary figures in the United States after the Civil War were the Realists. By the 1890s, Realism's most accomplished practitioners included Mark Twain and Henry James, but William Dean Howells had become the artistic director of the school. Through his magazine columns (the most

prominent was "The Editor's Study" in Harper's Monthly), through
the example he set in his novels and short stories, and through
the new writers whose work he promoted, Howells established
a good number of artistic principles for the postbellum generation of American fictionalists. Above all other considerations, he
stressed that writers ought to write about subjects, people, and
environments with which they were wholly familiar. Realists
should not impose their personal biases or philosophical, political, and ethical predispositions on the voice of a text's third-
person narrator. The world should be described as if one were
looking through a camera lens. The Realist should avoid pre-
senting portraits of people who reside at the extreme ends of
the human condition; those who occupy the center of American
society are fitter subjects for literary art. Thus, the goal of the
writer is to capture with fidelity that which typifies a society.

These and other like precepts pervaded the literary scene that
Crane encountered in New York during the early 1890s. They
became salient and valuable for him after he heard Hamlin
Garland lecture about Howells's work and influence in Avon,
New Jersey, in 1891. Crane published a newspaper piece about
the talk, which attracted Garland's notice. At that time, Garland,
ten years Crane's senior, was himself an emerging Realist of the
local-color school. Many American local colorists, who had
their aesthetic origins in Ivan Turgenev's seminal short-story
collection Sportsman's Notebook, published realistic fiction based
upon their regional experiences, chronicling the lives and manners of the people they grew up with or lived among for a long
time. Adherents to this approach included Sarah Orne Jewett,
Mary Wilkins Freeman, Rose Terry Cooke, Bret Harte, and
George Washington Cable. During the summer of 1891,
Garland himself contributed to this collective effort to portray
America region by region through publishing Main-Travelled Roads,
a story collection based on his family's farming experiences in
the Midwest. (Donna Campbell provides an excellent discussion
of Crane's tenuous relationship with the local-color movement
in her Resisting Regionalism: Gender and Naturalism in American Fiction,
1885–1915; see "For Further Reading.")

When Crane began to gather materials for Red Badge in 1893,

most of his immediate resources had realistic assumptions underlying their intentions. Matthew Brady's photographs of the Civil War had recorded with graphic accuracy the ghastliness of battle. Nonfictional reminiscences and novels such as Wilbur F. Hinman's *Corporal Si Klegg and His 'Pard'*, Joseph Kirkland's *The Captain of Company K*, and the novel that some critics believe marks the incipient moment of American Realism, John William De Forest's *Miss Ravenel's Conversion from Succession to Loyalty*, all share the desire to acquaint a civilian reader with the actualities of war and of military life.

Crane's most immediate source, however, owed its realistic intentions to another sort of discourse—history. In 1893 he borrowed from the mother of a former childhood playmate the multivolume work *Battles and Leaders of the Civil War* (1887), a compilation of a mammoth series of articles that had first appeared in *The Century* magazine years earlier. Here Crane found a rich vein of primary material, including essays by participating Union and Confederate officers, such as Generals Darius N. Couch, Alfred Pleasonton, Oliver O. Howard, and R. E. Colston. With these accounts, Crane began to understand the facts, tactics, and strategies of the Battle of Chancellorsville that he would integrate into his story. Despite the occasional note of nostalgia or bravado, despite the defensive tone adopted by a general in explaining the misdeeds of his troops, these historical sources on the whole do comply with the empirical spirit pursued by a new generation of nineteenth-century historians. These writers presented firsthand testimony when available and assembled all known facts in their correct chronological sequence in order to illustrate an historical event as accurately as the evidence allows.

For all his research in these and other historical texts, however, Crane could not compensate for his one obvious deficiency, one that challenged any claim he might make to call himself a Realist. Realists were supposed to confine their efforts to subjects they knew well and had experienced intimately. Born six years after the Civil War ended, Crane had never even seen a battle before he finished the manuscript for *Red Badge*. His mentor Howells would later chide him about this predicament, telling him that *Maggie* was more artistically successful because he based it upon what he had lived and observed directly, unlike *Red Badge*, which was constructed from the observations of others and Crane's own guesses. How ironic it was, after the latter novel was published, that the reading public hailed Crane as the nascent star of American Realism.

Nevertheless, many Civil War veterans attested to the validity of Henry Fleming's experiences in and reactions to combat. However, influenced by recent Russian literature, especially the works of Fyodor Dostoyevsky, American Realism was evolving. Crane had tapped into its new wellspring—a shift in emphasis from reporting physical truth to constructing narratives that explored psychological truth. Howells's colleague Henry James had already migrated toward this new direction, which manifested itself in subtler and more complex characterizations in each successive novel he undertook. Crane's immediate inspiration may have been iconoclastic writer and newspaperman Ambrose Bierce. Using his experiences as an officer in the Union army, Bierce published a dramatic series of Civil War horror tales in a San Francisco newspaper during the 1880s and 1890s. When he collected them in book form in 1891, he also included a number of stories about violent occurrences in civilian life and titled the volume *Tales of Soldiers and Civilians*. Bierce's premise was simple. By juxtaposing the atrocities of human experience in both war and peace, he shocked one generation out of its mistaken nostalgia about the war and another younger generation into realizing what war demands from the individual soul. If anyone wanted to comprehend the psychological essence of war, all he had to do was to observe and absorb the horror omnipresent in everyday life and then to project that vision onto a battle situation.

Crane took this lesson to heart. In an extraordinary way, *Red Badge* can be seen as an amalgam of his experiences in the slums of New York from 1891 to 1894. For instance, he would disguise himself as a derelict and stand in lines for bread or for a room for the night. These events show up directly in stories like "Men in the Storm," in which freezing men cannot understand why the managers of a flophouse make them wait as a snowstorm brews. In *Red Badge*, Crane transforms such psychological reactions and makes them the typical responses of Union privates who cannot comprehend the intentions of their generals. Likewise, Crane renders the conflicts over turf he saw waged in the Bowery into Henry Fleming's blood fever when his territorial instincts are aroused. The East Side of New York presented the young writer with a spectacle of the best and worst of human behavior.

The ultimate greatness of *Red Badge* may be not only that it tells a basic truth about war; it simultaneously distills the essence of a human will responding to any sort of crisis. In doing so, Crane creates an atmosphere of war with which an audience could readily connect, more so than they could with a text produced by a combat veteran. That veteran often had a subconscious misgiving that only soldiers who had experienced war could truly appreciate his account. With the swaggering confidence of a young writer, Crane made no such assumptions and instead trusted that pain and horror were universal enough so that all civilians could empathize with the plight of the soldier.

One other tactic existed in the game plan of an American Realist. As all good literary traditions had done before it, Realism rebelled against the aesthetic values of its predecessor—in this case, Romanticism. Popularized by writers such as James Fenimore Cooper, Ralph Waldo Emerson, Nathaniel Hawthorne, and Walt Whitman from the 1820s to the beginning of 1861, Romanticism and its beliefs, especially its pursuit for and contemplation of the ideal, had been severely tested by the savage realities of four bloody years of civil war. One postbellum consequence of this new national literary sensibility was that in their novels Realists often lampooned Romantic values. Oftentimes, the Realist would create an idealistic character with lofty beliefs and ambitions just so that the everyday realities of life could defeat him.

Like his Realist mentors, Crane challenged in his novel the Romantics' assumptions about war. Before his first taste of enemy gunfire, Fleming envisions war in terms of heroic struggles. Individual effort will be acknowledged and glorified in epic grandeur. The youth sees himself as a modern-day Achilles, perhaps destined to die but only after earning the accolades of his grateful comrades and cherished memorializing by his home town. Fleming soon finds out that war is a "blood-swollen god" who gobbles down human flesh, that individuals lose their identities in the great "blue demonstration," from endless drilling to the maneuvering of hapless men toward what to them seem to be meaningless battles.

Just as he could not free himself completely from the dogmatic aspect of his mother's religion, however, Crane likewise had difficulty in rejecting all dimensions of a Romantic sensibility. Long before the age of Sigmund Freud, British and American Romantics had explored (in a nonscientific way) the psychological basis of human behavior. Above all else, they valued the human mind and the individual it defined. The self became inviolable. For all of the onslaught by war, society, and fate upon his well-being, Fleming, during each reevaluation of his place, never surrenders his ego to the indifference of the universe, even at the end of the narrative:

> With this conviction came a store of assurance. He felt a quiet manhood, nonassertive but of sturdy and strong blood. He knew that he would no more quail before his guides wherever they should point. He had been to touch the great death, and found that, after all, it was but the great death. He was a man (p. 141).

I suspect that one reason Howells disapproved of *Red Badge* was that by the novel's end, all Henry Fleming had accomplished was to replace one set of antiquated Romantic values with another, more useful, conception that was still Romantic in character. Ironically, in "The Veteran," the short sequel Crane composed a year after the publication of *Red Badge*, Fleming, now an old man, dies the sort of hero's death he had Romantically imagined and then abandoned as a youthful private.

Crane was probably more comfortable in employing devices from Romanticism's literary cousin—Gothicism. Its chief antebellum practitioner in America was Edgar Allan Poe, whose tales Crane had studied intently in his fraternity library. The 1880s and 1890s proved to be a neo-Gothic era in literature, as evidenced by the publication of works such as Robert Louis Stevenson's *The Strange Case of Dr. Jekyll and Mr. Hyde,* Bram Stoker's *Dracula,* Oscar Wilde's *The Picture of Dorian Gray,* Arthur Conan Doyle's *The Hound of the Baskervilles,* and H. G. Wells's *The War of the Worlds.* American Realists of the period such as Bierce stripped Gothicism of its supernatural components and began to incorporate its other devices to depict the horror in everyday life. Ann Radcliffe, author of *The Mysteries of Udolpho* (1794), had suggested that there were two competing impulses in Gothicism: (1) Relying upon the literary device "suspense," *terror* aroused the intellect to a new level of awareness through dread. (2) Its opposite, *horror,* tried to annihilate thought by confronting the intellect with a multitude of terrible events in rapid succession. *Red Badge* fuses the two impulses. After standing his ground during the first skirmish, Fleming reacts with blind horror to the second Rebel assault, abandoning his position, his rifle, his comrades, and all of his Romantic preconceptions about war. Ultimately, however, terror does make its presence felt. Fleming dreads what his comrades might say when he returns to the regiment in chapter XIII. He remains in continual suspense about inevitable future battles, about how he will react to the next hostile encounter, and about what his place should be in such a threatening and uncaring environment. Crane combined these defining moments of horror and terror to illustrate the violent perceptual oscillations every soldier must cope with when he is first exposed to enemy fire.

Crane departed from pristine Realist conceptions not only by retreating to past traditions like Gothicism and Romanticism; he also integrated new ideas from emerging artistic schools, which during the 1890s were beginning to question the primacy of Realism in American letters. The strongest challenger was literary Naturalism. With philosophical assumptions arising from and encouraged by the biological theories of Charles Darwin, the political theories of Karl Marx, and, at a later time, the social theories of Herbert Spencer, Naturalism as a literary choice was first embraced by French writers during the latter half of the nineteenth century. Foremost among these was Émile Zola, whose novel about a Parisian prostitute, *Nana* (1880), likely inspired Crane to begin his American counterpart, *Maggie: A Girl of the Streets*. As a force, Naturalism did not reach American shores until a new generation of writers, eager to rebel against established literary values, burst upon the scene at the turn of the century—Frank Norris, Theodore Dreiser, Kate Chopin, and Jack London.

Naturalism is similar to Realism in its striving for objectivity in narration, yet it differs from its predecessor in its philosophical assumptions. Among other principles, it interpreted man's lot deterministically. Basically, it advocated that the individual is not in control of the forces that influence his or her behavior. These forces had two sources: one internal, the other external. At one extreme, millions of years of evolution have imprinted instincts in humans that manipulate our conduct. We share these subconscious desires with lower-class mammals—sexual urges, territorial impulses, the instinct to survive, etc. For example, when in chapter VII Fleming observes a squirrel flee when threatened, he equates this instinctual response with his own recent desertion under fire. For that one textual moment, nature provides him with a tentative explanation for his behavior, an example that seemingly relieves him of any responsibility.

At the other extreme, Naturalism also postulates that outside forces simultaneously govern human actions. In the great scheme of cosmic design, man becomes an isolated figure, hugely dwarfed by the environmental forces that surround him. He must travel along with society as it inexorably hurtles along a random path through time, or else he must be crushed by it. The "blue demonstration," whose metaphorical consequences change throughout the novel, limits Fleming's options time and again. For instance, after finally taking a Confederate position at an appalling human cost for both sides, Fleming's regiment is forced to abandon its hard-won gain. During the course of the final battle, the soldiers learn that their charge was just a diversion; elsewhere, the main body of Union forces had failed in its mission. When computed as part of the combined efforts of the entire Army of the Potomac, the achievements of the 304th New York and of Fleming himself mean very little. Consequently, he must follow society, as represented by the Union army, as it strategically retreats from Chancellorsville and from its cumulative failure. If nothing else, Naturalist premises fit neatly into Crane's developing view of a universe indifferent to individual presences.

Also opposing strict Realism, another aesthetic trend that emerged in American letters during the 1890s was literary Impressionism, which among other traits valued the psychological makeup of the artist in his or her rendering of a subject. Thus, the perspective of the artist should occupy the center of any interpretation of the work, whether it be a painting, a poem, or a novel. The artist pinpoints and depicts a small moment pregnant with meaning. Through the eyes of a barmaid working at the Folies-Bergère, Édouard Manet captures in paint an instant of ennui that speaks volumes about her life. On an Edgar Degas canvas, we witness a quiet and private moment when a ballerina perfects her position in an exercise. Crane's friend and mentor Hamlin Garland had intently studied the works and philosophy of the French Impressionists. He began to advocate that American literature ought to adopt some of their principles, which he renamed "veritism" in his 1894 book-length essay *Crumbling Idols*.

In *Red Badge*, Crane's psyche figures prominently at the center of many passages. One Impressionistic moment that is quintessentially Crane's comes during one of the 304th New York's unsuccessful advances. Through devices idiosyncratic to his prose technique, Crane dilates time itself. Throughout the battle scene, Fleming becomes the nexus of an apparent chaos of images, which are really all carefully orchestrated to recreate a terrified intellect coping with the most horrific of battle experiences. Afterward, Fleming marvels:

> They turned when they arrived at their old position to regard the ground over which they had charged.
>
> The youth in this contemplation was smitten with a large astonishment. He discovered that the distances, as compared with the brilliant measurings of his mind, were trivial and ridiculous. The stolid trees, where much had taken place, seemed incredibly near. The time, too, now that he reflected, he saw to have been

short. He wondered at the number of emotions and events that had been crowded into such little spaces. Elfin thoughts must have exaggerated and enlarged everything, he said (p. 123).

Like a good Impressionist Crane had distilled the attar of a defining moment. (In *Stephen Crane and Literary Impressionism*, James Nagel offers an authoritative overview of Crane's relationship with Impressionism.)

Aesthetically aligned with Impressionism is French Symbolism, a loose poetic school that flourished during the latter half of the nineteenth century. Both movements have some origins with the poet Charles Baudelaire, whose essays about the paintings of Eugène Delacroix and others allowed him to clarify how his Romantic proclivities were evolving into a more refined sensibility. Subsequently, Symbolist poets such as Stéphane Mallarmé, Arthur Rimbaud, and Paul Verlaine would explore the power of and relationship between symbols, realizing in the process the ability of poetry to create complex new symbols of its own. Though most often considered a Romantic by critics, Emily Dickinson had certainly anticipated a few Symbolist conceptions in her poetry. Some of those who embraced her work when it first appeared during the 1890s had been better prepared to comprehend it because they had already read Mallarmé's lavish sonnets.

Dickinson and Symbolism encouraged Crane to infuse prose with poetic devices. Symbols abound in *Red Badge*, from "the red sun . . . pasted in the sky like a wafer" to Wilson's "packet" that he instructs Fleming to send home if he should be killed. One significant recurring symbol is the battle standard of the regiment. Throughout the novel, Crane avoids interjecting a patriotic dimension. Instead, the text promotes both a functional and a philosophical purpose. Amid the confusion of a battlefield, a private desperately seeks for any sign of where he belongs and of what he should be doing. In such instances throughout *Red Badge*, the soldiers of the 304th follow not the orders of their superiors but the flag. When Fleming wrests the standard from the hands of a dying comrade, he symbolically tries to grab control of his environment. Through brute will, he leads the regiment in its final assault upon the Rebel stronghold. For a moment, he metaphorically masters his hostile environment—but only for a moment. More than anything else, Crane's Impressionistic uniqueness owes its character to his Symbolist eye for poetic concision and for the suggestive richness of images.

Stephen Crane's religious upbringing, his experiences among New York's poor, his encounters with Realism, Romanticism, Gothicism, Naturalism, Impressionism, and Symbolism, and many other influences are all present and carefully coordinated in this deceptively simple novel. For Crane, no one aesthetic, creed, philosophical presumption, or practical experience could consistently explain every second in an individual's life. One stifling event might lend itself to a Naturalist interpretation; the next might stolidly support a Realist perspective. Just as the correspondent of "The Open Boat" has the ability and responsibility to articulate the fear and frustration of his shipmates, the American writer has the capacity to reproduce in prose the riot of possibilities that the individual mind contemplates while trying to fathom its uncertain place in the universe. Fleming's sensibility shifts so often and so smoothly that we recognize how amazingly illuminating Crane was in portraying the restless nature of human thought.

After the composition of *Red Badge*, Crane went on to become a famous writer, a daring journalist, and a self-consuming traveler through life. From 1895 onward, his life reads like the script of an improbable biopic. Working as a roving correspondent for a New York newspaper, he effected a desperate escape to avoid being murdered by Mexican bandits, an experience that he later fictionalized in "One Dash—Horses." Later, back in New York City, he sided with a prostitute in her claim that she was falsely arrested. In doing so, Crane earned the rancor of all the police in the city to the degree that he had to flee New York to escape their unflagging harassment. Next, in Florida, he boarded a filibustering vessel laden with arms and rebels, so that he could report about the insurgency in Cuba. The next day, on the Atlantic, the boat sank. His precarious rescue later formed the basis for "The Open Boat." Back in Florida, he met and pursued a relationship with a flamboyant adventuress, Cora Taylor, who eventually became his common-law wife. He then covered a war between Turkey and Greece, discovering in the process that his insights about human behavior during combat in *Red Badge* were valid. He was living in England when the Spanish-American War broke out in 1898. He dragged Joseph Conrad all over London trying to book passage back to the United States. When he finally got to Cuba as a war correspondent, he took foolish risks in his continual investigation of the limits of his own bravery. All the while, his tuberculosis imposed an increasingly greater toll on his body. When he died in Germany on June 5, 1900, he was twenty-nine, having crowded a great deal of ferocious living and quality writing into a very brief span. The fact that most novelists do their best work during their thirties makes Crane's literary legacy all the more remarkable. We continue to read *The Red Badge of Courage* today not for its truth about the American Civil War but for its truth about all wars.

IV

What keeps a novel alive is that succeeding generations of readers find valid correspondences between its insights and their own experiences. I am writing this essay during September 2002, the one-year anniversary of the terrorist attacks upon the United States. The intended readers of this edition are most likely new to Crane and his fiction. In studying this novel for the umpteenth time, I was struck by the breadth of insight it offers—especially to young women and men trying to comprehend recent events. The parallels between *The Red Badge of Courage* and September 11, 2001, are chillingly remarkable—the impulse to flee, the adrenaline blood-rush of anger, the appetite for revenge, the confusion amid crisis, the impulse to do something, anything that might be useful, the nightmare of witnessing carnage, the helpless isolation of the individual lost in a hostile environment. Amid the bewilderment on that tragic day, we, like Henry Fleming and the 304th New York, looked toward the flag as a symbol of where we were supposed to be. And if anyone wants a glimmer of the psychological and spiritual price each American soldier has to pay in prosecuting the war against terrorism in Afghanistan and elsewhere, read *The Red Badge of Courage.*

Despite our collective pretense that civilization progresses, we will always have to contend with the realities of war and the threat of it. This circumstance inflicts upon the individual red-badge wounds of psychological extremity that can be dressed only by internal reflection. Even when pain is shared publicly, healing must remain private. If the universe is indeed indifferent, as Stephen Crane wrote, then we must each find our own capacity to judge the meaning of our lives.

Richard Fusco received his Ph.D. from Duke University in 1990. Since 1997 he has been an Assistant Professor of English at Saint Joseph's University in Philadelphia. A specialist in nineteenth-century American literature and in short-story narrative theory, he has published monographs about the works of a variety of American, British, and Continental literary figures, including Edgar Allan Poe, Guy de Maupassant, Henry James, Kate Chopin, Ambrose Bierce, O. Henry, Nathaniel Hawthorne, Jack London, John Reuben Thompson, Thomas Carlyle, Charles Dickens, Wilkie Collins, Arthur Conan Doyle, Dashiell Hammett, and Raymond Chandler. His major works of criticism include *Maupassant and the American Short Story: The Influence of Form at the Turn of the Century* (Pennsylvania State University Press, 1994) and Fin de millénaire: *Poe's Legacy for the Detective Story* (Enoch Pratt Free Library, 1993).

THE RED BADGE
OF COURAGE[1]
AN EPISODE OF THE
AMERICAN CIVIL WAR

CHAPTER I

THE COLD PASSED RELUCTANTLY from the earth, and the retiring fogs revealed an army stretched out on the hills, resting.[2] As the landscape changed from brown to green, the army awakened, and began to tremble with eagerness at the noise of rumors. It cast its eyes upon the roads, which were growing from long troughs of liquid mud to proper thoroughfares. A river, amber-tinted in the shadow of its banks, purled at the army's feet; and at night, when the stream had become of a sorrowful blackness, one could see across it the red, eyelike gleam of hostile campfires set in the low brows of distant hills.

Once a certain tall soldier[3] developed virtues and went resolutely to wash a shirt. He came flying back from a brook waving his garment bannerlike. He was swelled with a tale he had heard from a reliable friend, who had heard it from a truthful cavalryman, who had heard it from his trustworthy brother, one of the order-lies at division headquarters.[4] He adopted the important air of a herald in red and gold.

"We're goin' t' move t' morrah—sure," he said pompously to a group in the company street. "We're goin' 'way up the river, cut across, an' come around in behint 'em."

To his attentive audience he drew a loud and elaborate plan of a very brilliant campaign. When he had finished, the blue-clothed men scattered into small arguing groups between the rows of squat brown huts. A negro teamster who had been dancing upon a cracker box with the hilarious encouragement of twoscore soldiers was deserted. He sat mournfully down. Smoke drifted lazily from a multitude of quaint chimneys.

"It's a lie! that's all it is—a thunderin' lie!" said another private loudly. His smooth face was flushed, and his hands were thrust sulkily into his trousers' pockets. He took the matter as an affront to him. "I don't believe the derned old army's ever going to move. We're set. I've got ready to move eight times in the last two weeks, and we ain't moved yet."

The tall soldier felt called upon to defend the truth of a rumor he himself had introduced. He and the loud one came near to fighting over it.

A corporal began to swear before the assemblage. He had just put a costly board floor in his house, he said. During the early spring he had refrained from adding extensively to the comfort of his environment because he had felt that the army might start on the march at any moment. Of late, however, he had been impressed that they were in a sort of eternal camp.

Many of the men engaged in a spirited debate. One outlined in a peculiarly lucid manner all the plans of the commanding general. He was opposed by men who advocated that there were other plans of campaign. They clamored at each other, numbers making futile bids for the popular attention. Meanwhile, the soldier who had fetched the rumor bustled about with much importance. He was continually assailed by questions.

"What's up, Jim?"

"Th' army's goin' t' move."

"Ah, what yeh talkin' about? How yeh know it is?"

"Well, yeh kin b'lieve me er not, jest as yeh like. I don't care a hang."

There was much food for thought in the manner in which he replied. He came near to convincing them by disdaining to produce proofs. They grew much excited over it.

There was a youthful private who listened with eager ears to the words of the tall soldier and to the varied comments of his comrades. After receiving a fill of discussions concerning marches and attacks, he went to his hut and crawled through an intricate hole that served it as a door. He wished to be alone with some new thoughts that had lately come to him.

He lay down on a wide bunk that stretched across the end of the room. In the other end, cracker boxes were made to serve as furniture. They were grouped about the fireplace. A picture from an illustrated weekly was upon the log walls, and three rifles were paralleled on pegs. Equipments hung on handy projections, and some tin dishes lay upon a small pile of firewood. A folded tent was serving as a roof. The sunlight, without, beating upon it, made it glow a light yellow shade. A small window shot an oblique square of whiter light upon the cluttered floor. The smoke from the fire at times neglected the clay chimney and wreathed into the room, and this flimsy chimney of clay and sticks made endless threats to set ablaze the whole establishment.

The youth was in a little trance of astonishment. So they were at last going to fight. On the morrow, perhaps, there would be a battle, and he would be in it. For a time he was obliged to labor to make himself believe. He could not accept with assurance an omen that he was about to mingle in one of those great affairs of the earth.

He had, of course, dreamed of battles all his life—of vague and bloody conflicts that had thrilled him with their sweep and fire. In visions he had seen himself in many struggles. He had imagined peoples secure in the shadow of his eagle-eyed prowess. But awake he had regarded battles as crimson blotches on the pages of the past. He had put them as things of the bygone with his thought-images of heavy crowns and high castles. There was a portion of the world's history which he had regarded as the time of wars, but it, he thought, had been long gone over the horizon and had disappeared forever.

From his home his youthful eyes had looked upon the war in his own country with distrust. It must be some sort of a play affair. He had long despaired of witnessing a Greeklike struggle.[5] Such would be no more, he had said. Men were better, or more timid. Secular and religious education had effaced the throat-grappling instinct, or else firm finance held in check the passions.

He had burned several times to enlist. Tales of great movements shook the land. They might not be distinctly Homeric, but there seemed to be much glory in them. He had read of marches, sieges, conflicts, and he had longed to see it all. His busy mind had drawn for him large pictures extravagant in color, lurid with breathless deeds.

But his mother had discouraged him. She had affected to look with some contempt upon the quality of his war ardor and patriotism. She could calmly seat herself and with no apparent difficulty give him many hundreds of reasons why he was of vastly more importance on the farm than on the field of battle.

She had had certain ways of expression that told him that her statements on the subject came from a deep conviction. Moreover, on her side, was his belief that her ethical motive in the argument was impregnable.

At last, however, he had made firm rebellion against this yellow light thrown upon the color of his ambitions. The newspapers, the gossip of the village, his own picturings, had aroused him to an uncheckable degree. They were in truth fighting finely down there. Almost every day the newspapers printed accounts of a decisive victory.

One night, as he lay in bed, the winds had carried to him the clangoring of the church bell as some enthusiast jerked the rope frantically to tell the twisted news of a great battle. This voice of the people rejoicing in the night had made him shiver in a prolonged ecstasy of excitement. Later, he had gone down to his mother's room and had spoken thus: "Ma, I'm going to enlist."

"Henry, don't you be a fool," his mother had replied. She had then covered her face with the quilt. There was an end to the matter for that night.

Nevertheless, the next morning he had gone to a town that was near his mother's farm and had enlisted in a company that was forming there. When he had returned home his mother was milking the brindle cow. Four others stood waiting. "Ma, I've enlisted," he had said to her diffidently. There was a short silence. "The Lord's will be done, Henry," she had finally replied, and had then continued to milk the brindle cow.

When he had stood in the doorway with his soldier's clothes on his back, and with the light of excitement and expectancy in his eyes almost defeating the glow of regret for the home bonds, he had seen two tears leaving their trails on his mother's scarred cheeks.

Still, she had disappointed him by saying nothing whatever about returning with his shield or on it. He had privately primed himself for a beautiful scene. He had prepared certain sentences which he thought could be used with touching effect. But her words destroyed his plans. She had doggedly peeled potatoes and addressed him as follows: "You watch out, Henry, an' take good care of yerself in this here fighting business—you watch out, an' take good care of yerself. Don't go a-thinkin' you can lick the hull rebel army at the start, because yeh can't. Yer jest one little feller amongst a hull lot of others, and yeh've got to keep quiet an' do what they tell yeh. I know how you are, Henry.

"I've knet yeh eight pair of socks, Henry, and I've put in all yer best shirts, because I want my boy to be jest as warm and comf'able as anybody in the army. Whenever they get holes in 'em, I want yeh to send 'em right-away back to me, so's I kin dern 'em.

"An' allus be careful an' choose yer comp'ny. There's lots of bad men in the army, Henry. The army makes 'em wild, and they like nothing better than the job of leading off a young feller like you, as ain't never been away from home much and has allus had a mother, an' a-learning 'em to drink and swear. Keep clear of them folks, Henry. I don't want yeh to ever do anything, Henry, that yeh would be 'shamed to let me know about. Jest think as if I was a-watchin' yeh. If yeh keep that in yer mind allus, I guess yeh'll come out about right.

"Yeh must allus remember yer father, too, child, an' remember he never drunk a drop of licker in his life, and seldom swore a cross oath.

"I don't know what else to tell yeh, Henry, excepting that yeh must never do no shirking, child, on my account. If so be a time comes when yeh have to be kilt or do a mean thing, why, Henry, don't think of anything 'cept what's right, because there's many a woman has to bear up 'ginst sech things these times, and the Lord'll take keer of us all.

"Don't forget about the socks and the shirts, child; and I've put a cup of blackberry jam with yer bundle, because I know yeh like it above all things. Good-by, Henry. Watch out, and be a good boy."

He had, of course, been impatient under the ordeal of this speech. It had not been quite what he expected, and he had borne it with an air of irritation. He departed feeling vague relief.

Still, when he had looked back from the gate, he had seen his mother kneeling among the potato parings. Her brown face, upraised, was stained with tears, and her spare form was quivering. He bowed his head and went on, feeling suddenly ashamed of his purposes.

From his home he had gone to the seminary to bid adieu to many schoolmates. They had thronged about him with wonder and admiration. He had felt the gulf now between them and had swelled with calm pride. He and some of his fellows who had donned blue were quite overwhelmed with privileges for all of one afternoon, and it had been a very delicious thing. They had strutted.

A certain light haired girl had made vivacious fun at his martial spirit, but there was another and darker girl whom he had gazed at steadfastly, and he thought she grew demure and sad at sight of his blue and brass. As he had walked down the path between the rows of oaks, he had turned his head and detected her at a window watching his departure. As he perceived her, she had immediately begun to stare up through the high tree branches at the sky. He had seen a good deal of flurry and haste in her movement as she changed her attitude. He often thought of it.

On the way to Washington his spirit had soared. The regiment was fed and caressed at station after station until the youth had believed that he must be a hero. There was a lavish expenditure of bread and cold meats, coffee, and pickles and cheese. As he basked in the smiles of the girls and was patted and complimented by the old men, he had felt growing within him the strength to do mighty deeds of arms.

After complicated journeyings with many pauses, there had come months of monotonous life in a camp. He had had the belief that real war was a series of death struggles with small time in between for sleep and meals; but since his regiment had come to the field the army had done little but sit still and try to keep warm.

He was brought then gradually back to his old ideas. Greeklike struggles would be no more. Men were better, or more timid. Secular and religious education had effaced the throat-grappling instinct, or else firm finance held in check the passions.

He had grown to regard himself merely as a part of a vast

blue demonstration. His province was to look out, as far as he
could, for his personal comfort. For recreation he could twiddle
his thumbs and speculate on the thoughts which must agitate
the minds of the generals. Also, he was drilled and drilled and
reviewed, and drilled and drilled and reviewed.

The only foes he had seen were some pickets along the river
bank. They were a sun-tanned, philosophical lot, who sometimes shot reflectively at the blue pickets. When reproached for
this afterward, they usually expressed sorrow, and swore by
their gods that the guns had exploded without their permission.
The youth, on guard duty one night, conversed across the
stream with one of them.[6] He was a slightly ragged man, who
spat skillfully between his shoes and possessed a great fund of
bland and infantile assurance. The youth liked him personally.

"Yank," the other had informed him, "yer a right dum good
feller." This sentiment, floating to him upon the still air, had
made him temporarily regret war.

Various veterans had told him tales. Some talked of gray, be-
whiskered hordes who were advancing with relentless curses
and chewing tobacco with unspeakable valor; tremendous bodies of fierce soldiery who were sweeping along like the Huns.*
Others spoke of tattered and eternally hungry men who fired despondent powders. "They'll charge through hell's fire an' brimstone t' git a holt on a haversack, an' sech stomachs ain't a-lastin'
long," he was told. From the stories, the youth imagined the red,
live bones sticking out through slits in the faded uniforms.

Still, he could not put a whole faith in veterans' tales, for recruits were their prey. They talked much of smoke, fire, and
blood, but he could not tell how much might be lies. They persistently yelled "Fresh fish!"† at him, and were in no wise to be
trusted.

---

* Savage race from Asia that marauded throughout Europe during the
fourth and fifth centuries A.D. Also, an offensive term for people of
Germanic ancestry, significant here because Germans comprised a good
proportion of the troops in the Eleventh Corps.

† Military slang used by veterans to taunt new recruits about their inexperience.

However, he perceived now that it did not greatly matter what kind of soldiers he was going to fight, so long as they fought, which fact no one disputed. There was a more serious problem. He lay in his bunk pondering upon it. He tried to mathematically prove to himself that he would not run from a battle.

Previously he had never felt obliged to wrestle too seriously with this question. In his life he had taken certain things for granted, never challenging his belief in ultimate success, and bothering little about means and roads. But here he was confronted with a thing of moment. It had suddenly appeared to him that perhaps in a battle he might run. He was forced to admit that as far as war was concerned he knew nothing of himself.

A sufficient time before he would have allowed the problem to kick its heels at the outer portals of his mind, but now he felt compelled to give serious attention to it.

A little panic-fear grew in his mind. As his imagination went forward to a fight, he saw hideous possibilities. He contemplated the lurking menaces of the future, and failed in an effort to see himself standing stoutly in the midst of them. He recalled his visions of broken-bladed glory, but in the shadow of the impending tumult he suspected them to be impossible pictures.

He sprang from the bunk and began to pace nervously to and fro. "Good Lord, what's th' matter with me?" he said aloud.

He felt that in this crisis his laws of life were useless. Whatever he had learned of himself was here of no avail. He was an unknown quantity. He saw that he would again be obliged to experiment as he had in early youth. He must accumulate information of himself, and meanwhile he resolved to remain close upon his guard lest those qualities of which he knew nothing should everlastingly disgrace him. "Good Lord!" he repeated in dismay.

After a time the tall soldier slid dexterously through the hole. The loud private followed. They were wrangling.

"That's all right," said the tall soldier as he entered. He waved his hand expressively. "You can believe me or not, jest as you like. All you got to do is to sit down and wait as quiet as you can. Then pretty soon you'll find out I was right."

His comrade grunted stubbornly. For a moment he seemed to be searching for a formidable reply. Finally he said: "Well, you don't know everything in the world, do you?"

"Didn't say I knew everything in the world," retorted the other sharply. He began to stow various articles snugly into his knapsack.

The youth, pausing in his nervous walk, looked down at the busy figure. "Going to be a battle, sure, is there, Jim?" he asked.

"Of course there is," replied the tall soldier. "Of course there is. You jest wait 'til to-morrow, and you'll see one of the biggest battles ever was. You jest wait."

"Thunder!" said the youth.

"Oh, you'll see fighting this time, my boy, what'll be regular out-and-out fighting," added the tall soldier, with the air of a man who is about to exhibit a battle for the benefit of his friends.

"Huh!" said the loud one from a corner.

"Well," remarked the youth, "like as not this story'll turn out jest like them others did."

"Not much it won't," replied the tall soldier, exasperated. "Not much it won't. Didn't the cavalry all start this morning?"[7] He glared about him. No one denied his statement. "The cavalry started this morning," he continued. "They say there ain't hardly any cavalry left in camp. They're going to Richmond, or some place, while we fight all the Johnnies.* It's some dodge like that. The regiment's got orders, too. A feller what seen 'em go to headquarters told me a little while ago. And they're raising blazes all over camp—anybody can see that."

"Shucks!" said the loud one.

The youth remained silent for a time. At last he spoke to the tall soldier. "Jim!"

"What?"

"How do you think the reg'ment 'll do?"

---

* Short for Johnny Reb, slang for a Confederate soldier. The equivalent for a Union soldier was Billy Yank.

"Oh, they'll fight all right, I guess, after they once get into it,"
said the other with cold judgment. He made a fine use of the third
person. "There's been heaps of fun poked at 'em because they're
new, of course, and all that; but they'll fight all right, I guess."

"Think any of the boys 'll run?" persisted the youth.

"Oh, there may be a few of 'em run, but there's them kind in
every regiment, 'specially when they first goes under fire," said
the other in a tolerant way. "Of course it might happen that the
hull kit-and-boodle* might start and run, if some big fighting
came first-off, and then again they might stay and fight like fun.
But you can't bet on nothing. Of course they ain't never been under fire yet, and it ain't likely they'll lick the hull rebel army all-
to-oncet the first time; but I think they'll fight better than some,
if worse than others. That's the way I figger. They call the reg'ment
'Fresh fish' and everything; but the boys come of good stock, and
most of 'em 'll fight like sin after they oncet git shootin'," he
added, with a mighty emphasis on the last four words.

"Oh, you think you know——" began the loud soldier with
scorn.

The other turned savagely upon him. They had a rapid altercation, in which they fastened upon each other various strange
epithets.

The youth at last interrupted them. "Did you ever think you
might run yourself, Jim?" he asked. On concluding the sentence
he laughed as if he had meant to aim a joke. The loud soldier
also giggled.

The tall private waved his hand. "Well," said he profoundly,
"I've thought it might get too hot for Jim Conklin in some of
them scrimmages, and if a whole lot of boys started and run,
why, I s'pose I'd start and run. And if I once started to run, I'd
run like the devil, and no mistake. But if everybody was a-stand-
ing and a-fighting, why, I'd stand and fight. Be jiminey,† I
would. I'll bet on it."

---

* Dialect alteration of kit *and* caboodle, meaning "the whole thing."

† Mild oath probably originating in mythology—from Gemini, the
twins. Several linguists, however, believe that the expression derives
from a German phrase invoking Jesus.

"Huh!" said the loud one.

The youth of this tale felt gratitude for these words of his comrade. He had feared that all of the untried men possessed a great and correct confidence. He now was in a measure reassured.

CHAPTER II

THE NEXT MORNING THE youth discovered that his tall comrade had been the fast-flying messenger of a mistake. There was much scoffing at the latter by those who had yesterday been firm adherents of his views, and there was even a little sneering by men who had never believed the rumor. The tall one fought with a man from Chatfield Corners* and beat him severely.

The youth felt, however, that his problem was in no wise lifted from him. There was, on the contrary, an irritating prolongation. The tale had created in him a great concern for himself. Now, with the newborn question in his mind, he was compelled to sink back into his old place as part of a blue demonstration.[8]

For days he made ceaseless calculations, but they were all wondrously unsatisfactory. He found that he could establish nothing. He finally concluded that the only way to prove himself was to go into the blaze, and then figuratively to watch his legs to discover their merits and faults. He reluctantly admitted that he could not sit still and with a mental slate and pencil derive an answer. To gain it, he must have blaze, blood, and danger, even as a chemist requires this, that, and the other. So he fretted for an opportunity.

Meanwhile he continually tried to measure himself by his comrades. The tall soldier, for one, gave him some assurance. This man's serene unconcern dealt him a measure of confidence, for he had known him since childhood, and from his intimate knowledge he did not see how he could be capable of anything that was beyond him, the youth. Still, he thought that his comrade might be mistaken about himself. Or, on the other hand, he might be a man heretofore doomed to peace and obscurity, but, in reality, made to shine in war.

The youth would have liked to have discovered another who suspected himself. A sympathetic comparison of mental notes would have been a joy to him.

---

* Located in Saratoga County in upstate New York.

He occasionally tried to fathom a comrade with seductive sentences. He looked about to find men in the proper mood. All attempts failed to bring forth any statement which looked in any way like a confession to those doubts which he privately acknowledged in himself. He was afraid to make an open declaration of his concern, because he dreaded to place some unscrupulous confidant upon the high plane of the unconfessed from which elevation he could be derided.

In regard to his companions his mind wavered between two opinions, according to his mood. Sometimes he inclined to believing them all heroes. In fact, he usually admitted in secret the superior development of the higher qualities in others. He could conceive of men going very insignificantly about the world bearing a load of courage unseen, and although he had known many of his comrades through boyhood, he began to fear that his judgment of them had been blind. Then, in other moments, he flouted these theories, and assured himself that his fellows were all privately wondering and quaking.

His emotions made him feel strange in the presence of men who talked excitedly of a prospective battle as of a drama they were about to witness, with nothing but eagerness and curiosity apparent in their faces. It was often that he suspected them to be liars.

He did not pass such thoughts without severe condemnation of himself. He dinned reproaches at times. He was convicted by himself of many shameful crimes against the gods of traditions.

In his great anxiety his heart was continually clamoring at what he considered the intolerable slowness of the generals. They seemed content to perch tranquilly on the river bank, and leave him bowed down by the weight of a great problem. He wanted it settled forthwith. He could not long bear such a load, he said. Sometimes his anger at the commanders reached an acute stage, and he grumbled about the camp like a veteran.

One morning, however, he found himself in the ranks of his prepared regiment. The men were whispering speculations and recounting the old rumors. In the gloom before the break of the day their uniforms glowed a deep purple hue. From across the river the red eyes were still peering. In the eastern sky there was

a yellow patch like a rug laid for the feet of the coming sun; and
against it, black and patternlike, loomed the gigantic figure of
the colonel on a gigantic horse.[9]

From off in the darkness came the trampling of feet. The
youth could occasionally see dark shadows that moved like
monsters. The regiment stood at rest for what seemed a long
time. The youth grew impatient. It was unendurable the way
these affairs were managed. He wondered how long they were
to be kept waiting.

As he looked all about him and pondered upon the mystic
gloom, he began to believe that at any moment the ominous
distance might be aflare, and the rolling crashes of an engagement come to his ears. Staring once at the red eyes across the
river, he conceived them to be growing larger, as the orbs of a
row of dragons advancing. He turned toward the colonel and
saw him lift his gigantic arm and calmly stroke his mustache.

At last he heard from along the road at the foot of the hill the
clatter of a horse's galloping hoofs. It must be the coming of orders. He bent forward, scarce breathing. The exciting clickety-
click, as it grew louder and louder, seemed to be beating upon
his soul. Presently a horseman with jangling equipment drew
rein before the colonel of the regiment. The two held a short,
sharp-worded conversation. The men in the foremost ranks
craned their necks.

As the horseman wheeled his animal and galloped away he
turned to shout over his shoulder, "Don't forget that box of cigars!" The colonel mumbled in reply. The youth wondered what
a box of cigars had to do with war.

A moment later the regiment went swinging off into the
darkness. It was now like one of those moving monsters wend-
ing with many feet. The air was heavy, and cold with dew. A
mass of wet grass, marched upon, rustled like silk.

There was an occasional flash and glimmer of steel from the
backs of all these huge crawling reptiles. From the road came
creakings and grumblings as some surly guns were dragged away.

The men stumbled along still muttering speculations. There
was a subdued debate. Once a man fell down, and as he reached
for his rifle a comrade, unseeing, trod upon his hand. He of the

injured fingers swore bitterly and aloud. A low, tittering laugh went among his fellows.

Presently they passed into a roadway and marched forward with easy strides. A dark regiment moved before them, and from behind also came the tinkle of equipments on the bodies of marching men.

The rushing yellow of the developing day went on behind their backs. When the sunrays at last struck full and mellowingly upon the earth, the youth saw that the landscape was streaked with two long, thin, black columns which disappeared on the brow of a hill in front and rearward vanished in a wood. They were like two serpents crawling from the cavern of the night.

The river was not in view. The tall soldier burst into praises of what he thought to be his powers of perception.

Some of the tall one's companions cried with emphasis that they, too, had evolved the same thing, and they congratulated themselves upon it. But there were others who said that the tall one's plan was not the true one at all. They persisted with other theories. There was a vigorous discussion.

The youth took no part in them. As he walked along in careless line he was engaged with his own eternal debate. He could not hinder himself from dwelling upon it. He was despondent and sullen, and threw shifting glances about him. He looked ahead, often expecting to hear from the advance the rattle of firing.

But the long serpents crawled slowly from hill to hill without bluster of smoke. A dun-colored cloud of dust floated away to the right. The sky overhead was of a fairy blue.

The youth studied the faces of his companions, ever on the watch to detect kindred emotions. He suffered disappointment. Some ardor of the air which was causing the veteran commands to move with glee—almost with song—had infected the new regiment. The men began to speak of victory as of a thing they knew. Also, the tall soldier received his vindication. They were certainly going to come around in behind the enemy.[10] They expressed commiseration for that part of the army which had been left upon the river bank, felicitating themselves upon being a part of a blasting host.

The youth, considering himself as separated from the others, was saddened by the blithe and merry speeches that went from rank to rank. The company wags all made their best endeavors. The regiment tramped to the tune of laughter.

The blatant soldier often convulsed whole files by his biting sarcasms aimed at the tall one.

And it was not long before all the men seemed to forget their mission. Whole brigades grinned in unison, and regiments laughed.

A rather fat soldier attempted to pilfer a horse from a door-yard. He planned to load his knapsack upon it. He was escaping with his prize when a young girl rushed from the house and grabbed the animal's mane. There followed a wrangle. The young girl, with pink cheeks and shining eyes, stood like a dauntless statue.

The observant regiment, standing at rest in the roadway, whooped at once, and entered whole-souled upon the side of the maiden. The men became so engrossed in this affair that they entirely ceased to remember their own large war. They jeered the piratical private, and called attention to various defects in his personal appearance; and they were wildly enthusiastic in support of the young girl.

To her, from some distance, came bold advice. "Hit him with a stick."

There were crows and catcalls showered upon him when he retreated without the horse. The regiment rejoiced at his downfall. Loud and vociferous congratulations were showered upon the maiden, who stood panting and regarding the troops with defiance.

At nightfall the column broke into regimental pieces, and the fragments went into the fields to camp. Tents sprang up like strange plants. Camp fires, like red, peculiar blossoms, dotted the night.

The youth kept from intercourse with his companions as much as circumstances would allow him. In the evening he wandered a few paces into the gloom. From this little distance the many fires, with the black forms of men passing to and fro before the crimson rays, made weird and satanic effects.

He lay down in the grass. The blades pressed tenderly against his cheek. The moon had been lighted and was hung in a tree-top. The liquid stillness of the night enveloping him made him feel vast pity for himself. There was a caress in the soft winds; and the whole mood of the darkness, he thought, was one of sympathy for himself in his distress.

He wished, without reserve, that he was at home again making the endless rounds from the house to the barn, from the barn to the fields, from the fields to the barn, from the barn to the house. He remembered he had often cursed the brindle cow and her mates, and had sometimes flung milking stools. But, from his present point of view, there was a halo of happiness about each of their heads, and he would have sacrificed all the brass buttons on the continent to have been enabled to return to them. He told himself that he was not formed for a soldier. And he mused seriously upon the radical differences between himself and those men who were dodging implike around the fires.

As he mused thus he heard the rustle of grass, and, upon turning his head, discovered the loud soldier. He called out, "Oh, Wilson!"

The latter approached and looked down. "Why, hello, Henry; is it you? What you doing here?"

"Oh, thinking," said the youth.

The other sat down and carefully lighted his pipe. "You're getting blue, my boy. You're looking thundering peeked. What the dickens* is wrong with you?"

"Oh, nothing," said the youth.

The loud soldier launched then into the subject of the anticipated fight. "Oh, we've got 'em now!" As he spoke his boyish face was wreathed in a gleeful smile, and his voice had an exultant ring. "We've got 'em now. At last, by the eternal thunders, we'll lick 'em good!"

"If the truth was known," he added, more soberly, "*they've* licked *us* about every clip up to now;[11] but this time—this time—we'll lick 'em good!"

---

* Mild oath invoking the devil.

"I thought you was objecting to this march a little while ago," said the youth coldly.

"Oh, it wasn't that," explained the other. "I don't mind marching, if there's going to be fighting at the end of it. What I hate is this getting moved here and moved there, with no good coming of it, as far as I can see, excepting sore feet and damned short rations."

"Well, Jim Conklin says we'll get a plenty of fighting this time."

"He's right for once, I guess, though I can't see how it come. This time we're in for a big battle, and we've got the best end of it, certain sure. Gee rod!* how we will thump 'em!"

He arose and began to pace to and fro excitedly. The thrill of his enthusiasm made him walk with an elastic step. He was sprightly, vigorous, fiery in his belief in success. He looked into the future with clear, proud eye, and he swore with the air of an old soldier.

The youth watched him for a moment in silence. When he finally spoke his voice was as bitter as dregs. "Oh, you're going to do great things, I s'pose!"

The loud soldier blew a thoughtful cloud of smoke from his pipe. "Oh, I don't know," he remarked with dignity; "I don't know. I s'pose I'll do as well as the rest. I'm going to try like thunder." He evidently complimented himself upon the modesty of this statement.

"How do you know you won't run when the time comes?" asked the youth.

"Run?" said the loud one; "run?—of course not!" He laughed.

"Well," continued the youth, "lots of good-a-'nough men have thought they was going to do great things before the fight, but when the time come they skedaddled."

"Oh, that's all true, I s'pose," replied the other; "but I'm not

---

* Colloquialism for *Jesus' Rod*, invoking Christ's power and authority as shepherd. Some traditions believe that Christ possessed Moses' rod. Several religious denominations would consider this phrase used in such a context as blasphemous.

going to skedaddle.* The man that bets on my running will lose his money, that's all." He nodded confidently.

"Oh, shucks!" said the youth. "You ain't the bravest man in the world, are you?"

"No, I ain't," exclaimed the loud soldier indignantly; "and I didn't say I was the bravest man in the world, neither. I said I was going to do my share of fighting—that's what I said. And I am, too. Who are you, anyhow? You talk as if you thought you was Napoleon Bonaparte."[12] He glared at the youth for a moment, and then strode away.

The youth called in a savage voice after his comrade: "Well, you needn't git mad about it!" But the other continued on his way and made no reply.

He felt alone in space when his injured comrade had disappeared. His failure to discover any mite of resemblance in their view points made him more miserable than before. No one seemed to be wrestling with such a terrific personal problem. He was a mental outcast.

He went slowly to his tent and stretched himself on a blanket by the side of the snoring tall soldier. In the darkness he saw visions of a thousand-tongued fear that would babble at his back and cause him to flee, while others were going coolly about their country's business. He admitted that he would not be able to cope with this monster. He felt that every nerve in his body would be an ear to hear the voices, while other men would remain stolid and deaf.

And as he sweated with the pain of these thoughts, he could hear low, serene sentences. "I'll bid five." "Make it six." "Seven." "Seven goes."[13]

He stared at the red, shivering reflection of a fire on the white wall of his tent until, exhausted and ill from the monotony of his suffering, he fell asleep.

---

* The term *skedaddle*, meaning "desertion under fire," became popular early during the Civil War.

CHAPTER III

WHEN ANOTHER NIGHT CAME the columns, changed to purple streaks, filed across two pontoon bridges. A glaring fire wine-tinted the waters of the river. Its rays, shining upon the moving masses of troops, brought forth here and there sudden gleams of silver or gold. Upon the other shore a dark and mysterious range of hills was curved against the sky. The insect voices of the night sang solemnly.

After this crossing the youth assured himself that at any moment they might be suddenly and fearfully assaulted from the caves of the lowering woods. He kept his eyes watchfully upon the darkness.

But his regiment went unmolested to a camping place, and its soldiers slept the brave sleep of wearied men. In the morning they were routed out with early energy, and hustled along a narrow road that led deep into the forest.

It was during this rapid march that the regiment lost many of the marks of a new command.

The men had begun to count the miles upon their fingers, and they grew tired. "Sore feet an' damned short rations, that's all," said the loud soldier. There was perspiration and grumblings. After a time they began to shed their knapsacks. Some tossed them unconcernedly down; others hid them carefully, asserting their plans to return for them at some convenient time. Men extricated themselves from thick shirts. Presently few carried anything but their necessary clothing, blankets, haversacks, canteens, and arms and ammunition. "You can now eat and shoot," said the tall soldier to the youth. "That's all you want to do."

There was sudden change from the ponderous infantry of theory to the light and speedy infantry of practice. The regiment, relieved of a burden, received a new impetus. But there was much loss of valuable knapsacks, and, on the whole, very good shirts.[14]

But the regiment was not yet veteranlike in appearance.

Veteran regiments in the army were likely to be very small aggregations of men. Once, when the command had first come to the field, some perambula'ing veterans, noting the length of their column, had accosted them thus: "Hey, fellers, what brigade is that?" And when the men had replied that they formed a regiment and not a brigade, the older soldiers had laughed, and said, "O Gawd!"[15]

Also, there was too great a similarity in the hats. The hats of a regiment should properly represent the history of headgear for a period of years. And, moreover, there were no letters of faded gold speaking from the colors. They were new and beautiful, and the color bearer habitually oiled the pole.

Presently the army again sat down to think. The odor of the peaceful pines was in the men's nostrils. The sound of monotonous axe blows rang through the forest, and the insects, nodding upon their perches, crooned like old women. The youth returned to his theory of a blue demonstration.

One gray dawn, however, he was kicked in the leg by the tall soldier, and then, before he was entirely awake, he found himself running down a wood road in the midst of men who were panting from the first effects of speed. His canteen banged rhythmically upon his thigh, and his haversack bobbed softly. His musket bounced a trifle from his shoulder at each stride and made his cap feel uncertain upon his head.

He could hear the men whisper jerky sentences: "Say— what's all this—about?" "What th' thunder—we—skedaddlin' this way fer?" "Billie—keep off m' feet. Yeh run—like a cow." And the loud soldier's shrill voice could be heard: "What th' devil they in sich a hurry for?"

The youth thought the damp fog of early morning moved from the rush of a great body of troops. From the distance came a sudden spatter of firing.

He was bewildered. As he ran with his comrades he strenuously tried to think, but all he knew was that if he fell down those coming behind would tread upon him. All his faculties seemed to be needed to guide him over and past obstructions. He felt carried along by a mob.

The sun spread disclosing rays, and, one by one, regiments

burst into view like armed men just born of the earth. The youth perceived that the time had come. He was about to be measured. For a moment he felt in the face of his great trial like a babe, and the flesh over his heart seemed very thin. He seized time to look about him calculatingly.

But he instantly saw that it would be impossible for him to escape from the regiment. It inclosed him. And there were iron laws of tradition and law on four sides. He was in a moving box.

As he perceived this fact it occurred to him that he had never wished to come to the war. He had not enlisted of his free will. He had been dragged by the merciless government. And now they were taking him out to be slaughtered.

The regiment slid down a bank and wallowed across a little stream. The mournful current moved slowly on, and from the water, shaded black, some white bubble eyes looked at the men.

As they climbed the hill on the farther side artillery began to boom. Here the youth forgot many things as he felt a sudden impulse of curiosity. He scrambled up the bank with a speed that could not be exceeded by a bloodthirsty man.

He expected a battle scene.

There were some little fields girted and squeezed by a forest. Spread over the grass and in among the tree trunks, he could see knots and waving lines of skirmishers who were running hither and thither and firing at the landscape.[16] A dark battle line lay upon a sunstruck clearing that gleamed orange color. A flag fluttered.

Other regiments floundered up the bank. The brigade was formed in line of battle, and after a pause started slowly through the woods in the rear of the receding skirmishers, who were continually melting into the scene to appear again farther on. They were always busy as bees, deeply absorbed in their little combats.

The youth tried to observe everything. He did not use care to avoid trees and branches, and his forgotten feet were constantly knocking against stones or getting entangled in briers. He was aware that these battalions with their commotions were woven red and startling into the gentle fabric of softened greens and browns. It looked to be a wrong place for a battlefield.

The skirmishers in advance fascinated him. Their shots into thickets and at distant and prominent trees spoke to him of tragedies—hidden, mysterious, solemn.

Once the line encountered the body of a dead soldier. He lay upon his back staring at the sky. He was dressed in an awkward suit of yellowish brown. The youth could see that the soles of his shoes had been worn to the thinness of writing paper, and from a great rent in one the dead foot projected piteously. And it was as if fate had betrayed the soldier. In death it exposed to his enemies that poverty which in life he had perhaps concealed from his friends.

The ranks opened covertly to avoid the corpse. The invulnerable dead man forced a way for himself. The youth looked keenly at the ashen face. The wind raised the tawny beard. It moved as if a hand were stroking it. He vaguely desired to walk around and around the body and stare; the impulse of the living to try to read in dead eyes the answer to the Question.

During the march the ardor which the youth had acquired when out of view of the field rapidly faded to nothing. His curiosity was quite easily satisfied. If an intense scene had caught him with its wild swing as he came to the top of the bank, he might have gone roaring on. This advance upon Nature was too calm. He had opportunity to reflect. He had time in which to wonder about himself and to attempt to probe his sensations.

Absurd ideas took hold upon him. He thought that he did not relish the landscape. It threatened him. A coldness swept over his back, and it is true that his trousers felt to him that they were no fit for his legs at all.

A house standing placidly in distant fields had to him an ominous look. The shadows of the woods were formidable. He was certain that in this vista there lurked fierce-eyed hosts. The swift thought came to him that the generals did not know what they were about. It was all a trap. Suddenly those close forests would bristle with rifle barrels. Ironlike brigades would appear in the rear. They were all going to be sacrificed. The generals were stupids. The enemy would presently swallow the whole command. He glared about him, expecting to see the stealthy approach of his death.

He thought that he must break from the ranks and harangue his comrades. They must not all be killed like pigs; and he was sure it would come to pass unless they were informed of these dangers. The generals were idiots to send them marching into a regular pen. There was but one pair of eyes in the corps. He would step forth and make a speech. Shrill and passionate words came to his lips.

The line, broken into moving fragments by the ground, went calmly on through fields and woods. The youth looked at the men nearest him, and saw, for the most part, expressions of deep interest, as if they were investigating something that had fascinated them. One or two stepped with overvaliant airs as if they were already plunged into war. Others walked as upon thin ice. The greater part of the untested men appeared quiet and absorbed. They were going to look at war, the red animal—war, the blood-swollen god. And they were deeply engrossed in this march.

As he looked the youth gripped his outcry at his throat. He saw that even if the men were tottering with fear they would laugh at his warning. They would jeer him, and, if practicable, pelt him with missiles. Admitting that he might be wrong, a frenzied declamation of the kind would turn him into a worm.

He assumed, then, the demeanor of one who knows that he is doomed alone to unwritten responsibilities. He lagged, with tragic glances at the sky.

He was surprised presently by the young lieutenant of his company, who began heartily to beat him with a sword, calling out in a loud and insolent voice: "Come, young man, get up into ranks there. No skulking'll do here."[17] He mended his pace with suitable haste. And he hated the lieutenant, who had no appreciation of fine minds. He was a mere brute.

After a time the brigade was halted in the cathedral light of a forest.[18] The busy skirmishers were still popping. Through the aisles of the wood could be seen the floating smoke from their rifles. Sometimes it went up in little balls, white and compact.

During this halt many men in the regiment began erecting tiny hills in front of them. They used stones, sticks, earth, and anything they thought might turn a bullet. Some built comparatively large ones, while others seemed content with little ones.

This procedure caused a discussion among the men. Some wished to fight like duelists, believing it to be correct to stand erect and be, from their feet to their foreheads, a mark. They said they scorned the devices of the cautious. But the others scoffed in reply, and pointed to the veterans on the flanks who were digging at the ground like terriers. In a short time there was quite a barricade along the regimental fronts. Directly, however, they were ordered to withdraw from that place.

This astounded the youth. He forgot his stewing over the advance movement. "Well, then, what did they march us out here for?" he demanded of the tall soldier. The latter with calm faith began a heavy explanation, although he had been compelled to leave a little protection of stones and dirt to which he had devoted much care and skill.

When the regiment was aligned in another position each man's regard for his safety caused another line of small intrenchments. They ate their noon meal behind a third one. They were moved from this one also. They were marched from place to place with apparent aimlessness.

The youth had been taught that a man became another thing in a battle. He saw his salvation in such a change. Hence this waiting was an ordeal to him. He was in a fever of impatience. He considered that there was denoted a lack of purpose on the part of the generals. He began to complain to the tall soldier. "I can't stand this much longer," he cried. "I don't see what good it does to make us wear out our legs for nothin'." He wished to return to camp, knowing that this affair was a blue demonstration; or else to go into a battle and discover that he had been a fool in his doubts, and was, in truth, a man of traditional courage. The strain of present circumstances he felt to be intolerable.

The philosophical tall soldier measured a sandwich of cracker and pork and swallowed it in a nonchalant manner. "Oh, I suppose we must go reconnoitering around the country jest to keep 'em from getting too close, or to develop 'em, or something."

"Huh!" said the loud soldier.

"Well," cried the youth, still fidgeting, "I'd rather do anything 'most than go tramping 'round the country all day doing no good to nobody and jest tiring ourselves out."

"So would I," said the loud soldier. "It ain't right. I tell you if anybody with any sense was a-runnin' this army it——"

"Oh, shut up!" roared the tall private. "You little fool. You little damn' cuss.* You ain't had that there coat and them pants on for six months, and yet you talk as if——"

"Well, I wanta do some fighting anyway," interrupted the other. "I didn't come here to walk. I could 'ave walked to home—'round an 'round the barn, if I jest wanted to walk."

The tall one, red-faced, swallowed another sandwich as if taking poison in despair.

But gradually, as he chewed, his face became again quiet and contented. He could not rage in fierce argument in the presence of such sandwiches. During his meals he always wore an air of blissful contemplation of the food he had swallowed. His spirit seemed then to be communing with the viands.

He accepted new environment and circumstance with great coolness, eating from his haversack at every opportunity. On the march he went along with the stride of a hunter, objecting to neither gait nor distance. And he had not raised his voice when he had been ordered away from three little protective piles of earth and stone, each of which had been an engineering feat worthy of being made sacred to the name of his grandmother.

In the afternoon the regiment went out over the same ground it had taken in the morning. The landscape then ceased to threaten the youth. He had been close to it and become familiar with it.

When, however, they began to pass into a new region, his old fears of stupidity and incompetence reassailed him, but this time he doggedly let them babble. He was occupied with his problem, and in his desperation he concluded that the stupidity did not greatly matter.

Once he thought he had concluded that it would be better to

---

* Informal term for a man, derived from either *curse* or *customer*.

get killed directly and end his troubles. Regarding death thus out of the corner of his eye, he conceived it to be nothing but rest, and he was filled with a momentary astonishment that he should have made an extraordinary commotion over the mere matter of getting killed. He would die; he would go to some place where he would be understood. It was useless to expect appreciation of his profound and fine senses from such men as the lieutenant. He must look to the grave for comprehension.

The skirmish fire increased to a long clattering sound. With it was mingled far-away cheering. A battery spoke.

Directly the youth would see the skirmishers running. They were pursued by the sound of musketry fire. After a time the hot, dangerous flashes of the rifles were visible. Smoke clouds went slowly and insolently across the fields like observant phantoms. The din became crescendo, like the roar of an oncoming train.

A brigade ahead of them and on the right went into action with a rending roar. It was as if it had exploded. And thereafter it lay stretched in the distance behind a long gray wall, that one was obliged to look twice at to make sure that it was smoke.

The youth, forgetting his neat plan of getting killed, gazed spell bound. His eyes grew wide and busy with the action of the scene. His mouth was a little ways open.

Of a sudden he felt a heavy and sad hand laid upon his shoulder. Awakening from his trance of observation he turned and beheld the loud soldier.

"It's my first and last battle, old boy," said the latter, with intense gloom. He was quite pale and his girlish lip was trembling.

"Eh?" murmured the youth in great astonishment.

"It's my first and last battle, old boy," continued the loud soldier. "Something tells me——"

"What?"

"I'm a gone coon* this first time and—and I w-want you to take these here things—to—my—folks." He ended in a quavering

---

* Person in a hopeless situation; several linguists believe this meaning derives from the word's use as a racist term for an African American.

sob of pity for himself. He handed the youth a little packet done up in a yellow envelope.

"Why, what the devil——" began the youth again.

But the other gave him a glance as from the depths of a tomb, and raised his limp hand in a prophetic manner and turned away.

CHAPTER IV

THE BRIGADE WAS HALTED in the fringe of a grove. The men crouched among the trees and pointed their restless guns out at the fields. They tried to look beyond the smoke.

Out of this haze they could see running men. Some shouted information and gestured as they hurried.

The men of the new regiment watched and listened eagerly, while their tongues ran on in gossip of the battle. They mouthed rumors that had flown like birds out of the unknown.

"They say Perry has been driven in with big loss."

"Yes, Carrott went t' th' hospital. He said he was sick. That smart lieutenant is commanding 'G' Company.[19] Th' boys say they won't be under Carrott no more if they all have t' desert. They allus knew he was a——"

"Hannises' batt'ry is took."[20]

"It ain't either. I saw Hannises' batt'ry off on th' left not more'n fifteen minutes ago."

"Well——"

"Th' general, he ses he is goin' t' take th' hull cammand of th' 304th when we go inteh action, an' then he ses we'll do sech fightin' as never another one reg'ment done."[21]

"They say we're catchin' it over on th' left. They say th' enemy driv' our line inteh a devil of a swamp an' took Hannises' batt'ry."

"No sech thing. Hannises' batt'ry was 'long here 'bout a minute ago."

"That young Hasbrouck, he makes a good off'cer. He ain't afraid 'a nothin'."

"I met one of th' 148th Maine boys an' he ses his brigade fit th' hull rebel army fer four hours over on th' turnpike road* an' killed about five thousand of 'em. He ses one more sech fight as that an' th' war 'll be over."

---

*The Orange Turnpike, an east–west road between Orange Court House and Fredericksburg.

"Bill wasn't scared either. No, sir! It wasn't that. Bill ain't a-gittin' scared easy. He was jest mad, that's what he was. When that feller trod on his hand, he up an' sed that he was willin' t' give his hand t' his country, but he be dumbed if he was goin' t' have every dumb bushwhacker in th' kentry walkin' 'round on it. Se he went t' th' hospital disregardless of th' fight. Three fingers was crunched. Th' dern doctor wanted t' amputate 'm, an' Bill, he raised a heluva row, I hear. He's a funny feller."

The din in front swelled to a tremendous chorus. The youth and his fellows were frozen to silence. They could see a flag that tossed in the smoke angrily. Near it were the blurred and agitated forms of troops. There came a turbulent stream of men across the fields. A battery changing position at a frantic gallop scattered the stragglers right and left.

A shell screaming like a storm banshee* went over the huddled heads of the reserves. It landed in the grove, and exploding redly flung the brown earth. There was a little shower of pine needles.

Bullets began to whistle among the branches and nip at the trees. Twigs and leaves came sailing down. It was as if a thousand axes, wee and invisible, were being wielded. Many of the men were constantly dodging and ducking their heads.

The lieutenant of the youth's company was shot in the hand. He began to swear so wondrously that a nervous laugh went along the regimental line. The officer's profanity sounded conventional. It relieved the tightened senses of the new men. It was as if he had hit his fingers with a tack hammer at home.

He held the wounded member carefully away from his side so that the blood would not drip upon his trousers.

The captain of the company, tucking his sword under his arm, produced a handkerchief and began to bind with it the lieutenant's wound. And they disputed as to how the binding should be done.

The battle flag in the distance jerked about madly. It seemed

---

* In Irish and Scottish folklore, a female spirit whose wailing under a window portends a death in the family.

to be struggling to free itself from an agony. The billowing smoke was filled with horizontal flashes.

Men running swiftly emerged from it. They grew in numbers until it was seen that the whole command was fleeing. The flag suddenly sank down as if dying. Its motion as it fell was a gesture of despair.

Wild yells came from behind the walls of smoke. A sketch in gray and red dissolved into a moblike body of men who galloped like wild horses.

The veteran regiments on the right and left of the 304th immediately began to jeer. With the passionate song of the bullets and the banshee shrieks of shells were mingled loud catcalls and bits of facetious advice concerning places of safety.

But the new regiment was breathless with horror. "Gawd! Saunders's got crushed!" whispered the man at the youth's elbow. They shrank back and crouched as if compelled to await a flood.

The youth shot a swift glance along the blue ranks of the regiment. The profiles were motionless, carven; and afterward he remembered that the color sergeant was standing with his legs apart, as if he expected to be pushed to the ground.

The following throng went whirling around the flank. Here and there were officers carried along on the stream like exasperated chips. They were striking about them with their swords and with their left fists, punching every head they could reach. They cursed like highwaymen.

A mounted officer displayed the furious anger of a spoiled child. He raged with his head, his arms, and his legs.

Another, the commander of the brigade, was galloping about bawling. His hat was gone and his clothes were awry. He resembled a man who has come from bed to go to a fire. The hoofs of his horse often threatened the heads of the running men, but they scampered with singular fortune. In this rush they were apparently all deaf and blind. They heeded not the largest and longest of the oaths that were thrown at them from all directions.

Frequently over this tumult could be heard the grim jokes of the critical veterans; but the retreating men apparently were not even conscious of the presence of an audience.

The battle reflection that shone for an instant in the faces on the mad current made the youth feel that forceful hands from heaven would not have been able to have held him in place if he could have got intelligent control of his legs.

There was an appalling imprint upon these faces. The struggle in the smoke had pictured an exaggeration of itself on the bleached cheeks and in the eyes wild with one desire.

The sight of this stampede exerted a floodlike force that seemed able to drag sticks and stones and men from the ground. They of the reserves had to hold on. They grew pale and firm, and red and quaking.

The youth achieved one little thought in the midst of this chaos. The composite monster which had caused the other troops to flee had not then appeared. He resolved to get a view of it, and then, he thought he might very likely run better than the best of them.

CHAPTER V

THERE WERE MOMENTS OF waiting. The youth thought of the village street at home before the arrival of the circus parade on a day in the spring. He remembered how he had stood, a small, thrillful boy, prepared to follow the dingy lady upon the white horse, or the band in its faded chariot. He saw the yellow road, the lines of expectant people, and the sober houses. He particularly remembered an old fellow who used to sit upon a cracker box in front of the store and feign to despise such exhibitions. A thousand details of color and form surged in his mind. The old fellow upon the cracker box appeared in middle prominence.

Some one cried, "Here they come!"

There was rustling and muttering among the men. They displayed a feverish desire to have every possible cartridge ready to their hands. The boxes were pulled around into various positions, and adjusted with great care. It was as if seven hundred new bonnets were being tried on.

The tall soldier, having prepared his rifle, produced a red handkerchief of some kind. He was engaged in knitting it about his throat with exquisite attention to its position, when the cry was repeated up and down the line in a muffled roar of sound.

"Here they come! Here they come!" Gun locks clicked.

Across the smoke-infested fields came a brown swarm of running men who were giving shrill yells. They came on, stooping and swinging their rifles at all angles. A flag, tilted forward, sped near the front.

As he caught sight of them the youth was momentarily startled by a thought that perhaps his gun was not loaded. He stood trying to rally his faltering intellect so that he might recollect the moment when he had loaded, but he could not.

A hatless general pulled his dripping horse to a stand near the colonel of the 304th. He shook his fist in the other's face. "You've got to hold 'em back!" he shouted, savagely; "you've got to hold 'em back!"[22]

In his agitation the colonel began to stammer. "A-all r-right,

35

General, all right, by Gawd! We-we'll do our—we-we'll d-d-
do—do our best, General." The general made a passionate gesture and galloped away. The colonel, perchance to relieve his
feelings, began to scold like a wet parrot. The youth, turning
swiftly to make sure that the rear was unmolested, saw the commander regarding his men in a highly resentful manner, as if he
regretted above everything his association with them.

The man at the youth's elbow was mumbling, as if to himself: "Oh, we're in for it now! oh, we're in for it now!"

The captain of the company had been pacing excitedly to
and fro in the rear. He coaxed in schoolmistress fashion, as to a
congregation of boys with primers. His talk was an endless rep-
etition. "Reserve your fire, boys—don't shoot till I tell you—
save your fire—wait till they get close up—don't be damned
fools——"

Perspiration streamed down the youth's face, which was
soiled like that of a weeping urchin. He frequently, with a nervous movement, wiped his eyes with his coat sleeve. His mouth
was still a little way open.

He got the one glance at the foe-swarming field in front of
him, and instantly ceased to debate the question of his piece being loaded.[23] Before he was ready to begin—before he had announced to himself that he was about to fight—he threw the
obedient, well-balanced rifle into position and fired a first wild
shot. Directly he was working at his weapon like an automatic
affair.

He suddenly lost concern for himself, and forgot to look at a
menacing fate. He became not a man but a member. He felt that
something of which he was a part—a regiment, an army, a
cause, or a country—was in a crisis. He was welded into a common personality which was dominated by a single desire. For
some moments he could not flee no more than a little finger can
commit a revolution from a hand.

If he had thought the regiment was about to be annihilated
perhaps he could have amputated himself from it. But its noise
gave him assurance. The regiment was like a firework that, once
ignited, proceeds superior to circumstances until its blazing vi-

tality fades. It wheezed and banged with a mighty power. He pictured the ground before it as strewn with the discomfited.

There was a consciousness always of the presence of his comrades about him. He felt the subtle battle brotherhood more potent even than the cause for which they were fighting. It was a mysterious fraternity born of the smoke and danger of death.

He was at a task. He was like a carpenter who has made many boxes, making still another box, only there was furious haste in his movements. He, in his thought, was careering off in other places, even as the carpenter who as he works whistles and thinks of his friend or his enemy, his home or a saloon. And these jolted dreams were never perfect to him afterward, but remained a mass of blurred shapes.

Presently he began to feel the effects of the war atmosphere—a blistering sweat, a sensation that his eyeballs were about to crack like hot stones. A burning roar filled his ears.

Following this came a red rage. He developed the acute exasperation of a pestered animal, a well-meaning cow worried by dogs. He had a mad feeling against his rifle, which could only be used against one life at a time. He wished to rush forward and strangle with his fingers. He craved a power that would enable him to make a world-sweeping gesture and brush all back. His impotency appeared to him, and made his rage into that of a driven beast.

Buried in the smoke of many rifles his anger was directed not so much against the men whom he knew were rushing toward him as against the swirling battle phantoms which were choking him, stuffing their smoke robes down his parched throat. He fought frantically for respite for his senses, for air, as a babe being smothered attacks the deadly blankets.

There was a blare of heated rage mingled with a certain expression of intentness on all faces. Many of the men were making low-toned noises with their mouths, and these subdued cheers, snarls, imprecations, prayers, made a wild, barbaric song that went as an undercurrent of sound, strange and chantlike with the resounding chords of the war march. The man at the youth's elbow was babbling. In it there was something soft and tender like the monologue of a babe. The tall soldier was swearing in a loud voice. From his lips came a black procession of curious oaths. Of a sudden another broke out in a querulous way like a man who has mislaid his hat. "Well, why don't they support us? Why don't they send supports? Do they think——"

The youth in his battle sleep heard this as one who dozes hears.

There was a singular absence of heroic poses. The men bending and surging in their haste and rage were in every impossible attitude. The steel ramrods clanked and clanged with incessant din as the men pounded them furiously into the hot rifle barrels. The flaps of the cartridge boxes were all unfastened, and bobbed idiotically with each movement. The rifles, once loaded, were jerked to the shoulder and fired without apparent aim into the smoke or at one of the blurred and shifting forms which upon the field before the regiment had been growing larger and larger like puppets under a magician's hand.

The officers, at their intervals, rearward, neglected to stand in picturesque attitudes. They were bobbing to and fro roaring directions and encouragements. The dimensions of their howls were extraordinary. They expended their lungs with prodigal wills. And often they nearly stood upon their heads in their anxiety to observe the enemy on the other side of the tumbling smoke.

The lieutenant of the youth's company had encountered a soldier who had fled screaming at the first volley of his comrades. Behind the lines these two were acting a little isolated scene. The man was blubbering and staring with sheeplike eyes at the lieutenant, who had seized him by the collar and was pommeling him. He drove him back into the ranks with many blows. The soldier went mechanically, dully, with his animal-like eyes upon the officer. Perhaps there was to him a divinity expressed in the voice of the other—stern, hard, with no reflection of fear in it. He tried to reload his gun, but his shaking hands prevented. The lieutenant was obliged to assist him. •

The men dropped here and there like bundles. The captain of the youth's company had been killed in an early part of the action. His body lay stretched out in the position of a tired man resting, but upon his face there was an astonished and sorrow-

ful look, as if he thought some friend had done him an ill turn.
The babbling man was grazed by a shot that made the blood
stream widely down his face. He clapped both hands to his
head. "Oh!" he said, and ran. Another grunted suddenly as if he
had been struck by a club in the stomach. He sat down and
gazed ruefully. In his eyes there was mute, indefinite reproach.
Farther up the line a man, standing behind a tree, had had his
knee joint splintered by a ball. Immediately he had dropped his
rifle and gripped the tree with both arms. And there he remained, clinging desperately and crying for assistance that he
might withdraw his hold upon the tree.

At last an exultant yell went along the quivering line. The firing dwindled from an uproar to a last vindictive popping. As the
smoke slowly eddied away, the youth saw that the charge had
been repulsed. The enemy were scattered into reluctant groups.
He saw a man climb to the top of the fence, straddle the rail, and
fire a parting shot. The waves had receded, leaving bits of dark
débris upon the ground.

Some in the regiment began to whoop frenziedly. Many
were silent. Apparently they were trying to contemplate themselves.

After the fever had left his veins, the youth thought that at
last he was going to suffocate. He became aware of the foul atmosphere in which he had been struggling. He was grimy and
dripping like a laborer in a foundry. He grasped his canteen and
took a long swallow of the warmed water.

A sentence with variations went up and down the line.
"Well, we've helt 'em back. We've helt 'em back; derned if we
haven't." The men said it blissfully, leering at each other with
dirty smiles.

The youth turned to look behind him and off to the right
and off to the left. He experienced the joy of a man who at last
finds leisure in which to look about him.

Under foot there were a few ghastly forms motionless. They
lay twisted in fantastic contortions. Arms were bent and heads
were turned in incredible ways. It seemed that the dead men
must have fallen from some great height to get into such posi-

tions. They looked to be dumped out upon the ground from the sky.

From a position in the rear of the grove a battery was throwing shells over it. The flash of the guns startled the youth at first. He thought they were aimed directly at him. Through the trees he watched the black figures of the gunners as they worked swiftly and intently. Their labor seemed a complicated thing. He wondered how they could remember its formula in the midst of confusion.

The guns squatted in a row like savage chiefs. They argued with abrupt violence. It was a grim pow-wow. Their busy servants ran hither and thither.

A small procession of wounded men were going drearily toward the rear. It was a flow of blood from the torn body of the brigade.

To the right and to the left were the dark lines of other troops. Far in front he thought he could see lighter masses protruding in points from the forest. They were suggestive of unnumbered thousands.

Once he saw a tiny battery go dashing along the line of the horizon. The tiny riders were beating the tiny horses.

From a sloping hill came the sound of cheerings and clashes. Smoke welled slowly through the leaves.

Batteries were speaking with thunderous oratorical effort. Here and there were flags, the red in the stripes dominating. They splashed bits of warm color upon the dark lines of troops.

The youth felt the old thrill at the sight of the emblem. They were like beautiful birds strangely undaunted in a storm.

As he listened to the din from the hillside, to a deep pulsating thunder that came from afar to the left, and to the lesser clamors which came from many directions, it occurred to him that they were fighting, too, over there, and over there, and over there. Heretofore he had supposed that all the battle was directly under his nose.

As he gazed around him the youth felt a flash of astonishment at the blue, pure sky and the sun gleamings on the trees and fields. It was surprising that Nature had gone tranquilly on with her golden process in the midst of so much devilment.

CHAPTER VI

THE YOUTH AWAKENED SLOWLY. He came gradually back to a position from which he could regard himself. For moments he had been scrutinizing his person in a dazed way as if he had never before seen himself. Then he picked up his cap from the ground. He wriggled in his jacket to make a more comfortable fit, and kneeling relaced his shoe. He thoughtfully mopped his reeking features.

So it was all over at last! The supreme trial had been passed. The red, formidable difficulties of war had been vanquished.

He went into an ecstasy of self-satisfaction. He had the most delightful sensations of his life. Standing as if apart from himself, he viewed that last scene. He perceived that the man who had fought thus was magnificent.

He felt that he was a fine fellow. He saw himself even with those ideals which he had considered as far beyond him. He smiled in deep gratification.

Upon his fellows he beamed tenderness and good will. "Gee! ain't it hot, hey?" he said affably to a man who was polishing his streaming face with his coat sleeves.

"You bet!" said the other, grinning sociably. "I never seen sech dumb hotness." He sprawled out luxuriously on the ground. "Gee, yes! An' I hope we don't have no more fightin' till a week from Monday."

There were some handshakings and deep speeches with men whose features were familiar, but with whom the youth now felt the bonds of tied hearts. He helped a cursing comrade to bind up a wound of the shin.

But, of a sudden, cries of amazement broke out along the ranks of the new regiment. "Here they come ag'in! Here they come ag'in!" The man who had sprawled upon the ground started up and said, "Gosh!"

The youth turned quick eyes upon the field. He discerned forms begin to swell in masses out of a distant wood. He again saw the tilted flag speeding forward.

41

The shells, which had ceased to trouble the regiment for a time, came swirling again, and exploded in the grass or among the leaves of the trees. They looked to be strange war flowers bursting into fierce bloom.

The men groaned. The luster faded from their eyes. Their smudged countenances now expressed a profound dejection. They moved their stiffened bodies slowly, and watched in sullen mood the frantic approach of the enemy. The slaves toiling in the temple of this god began to feel rebellion at his harsh tasks.

They fretted and complained each to each. "Oh, say, this is too much of a good thing! Why can't somebody send us supports?"

"We ain't never goin' to stand this second banging. I didn't come here to fight the hull damn' rebel army."

There was one who raised a doleful cry. "I wish Bill Smithers had trod on my hand, insteader me treddin' on his'n." The sore joints of the regiment creaked as it painfully floundered into position to repulse.

The youth stared. Surely, he thought, this impossible thing was not about to happen. He waited as if he expected the enemy to suddenly stop, apologize, and retire bowing. It was all a mistake.

But the firing began somewhere on the regimental line and ripped along in both directions. The level sheets of flame developed great clouds of smoke that tumbled and tossed in the mild wind near the ground for a moment, and then rolled through the ranks as through a gate. The clouds were tinged an earthlike yellow in the sunrays and in the shadow were a sorry blue. The flag was sometimes eaten and lost in this mass of vapor, but more often it projected, sun-touched, resplendent.

Into the youth's eyes there came a look that one can see in the orbs of a jaded horse. His neck was quivering with nervous weakness and the muscles of his arms felt numb and bloodless. His hands, too, seemed large and awkward as if he was wearing invisible mittens. And there was a great uncertainty about his knee joints.

The words that comrades had uttered previous to the firing began to recur to him. "Oh, say, this is too much of a good thing! What do they take us for—why don't they send supports? I didn't come here to fight the hull damned rebel army."

He began to exaggerate the endurance, the skill, and the valor of those who were coming. Himself reeling from exhaustion, he was astonished beyond measure at such persistency. They must be machines of steel. It was very gloomy struggling against such affairs, wound up perhaps to fight until sundown.

He slowly lifted his rifle and catching a glimpse of the thick-spread field he blazed at a cantering cluster. He stopped then and began to peer as best he could through the smoke. He caught changing views of the ground covered with men who were all running like pursued imps, and yelling.

To the youth it was an onslaught of redoubtable dragons. He became like the man who lost his legs at the approach of the red and green monster. He waited in a sort of a horrified, listening attitude. He seemed to shut his eyes and wait to be gobbled.

A man near him who up to this time had been working feverishly at his rifle suddenly stopped and ran with howls. A lad whose face had borne an expression of exalted courage, the majesty of he who dares give his life, was, at an instant, smitten abject. He blanched like one who has come to the edge of a cliff at midnight and is suddenly made aware. There was a revelation. He, too, threw down his gun and fled. There was no shame in his face. He ran like a rabbit.

Others began to scamper away through the smoke. The youth turned his head, shaken from his trance by this movement as if the regiment was leaving him behind. He saw the few fleeting forms.

He yelled then with fright and swung about. For a moment, in the great clamor, he was like a proverbial chicken. He lost the direction of safety. Destruction threatened him from all points.

Directly he began to speed toward the rear in great leaps. His rifle and cap were gone. His unbuttoned coat bulged in the wind. The flap of his cartridge box bobbed wildly, and his canteen, by its slender cord, swung out behind. On his face was all the horror of those things which he imagined.

The lieutenant sprang forward bawling. The youth saw his features wrathfully red, and saw him make a dab with his sword. His one thought of the incident was that the lieutenant was a peculiar creature to feel interested in such matters upon this occasion.

He ran like a blind man. Two or three times he fell down. Once he knocked his shoulder so heavily against a tree that he went headlong.

Since he had turned his back upon the fight his fears had been wondrously magnified. Death about to thrust him between the shoulder blades was far more dreadful than death about to smite him between the eyes. When he thought of it later, he conceived the impression that it is better to view the appalling than to be merely within hearing. The noises of the battle were like stones; he believed himself liable to be crushed.

As he ran on he mingled with others. He dimly saw men on his right and on his left, and he heard footsteps behind him. He thought that all the regiment was fleeing, pursued by these ominous crashes.

In his flight the sound of these following footsteps gave him his one meager relief. He felt vaguely that death must make a first choice of the men who were nearest; the initial morsels for the dragons would be then those who were following him. So he displayed the zeal of an insane sprinter in his purpose to keep them in the rear. There was a race.

As he, leading, went across a little field, he found himself in a region of shells. They hurtled over his head with long wild screams. As he listened he imagined them to have rows of cruel teeth that grinned at him. Once one lit before him and the livid lightning of the explosion effectually barred the way in his chosen direction. He groveled on the ground and then springing up went careering off through some bushes.

He experienced a thrill of amazement when he came within view of a battery in action. The men there seemed to be in conventional moods, altogether unaware of the impending annihilation. The battery was disputing with a distant antagonist and the gunners were wrapped in admiration of their shooting. They were continually bending in coaxing postures over the guns. They seemed to be patting them on the back and encouraging them with words. The guns, stolid and undaunted, spoke with dogged valor.

The precise gunners were coolly enthusiastic. They lifted their eyes every chance to the smoke-wreathed hillock from whence the hostile battery addressed them. The youth pitied them as he ran. Methodical idiots! Machine-like fools! The refined joy of planting shells in the midst of the other battery's formation would appear a little thing when the infantry came swooping out of the woods.

The face of a youthful rider, who was jerking his frantic horse with an abandon of temper he might display in a placid barnyard, was impressed deeply upon his mind. He knew that he looked upon a man who would presently be dead.

Too, he felt a pity for the guns, standing, six good comrades, in a bold row.

He saw a brigade going to the relief of its pestered fellows. He scrambled upon a wee hill and watched it sweeping finely, keeping formation in difficult places. The blue of the line was crusted with steel color, and the brilliant flags projected. Officers were shouting.

This sight also filled him with wonder. The brigade was hurrying briskly to be gulped into the infernal mouths of the war god. What manner of men were they, anyhow? Ah, it was some wondrous breed! Or else they didn't comprehend—the fools.

A furious order caused commotion in the artillery. An officer on a bounding horse made maniacal motions with his arms. The teams went swinging up from the rear, the guns were whirled about, and the battery scampered away. The cannon with their noses poked slantingly at the ground grunted and grumbled like stout men, brave but with objections to hurry.

The youth went on, moderating his pace since he had left the place of noises.

Later he came upon a general of division seated upon a horse that pricked its ears in an interested way at the battle.[24] There was a great gleaming of yellow and patent leather about the saddle and bridle. The quiet man astride looked mouse-colored upon such a splendid charger.

A jingling staff was galloping hither and thither. Sometimes the general was surrounded by horsemen and at other times he was quite alone. He looked to be much harassed. He had the appearance of a business man whose market is swinging up and down.

The youth went slinking around this spot. He went as near as he dared trying to overhear words. Perhaps the general, unable to comprehend chaos, might call upon him for information. And he could tell him. He knew all concerning it. Of a surety the force was in a fix, and any fool could see that if they did not retreat while they had opportunity—why——

He felt that he would like to thrash the general, or at least approach and tell him in plain words exactly what he thought him to be. It was criminal to stay calmly in one spot and make no effort to stay destruction. He loitered in a fever of eagerness for the division commander to apply to him.

As he warily moved about, he heard the general call out irritably: "Tompkins, go over an' see Taylor, an' tell him not t' be in such an all-fired hurry; tell him t' halt his brigade in th' edge of th' woods; tell him t' detach a reg'ment—say I think th' center 'll break if we don't help it out some; tell him t' hurry up."

A slim youth on a fine chestnut horse caught these swift words from the mouth of his superior. He made his horse bound into a gallop almost from a walk in his haste to go upon his mission. There was a cloud of dust.

A moment later the youth saw the general bounce excitedly in his saddle.

"Yes, by heavens, they have!" The officer leaned forward. His face was aflame with excitement. "Yes, by heavens, they've held 'im! They've held 'im!"

He began to blithely roar at his staff: "We'll wallop 'im now. We'll wallop 'im now. We've got 'em sure." He turned suddenly upon an aid: "Here—you—Jones—quick—ride after Tompkins—see Taylor—tell him t' go in—everlastingly—like blazes—anything."

As another officer sped his horse after the first messenger, the general beamed upon the earth like a sun. In his eyes was a desire to chant a pæan. He kept repeating, "They've held 'em, by heavens!"

His excitement made his horse plunge, and he merrily kicked and swore at it. He held a little carnival of joy on horseback.

CHAPTER VII

THE YOUTH CRINGED AS if discovered in a crime. By heavens, they had won after all! The imbecile line had remained and become victors. He could hear cheering.

He lifted himself upon his toes and looked in the direction of the fight. A yellow fog lay wallowing on the treetops. From beneath it came the clatter of musketry. Hoarse cries told of an advance.

He turned away amazed and angry. He felt that he had been wronged.

He had fled, he told himself, because annihilation approached. He had done a good part in saving himself, who was a little piece of the army. He had considered the time, he said, to be one in which it was the duty of every little piece to rescue itself if possible. Later the officers could fit the little pieces together again, and make a battle front. If none of the little pieces were wise enough to save themselves from the flurry of death at such a time, why, then, where would be the army? It was all plain that he had proceeded according to very correct and commendable rules. His actions had been sagacious things. They had been full of strategy. They were the work of a master's legs.

Thoughts of his comrades came to him. The brittle blue line had withstood the blows and won. He grew bitter over it. It seemed that the blind ignorance and stupidity of those little pieces had betrayed him. He had been overturned and crushed by their lack of sense in holding the position, when intelligent deliberation would have convinced them that it was impossible. He, the enlightened man who looks afar in the dark, had fled because of his superior perceptions and knowledge. He felt a great anger against his comrades. He knew it could be proved that they had been fools.

He wondered what they would remark when later he appeared in camp. His mind heard howls of derision. Their density would not enable them to understand his sharper point of view.

He began to pity himself acutely. He was ill used. He was

trodden beneath the feet of an iron injustice. He had proceeded with wisdom and from the most righteous motives under heaven's blue only to be frustrated by hateful circumstances.

A dull, animal-like rebellion against his fellows, war in the abstract, and fate grew within him. He shambled along with bowed head, his brain in a tumult of agony and despair. When he looked loweringly up, quivering at each sound, his eyes had the expression of those of a criminal who thinks his guilt and his punishment great, and knows that he can find no words.

He went from the fields into a thick wood, as if resolved to bury himself. He wished to get out of hearing of the crackling shots which were to him like voices.

The ground was cluttered with vines and bushes, and the trees grew close and spread out like bouquets. He was obliged to force his way with much noise. The creepers, catching against his legs, cried out harshly as their sprays were torn from the barks of trees. The swishing saplings tried to make known his presence to the world. He could not conciliate the forest. As he made his way, it was always calling out protestations. When he separated embraces of trees and vines the disturbed foliages waved their arms and turned their face leaves toward him. He dreaded lest these noisy motions and cries should bring men to look at him. So he went far, seeking dark and intricate places.

After a time the sound of musketry grew faint and the cannon boomed in the distance. The sun, suddenly apparent, blazed among the trees. The insects were making rhythmical noises. They seemed to be grinding their teeth in unison. A woodpecker stuck his impudent head around the side of a tree. A bird flew on lighthearted wing.

Off was the rumble of death. It seemed now that Nature had no ears.

This landscape gave him assurance. A fair field holding life. It was the religion of peace. It would die if its timid eyes were compelled to see blood. He conceived Nature to be a woman with a deep aversion to tragedy.

He threw a pine cone at a jovial squirrel, and he ran with chattering fear. High in a treetop he stopped, and, poking his head cautiously from behind a branch, looked down with a air of trepidation.

The youth felt triumphant at this exhibition. There was the law, he said. Nature had given him a sign. The squirrel, immediately upon recognizing danger, had taken to his legs without ado. He did not stand stolidly baring his furry belly to the missile, and die with an upward glance at the sympathetic heavens. On the contrary, he had fled as fast as his legs could carry him; and he was but an ordinary squirrel, too—doubtless no philosopher of his race. The youth wended, feeling that Nature was of his mind. She re-enforced his argument with proofs that lived where the sun shone.

Once he found himself almost into a swamp. He was obliged to walk upon bog tufts and watch his feet to keep from the oily mire. Pausing at one time to look about him he saw, out at some black water, a small animal pounce in and emerge directly with a gleaming fish.

The youth went again into the deep thickets. The brushed branches made a noise that drowned the sounds of cannon. He walked on, going from obscurity into promises of a greater obscurity.

At length he reached a place where the high, arching boughs made a chapel. He softly pushed the green doors aside and entered. Pine needles were a gentle brown carpet. There was a religious half light.

Near the threshold he stopped, horror-stricken at the sight of a thing.

He was being looked at by a dead man who was seated with his back against a columnlike tree. The corpse was dressed in a uniform that once had been blue, but was now faded to a melancholy shade of green. The eyes, staring at the youth, had changed to the dull hue to be seen on the side of a dead fish. The mouth was open. Its red had changed to an appalling yellow. Over the gray skin of the face ran little ants. One was trundling some sort of a bundle along the upper lip.

The youth gave a shriek as he confronted the thing. He was for moments turned to stone before it. He remained staring into the liquid-looking eyes. The dead man and the living man exchanged a long look. Then the youth cautiously put one hand behind him and brought it against a tree. Leaning upon this he retreated, step by step, with his face still toward the thing. He feared that if he turned his back the body might spring up and stealthily pursue him.

The branches, pushing against him, threatened to throw him over upon it. His unguided feet, too, caught aggravatingly in brambles; and with it all he received a subtle suggestion to touch the corpse. As he thought of his hand upon it he shuddered profoundly.

At last he burst the bonds which had fastened him to the spot and fled, unheeding the underbrush. He was pursued by a sight of the black ants swarming greedily upon the gray face and venturing horribly near to the eyes.

After a time he paused, and, breathless and panting, listened. He imagined some strange voice would come from the dead throat and squawk after him in horrible menaces.

The trees about the portal of the chapel moved soughingly in a soft wind. A sad silence was upon the little guarding edifice.

CHAPTER VIII

THE TREES BEGAN SOFTLY to sing a hymn of twilight. The sun sank until slanted bronze rays struck the forest. There was a lull in the noises of insects as if they had bowed their beaks and were making a devotional pause. There was silence save for the chanted chorus of the trees.

Then, upon this stillness, there suddenly broke a tremendous clangor of sounds. A crimson roar came from the distance.

The youth stopped. He was transfixed by this terrific medley of all noises. It was as if worlds were being rended. There was the ripping sound of musketry and the breaking crash of the artillery.

His mind flew in all directions. He conceived the two armies to be at each other panther fashion. He listened for a time. Then he began to run in the direction of the battle. He saw that it was an ironical thing for him to be running thus toward that which he had been at such pains to avoid. But he said, in substance, to himself that if the earth and the moon were about to clash, many persons would doubtless plan to get upon the roofs to witness the collision.

As he ran, he became aware that the forest had stopped its music, as if at last becoming capable of hearing the foreign sounds. The trees hushed and stood motionless. Everything seemed to be listening to the crackle and clatter and ear-shaking thunder. The chorus pealed over the still earth.

It suddenly occurred to the youth that the fight in which he had been was, after all, but perfunctory popping. In the hearing of this present din he was doubtful if he had seen real battle scenes. This uproar explained a celestial battle; it was tumbling hordes a-struggle in the air.

Reflecting, he saw a sort of a humor in the point of view of himself and his fellows during the late encounter. They had taken themselves and the enemy very seriously and had imagined that they were deciding the war. Individuals must have supposed that they were cutting the letters of their names deep into everlasting tablets of brass, or enshrining their reputations forever in the hearts of their countrymen, while, as to fact, the affair would appear in printed reports under a meek and immaterial title. But he saw that it was good, else, he said, in battle every one would surely run save forlorn hopes and their ilk.

He went rapidly on. He wished to come to the edge of the forest that he might peer out.

As he hastened, there passed through his mind pictures of stupendous conflicts. His accumulated thought upon such subjects was used to form scenes. The noise was as the voice of an eloquent being, describing.

Sometimes the brambles formed chains and tried to hold him back. Trees, confronting him, stretched out their arms and forbade him to pass. After its previous hostility this new resistance of the forest filled him with a fine bitterness. It seemed that Nature could not be quite ready to kill him.

But he obstinately took roundabout ways, and presently he was where he could see long gray walls of vapor where lay battle lines. The voices of cannon shook him. The musketry sounded in long irregular surges that played havoc with his ears. He stood regardant for a moment. His eyes had an awestruck expression. He gawked in the direction of the fight.

Presently he proceeded again on his forward way. The battle was like the grinding of an immense and terrible machine to him. Its complexities and powers, its grim processes, fascinated him. He must go close and see it produce corpses.

He came to a fence and clambered over it. On the far side, the ground was littered with clothes and guns. A newspaper, folded up, lay in the dirt. A dead soldier was stretched with his face hidden in his arm. Farther off there was a group of four or five corpses keeping mournful company. A hot sun had blazed upon the spot.

In this place the youth felt that he was an invader. This forgotten part of the battle ground was owned by the dead men, and he hurried, in the vague apprehension that one of the swollen forms would rise and tell him to begone.

He came finally to a road from which he could see in the distance dark and agitated bodies of troops, smoke-fringed. In the lane was a blood-stained crowd streaming to the rear. The wounded men were cursing, groaning, and wailing. In the air, always, was a mighty swell of sound that it seemed could sway the earth. With the courageous words of the artillery and the spiteful sentences of the musketry mingled red cheers. And from this region of noises came the steady current of the maimed.

One of the wounded men had a shoeful of blood. He hopped like a schoolboy in a game. He was laughing hysterically.

One was swearing that he had been shot in the arm through the commanding general's mismanagement of the army. One was marching with an air imitative of some sublime drum major.[25] Upon his features was an unholy mixture of merriment and agony. As he marched he sang a bit of doggerel in a high and quavering voice:

> "Sing a song 'a vic'try,
> A pocketful 'a bullets,
> Five an' twenty dead men
> Baked in a—pie."[26]

Parts of the procession limped and staggered to this tune.

Another had the gray seal of death already upon his face. His lips were curled in hard lines and his teeth were clinched. His hands were bloody from where he had pressed them upon his wound. He seemed to be awaiting the moment when he should pitch headlong. He stalked like the specter of a soldier, his eyes burning with the power of a stare into the unknown.[27]

There were some who proceeded sullenly, full of anger at their wounds, and ready to turn upon anything as an obscure cause.

An officer was carried along by two privates. He was peevish. "Don't joggle so, Johnson, yeh fool," he cried. "Think m' leg is made of iron? If yeh can't carry me decent, put me down an' let someone else do it."

He bellowed at the tottering crowd who blocked the quick

march of his bearers. "Say, make way there, can't yeh? Make way, dickens take it all."

They sulkily parted and went to the roadsides. As he was carried past they made pert remarks to him. When he raged in reply and threatened them, they told him to be damned.

The shoulder of one of the tramping bearers knocked heavily against the spectral soldier who was staring into the unknown.

The youth joined this crowd and marched along with it. The torn bodies expressed the awful machinery in which the men had been entangled.

Orderlies and couriers occasionally broke through the throng in the roadway, scattering wounded men right and left, galloping on followed by howls. The melancholy march was continually disturbed by the messengers, and sometimes by bustling batteries that came swinging and thumping down upon them, the officers shouting orders to clear the way.

There was a tattered man, fouled with dust, blood and powder stain from hair to shoes, who trudged quietly at the youth's side.[28] He was listening with eagerness and much humility to the lurid descriptions of a bearded sergeant. His lean features wore an expression of awe and admiration. He was like a listener in a country store to wondrous tales told among the sugar barrels. He eyed the story-teller with unspeakable wonder. His mouth was agape in yokel fashion.

The sergeant, taking note of this, gave pause to his elaborate history while he administered a sardonic comment. "Be keerful, honey, you'll be a-ketchin' flies," he said.

The tattered man shrank back abashed.

After a time he began to sidle near to the youth, and in a different way try to make him a friend. His voice was gentle as a girl's voice and his eyes were pleading. The youth saw with surprise that the soldier had two wounds, one in the head, bound with a blood-soaked rag, and the other in the arm, making that member dangle like a broken bough.

After they had walked together for some time the tattered man mustered sufficient courage to speak. "Was pretty good fight, wa'n't it?" he timidly said. The youth, deep in thought, glanced up at the bloody and grim figure with its lamblike eyes. "What?"

"Was pretty good fight, wa'n't it?"

"Yes," said the youth shortly. He quickened his pace.

But the other hobbled industriously after him. There was an air of apology in his manner, but he evidently thought that he needed only to talk for a time, and the youth would perceive that he was a good fellow.

"Was pretty good fight, wa'n't it?" he began in a small voice, and then he achieved the fortitude to continue. "Dern me if I ever see fellers fight so. Laws,* how they did fight! I knowed th' boys 'd like when they onct got square at it. Th' boys ain't had no fair chanct up t' now, but this time they showed what they was. I knowed it'd turn out this way. Yeh can't lick them boys. No, sir! They're fighters, they be."

He breathed a deep breath of humble admiration. He had looked at the youth for encouragement several times. He received none, but gradually he seemed to get absorbed in his subject.

"I was talkin' 'cross pickets with a boy from Georgie, onct, an' that boy, he ses, 'Your fellers 'll all run like hell when they onct hearn a gun,' he ses. 'Mebbe they will,' I ses, 'but I don't b'lieve none of it,' I ses; 'an' b'jiminey,' I ses back t' 'um, 'mebbe your fellers 'll all run like hell when they onct hearn a gun,' I ses. He larfed. Well, they didn't run t' day, did they, hey? No, sir! They fit, an' fit, an' fit."

His homely face was suffused with a light of love for the army which was to him all things beautiful and powerful.

After a time he turned to the youth. "Where yeh hit, ol' boy?" he asked in a brotherly tone.

The youth felt instant panic at this question, although at first its full import was not borne in upon him.

"What?" he asked.

"Where yeh hit?" repeated the tattered man.

"Why," began the youth, "I—I—that is—why—I——"

---

* Colloquialism for the mild oath Lord!

He turned away suddenly and slid through the crowd. His brow was heavily flushed, and his fingers were picking nervously at one of his buttons. He bent his head and fastened his eyes studiously upon the button as if it were a little problem.

The tattered man looked after him in astonishment.

CHAPTER IX

THE YOUTH FELL BACK in the procession until the tattered soldier was not in sight. Then he started to walk on with the others.

But he was amid wounds. The mob of men was bleeding. Because of the tattered soldier's question he now felt that his shame could be viewed. He was continually casting sidelong glances to see if the men were contemplating the letters of guilt he felt burned into his brow.

At times he regarded the wounded soldiers in an envious way. He conceived persons with torn bodies to be peculiarly happy. He wished that he, too, had a wound, a red badge of courage.

The spectral soldier was at his side like a stalking reproach. The man's eyes were still fixed in a stare into the unknown. His gray, appalling face had attracted attention in the crowd, and men, slowing to his dreary pace, were walking with him. They were discussing his plight, questioning him and giving him advice. In a dogged way he repelled them, signing to them to go on and leave him alone. The shadows of his face were deepening and his tight lips seemed holding in check the moan of great despair. There could be seen a certain stiffness in the movements of his body, as if he were taking infinite care not to arouse the passion of his wounds. As he went on, he seemed always looking for a place, like one who goes to choose a grave.

Something in the gesture of the man as he waved the bloody and pitying soldiers away made the youth start as if bitten. He yelled in horror. Tottering forward he laid a quivering hand upon the man's arm. As the latter slowly turned his waxlike features toward him, the youth screamed:

"Gawd! Jim Conklin!"

The tall soldier made a little commonplace smile. "Hello, Henry," he said.

The youth swayed on his legs and glared strangely. He stuttered and stammered. "Oh, Jim—oh, Jim—oh, Jim——"

The tall soldier held out his gory hand. There was a curious red and black combination of new blood and old blood upon it.

"Where yeh been, Henry?" he asked. He continued in a monot-onous voice, "I thought mebbe yeh got keeled over. There's been thunder t' pay t'-day. I was worryin' about it a good deal."

The youth still lamented. "Oh, Jim—oh, Jim—oh, Jim——"

"Yeh know," said the tall soldier, "I was out there." He made a careful gesture. "An', Lord, what a circus! An', b'jiminey, I got shot—I got shot. Yes, b'jiminey, I got shot." He reiterated this fact in a bewildered way, as if he did not know how it came about.

The youth put forth anxious arms to assist him, but the tall soldier went firmly on as if propelled. Since the youth's arrival as a guardian for his friend, the other wounded men had ceased to display much interest. They occupied themselves again in dragging their own tragedies toward the rear.

Suddenly, as the two friends marched on, the tall soldier seemed to be overcome by a terror. His face turned to a sem-blance of gray paste. He clutched the youth's arm and looked all about him, as if dreading to be overheard. Then he began to speak in a shaking whisper:

"I tell yeh what I'm 'fraid of, Henry—I'll tell yeh what I'm 'fraid of. I'm 'fraid I'll fall down—an' then yeh know—them damned artillery wagons—they like as not 'll run over me. That's what I'm 'fraid of——"

The youth cried out to him hysterically: "I'll take care of yeh, Jim! I'll take care of yeh! I swear t' Gawd I will!"

"Sure—will yeh, Henry?" the tall soldier beseeched.

"Yes—yes—I tell yeh—I'll take care of yeh, Jim!" protested the youth. He could not speak accurately because of the gulp-ings in his throat.

But the tall soldier continued to beg in a lowly way. He now hung babelike to the youth's arm. His eyes rolled in the wild-ness of his terror. "I was allus a good friend t' yeh, wa'n't I, Henry? I've allus been a pretty good feller, ain't I? An' it ain't much t' ask, is it? Jest t' pull me along outer th' road? I'd do it fer you, wouldn't I, Henry?"

He paused in piteous anxiety to await his friend's reply.

The youth had reached an anguish where the sobs scorched him. He strove to express his loyalty, but he could only make fantastic gestures.

However, the tall soldier seemed suddenly to forget all those fears. He became again the grim, stalking specter of a soldier. He went stonily forward. The youth wished his friend to lean upon him, but the other always shook his head and strangely protested. "No—no—no—leave me be—leave me be——"

His look was fixed again upon the unknown. He moved with mysterious purpose, and all of the youth's offers he brushed aside. "No—no—leave me be—leave me be——"

The youth had to follow.

Presently the latter heard a voice talking softly near his shoulders. Turning he saw that it belonged to the tattered soldier. "Ye'd better take 'im outa th' road, pardner. There's a batt'ry comin' helitywhoop* down th' road an' he'll git runned over. He's a goner anyhow in about five minutes—yeh kin see that. Ye'd better take 'im outa th' road. Where th' blazes does he git his stren'th from?"

"Lord knows!" cried the youth. He was shaking his hands helplessly.

He ran forward presently and grasped the tall soldier by the arm. "Jim! Jim!" he coaxed, "come with me."

The tall soldier weakly tried to wrench himself free. "Huh," he said vacantly. He stared at the youth for a moment. At last he spoke as if dimly comprehending. "Oh! Inteh th' fields? Oh!"

He started blindly through the grass.

The youth turned once to look at the lashing riders and jouncing guns of the battery. He was startled from this view by a shrill outcry from the tattered man.

"Gawd! He's runnin'!"

Turning his head swiftly, the youth saw his friend running in a staggering and stumbling way toward a little clump of bushes. His heart seemed to wrench itself almost free from his body at this sight. He made a noise of pain. He and the tattered man began a pursuit. There was a singular race.

When he overtook the tall soldier he began to plead with all the words he could find. "Jim—Jim—what are you doing— what makes you do this way—you'll hurt yerself."

---

*Variation of the dialect term *hellwhoop*; means "at great speed."

The same purpose was in the tall soldier's face. He protested in a dulled way, keeping his eyes fastened on the mystic place of his intentions. "No—no—don't tech me—leave me be—leave me be——"

The youth, aghast and filled with wonder at the tall soldier, began quaveringly to question him. "Where yeh goin', Jim? What you thinking about? Where you going? Tell me, won't you, Jim?"

The tall soldier faced about as upon relentless pursuers. In his eyes there was a great appeal. "Leave me be, can't yeh? Leave me be fer a minnit."

The youth recoiled. "Why, Jim," he said, in a dazed way, "what's the matter with you?"

The tall soldier turned and, lurching dangerously, went on. The youth and the tattered soldier followed, sneaking as if whipped, feeling unable to face the stricken man if he should again confront them. They began to have thoughts of a solemn ceremony. There was something rite-like in these movements of the doomed soldier. And there was a resemblance in him to a devotee of a mad religion, blood-sucking, muscle-wrenching, bone-crushing. They were awed and afraid. They hung back lest he have at command a dreadful weapon.

At last, they saw him stop and stand motionless. Hastening up, they perceived that his face wore an expression telling that he had at last found the place for which he had struggled. His spare figure was erect; his bloody hands were quietly at his side. He was waiting with patience for something that he had come to meet. He was at the rendezvous. They paused and stood, expectant.

There was a silence.

Finally, the chest of the doomed soldier began to heave with a strained motion. It increased in violence until it was as if an animal was within and was kicking and tumbling furiously to be free.

This spectacle of gradual strangulation made the youth writhe, and once as his friend rolled his eyes, he saw something in them that made him sink wailing to the ground. He raised his voice in a last supreme call.

"Jim—Jim—Jim——"

The tall soldier opened his lips and spoke. He made a gesture. "Leave me be—don't tech me—leave me be——"

There was another silence while he waited.

Suddenly, his form stiffened and straightened. Then it was shaken by a prolonged ague. He stared into space. To the two watchers there was a curious and profound dignity in the firm lines of his awful face.

He was invaded by a creeping strangeness that slowly enveloped him. For a moment the tremor of his legs caused him to dance a sort of hideous hornpipe.* His arms beat wildly about his head in expression of implike enthusiasm.

His tall figure stretched itself to its full height. There was a slight rending sound. Then it began to swing forward, slow and straight, in the manner of a falling tree. A swift muscular contortion made the left shoulder strike the ground first.

The body seemed to bounce a little way from the earth. "God!" said the tattered soldier.

The youth had watched, spellbound, this ceremony at the place of meeting. His face had been twisted into an expression of every agony he had imagined for his friend.

He now sprang to his feet and, going closer, gazed upon the pastelike face. The mouth was open and the teeth showed in a laugh.

As the flap of the blue jacket fell away from the body, he could see that the side looked as if it had been chewed by wolves.

The youth turned, with sudden, livid rage, toward the battlefield. He shook his fist. He seemed about to deliver a philippic.†

"Hell——"

The red sun was pasted in the sky like a wafer.[29]

---

* Lively folk dance, usually performed alone and so named because it was originally accompanied by a musical instrument called a hornpipe; once popular among British sailors.

† A particularly derisive denunciation.

CHAPTER X

THE TATTERED MAN STOOD musing.

"Well, he was reg'lar jim-dandy* fer nerve, wa'n't he," said he finally in a little awestruck voice. "A reg'lar jim-dandy." He thoughtfully poked one of the docile hands with his foot. "I wonner where he got 'is stren'th from? I never seen a man do like that before. It was a funny thing. Well, he was a reg'lar jim-dandy."

The youth desired to screech out his grief. He was stabbed, but his tongue lay dead in the tomb of his mouth. He threw himself again upon the ground and began to brood.

The tattered man stood musing.

"Look-a-here, pardner," he said, after a time. He regarded the corpse as he spoke. "He's up an' gone, ain't 'e, an' we might as well begin t' look out fer ol' number one. This here thing is all over. He's up an' gone, ain't 'e? An' he's all right here. Nobody won't bother 'im. An' I must say I ain't enjoying any great health m'self these days."

The youth, awakened by the tattered soldier's tone, looked quickly up. He saw that he was swinging uncertainly on his legs and that his face had turned to a shade of blue.

"Good Lord!" he cried, "you ain't goin' t'—not you, too."

The tattered man waved his hand. "Nary die," he said. "All I want is some pea soup an' a good bed. Some pea soup," he repeated dreamfully.

The youth arose from the ground. "I wonder where he came from. I left him over there." He pointed. "And now I find 'im here. And he was coming from over there, too." He indicated a new direction. They both turned toward the body as if to ask of it a question.

---

* Popular slang for "exceedingly fine," from the nineteenth-century aesthetic movement that affected extravagant elegance in dress and deportment.

"Well," at length spoke the tattered man, "there ain't no use in our stayin' here an' tryin' t' ask him anything."

The youth nodded an assent wearily. They both turned to gaze for a moment at the corpse.

The youth murmured something.

"Well, he was a jim-dandy, wa'n't 'e?" said the tattered man as if in response.

They turned their backs upon it and started away. For a time they stole softly, treading with their toes. It remained laughing there in the grass.

"I'm commencin' t' feel pretty bad," said the tattered man, suddenly breaking one of his little silences. "I'm commencin' t' feel pretty damn' bad."

The youth groaned. "O Lord!" He wondered if he was to be the tortured witness of another grim encounter.

But his companion waved his hand reassuringly. "Oh, I'm not goin' t' die yit! There too much dependin' on me fer me t' die yit. No, sir! Nary die! I *can't*! Ye'd oughta see th' swad* a' chil'ren I've got, an' all like that."

The youth glancing at his companion could see by the shadow of a smile that he was making some kind of fun.

As they plodded on the tattered soldier continued to talk. "Besides, if I died, I wouldn't die th' way that feller did. That was th' funniest thing. I'd jest flop down, I would. I never seen a feller die th' way that feller did.

"Yeh know Tom Jamison, he lives next door t' me up home. He's a nice feller, he is, an' we was allus good friends. Smart, too. Smart as a steel trap. Well, when we was a-fightin' this afternoon, all-of-a-sudden he begin t' rip up an' cuss an' beller at me. 'Yer shot, yeh blamed infernal!'—he swear horrible—he ses t' me. I put up m' hand t' m' head an' when I looked at m' fingers, I seen, sure 'nough, I was shot. I give a holler an' begin t' run, but b'fore I could git away another one hit me in th' arm an' whirl' me clean 'round. I got skeared when they was all a-shootin' b'hind me an' I run t' beat all, but I cotch it pretty bad. I've an idee I'd a' been fightin' yit, if t'was n't fer Tom Jamison."

---

* American colloquialism for "a bunch."

Then he made a calm announcement: "There's two of 'em—little ones—but they're beginnin' t' have fun with me now. I don't b'lieve I kin walk much furder."

They went slowly on in silence. "Yeh look pretty peek-ed yerself," said the tattered man at last. "I bet yeh've got a worser one than yeh think. Ye'd better take keer of yer hurt. It don't do t' let sech things go. It might be inside mostly, an' them plays thunder. Where is it located?" But he continued his harangue without waiting for a reply. "I see 'a feller git hit plum in th' head when my reg'ment was a-standin' at ease onct. An' everybody yelled out to 'im: Hurt, John? Are yeh hurt much? 'No,' ses he. He looked kinder surprised, an' he went on tellin' 'em how he felt. He sed he didn't feel nothin'. But, by dad, th' first thing that feller knowed he was dead. Yes, he was dead—stone dead. So, yeh wanta watch out. Yeh might have some queer kind 'a hurt yerself. Yeh can't never tell. Where is your'n located?"

The youth had been wriggling since the introduction of this topic. He now gave a cry of exasperation and made a furious motion with his hand. "Oh, don't bother me!" he said. He was enraged against the tattered man, and could have strangled him. His companions seemed ever to play intolerable parts. They were ever upraising the ghost of shame on the stick of their curiosity. He turned toward the tattered man as one at bay. "Now, don't bother me," he repeated with desperate menace.

"Well, Lord knows I don't wanta bother anybody," said the other. There was a little accent of despair in his voice as he replied, "Lord knows I've gota 'nough m' own t' tend to."

The youth, who had been holding a bitter debate with himself and casting glances of hatred and contempt at the tattered man, here spoke in a hard voice. "Good-by," he said.

The tattered man looked at him in gaping amazement. "Why—why, pardner, where yeh goin'?" he asked unsteadily. The youth looking at him, could see that he, too, like that other one, was beginning to act dumb and animal-like. His thoughts seemed to be floundering about in his head. "Now—now—look—a—here, you Tom Jamison—now—I won't have this—this here won't do. Where—where yeh goin'?"

The youth pointed vaguely. "Over there," he replied.

"Well, now look—a—here—now," said the tattered man, rambling on in idiot fashion. His head was hanging forward and his words were slurred. "This thing won't do, now, Tom Jamison. It won't do. I know yeh, yeh pig-headed devil. Yeh wanta go trompin' off with a bad hurt. It ain't right—now— Tom Jamison—it ain't. Yeh wanta leave me take keer of yeh, Tom Jamison. It ain't—right—it ain't—fer yeh t' go—trompin' off—with a bad hurt—it ain't—ain't—ain't right—it ain't."

In reply the youth climbed a fence and started away. He could hear the tattered man bleating plaintively.

Once he faced about angrily. "What?"

"Look—a—here, now, Tom Jamison—now—it ain't——"

The youth went on. Turning at a distance he saw the tattered man wandering about helplessly in the field.

He now thought that he wished he was dead. He believed that he envied those men whose bodies lay strewn over the grass of the fields and on the fallen leaves of the forest.

The simple questions of the tattered man had been knife thrusts to him. They asserted a society that probes pitilessly at secrets until all is apparent. His late companion's chance persistency made him feel that he could not keep his crime concealed in his bosom. It was sure to be brought plain by one of those arrows which cloud the air and are constantly pricking, discovering, proclaiming those things which are willed to be forever hidden. He admitted that he could not defend himself against this agency. It was not within the power of vigilance.

CHAPTER XI

HE BECAME AWARE THAT the furnace roar of the battle was growing louder. Great brown clouds had floated to the still heights of air before him. The noise, too, was approaching. The woods filtered men and the fields became dotted.

As he rounded a hillock, he perceived that the roadway was now a crying mass of wagons, teams, and men. From the heaving tangle issued exhortations, commands, imprecations. Fear was sweeping it all along. The cracking whips bit and horses plunged and tugged. The white-topped wagons strained and stumbled in their exertions like fat sheep.

The youth felt comforted in a measure by this sight. They were all retreating. Perhaps, then, he was not so bad after all. He seated himself and watched the terror-stricken wagons. They fled like soft, ungainly animals. All the roarers and lashers served to help him to magnify the dangers and horrors of the engagement that he might try to prove to himself that the thing with which men could charge him was in truth a symmetrical act. There was an amount of pleasure to him in watching the wild march of this vindication.

Presently the calm head of a forward-going column of infantry appeared in the road. It came swiftly on. Avoiding the obstructions gave it the sinuous movement of a serpent. The men at the head butted mules with their musket stocks. They prodded teamsters indifferent to all howls. The men forced their way through parts of the dense mass by strength. The blunt head of the column pushed. The raving teamsters swore many strange oaths.

The commands to make way had the ring of a great importance in them. The men were going forward to the heart of the din. They were to confront the eager rush of the enemy. They felt the pride of their onward movement when the remainder of the army seemed trying to dribble down this road. They tumbled teams about with a fine feeling that it was no matter so long as their column got to the front in time. This importance made their faces grave and stern. And the backs of the officers were very rigid.

As the youth looked at them the black weight of his woe returned to him. He felt that he was regarding a procession of chosen beings. The separation was as great to him as if they had marched with weapons of flame and banners of sunlight. He could never be like them. He could have wept in his longings.

He searched about in his mind for an adequate malediction for the indefinite cause, the thing upon which men turn the words of final blame. It—whatever it was—was responsible for him, he said. There lay the fault.

The haste of the column to reach the battle seemed to the forlorn young man to be something much finer than stout fighting. Heroes, he thought, could find excuses in that long seething lane. They could retire with perfect self-respect and make excuses to the stars.

He wondered what those men had eaten that they could be in such haste to force their way to grim chances of death. As he watched his envy grew until he thought that he wished to change lives with one of them. He would have liked to have used a tremendous force, he said, throw off himself and become a better. Swift pictures of himself, apart, yet in himself, came to him—a blue desperate figure leading lurid charges with one knee forward and a broken blade high—a blue, determined figure standing before a crimson and steel assault, getting calmly killed on a high place before the eyes of all. He thought of the magnificent pathos of his dead body.

These thoughts uplifted him. He felt the quiver of war desire. In his ears, he heard the ring of victory. He knew the frenzy of a rapid successful charge. The music of the trampling feet, the sharp voices, the clanking arms of the column near him made him soar on the red wings of war. For a few moments he was sublime.

He thought that he was about to start for the front. Indeed, he saw a picture of himself, dust-stained, haggard, panting, flying to the front at the proper moment to seize and throttle the dark, leering witch of calamity.

Then the difficulties of the thing began to drag at him. He hesitated, balancing awkwardly on one foot.

He had no rifle; he could not fight with his hands, said he resentfully to his plan. Well, rifles could be had for the picking. They were extraordinarily profuse.

Also, he continued, it would be a miracle if he found his regiment. Well, he could fight with any regiment.

He started forward slowly. He stepped as if he expected to tread upon some explosive thing. Doubts and he were struggling.

He would truly be a worm if any of his comrades should see him returning thus, the marks of his flight upon him. There was a reply that the intent fighters did not care for what happened rearward saving that no hostile bayonets appeared there. In the battle-blur his face would, in a way be hidden, like the face of a cowled man.

But then he said that his tireless fate would bring forth, when the strife lulled for a moment, a man to ask of him an explanation. In imagination he felt the scrutiny of his companions as he painfully labored through some lies.

Eventually, his courage expended itself upon these objections. The debates drained him of his fire.

He was not cast down by this defeat of his plan, for, upon studying the affair carefully, he could not but admit that the objections were very formidable.

Furthermore, various ailments had begun to cry out. In their presence he could not persist in flying high with the wings of war; they rendered it almost impossible for him to see himself in a heroic light. He tumbled headlong.

He discovered that he had a scorching thirst. His face was so dry and grimy that he thought he could feel his skin crackle. Each bone of his body had an ache in it, and seemingly threatened to break with each movement. His feet were like two sores. Also, his body was calling for food. It was more powerful than a direct hunger. There was a dull, weight like feeling in his stomach, and, when he tried to walk, his head swayed and he tottered. He could not see with distinctness. Small patches of green mist floated before his vision.

While he had been tossed by many emotions, he had not been aware of ailments. Now they beset him and made clamor. As he was at last compelled to pay attention to them, his capacity for self-hate was multiplied. In despair, he declared that he was not like those others. He now conceded it to be impossible that he should ever become a hero. He was a craven loon.* Those pictures of glory were piteous things. He groaned from his heart and went staggering off.

A certain mothlike quality within him kept him in the vicinity of the battle. He had a great desire to see, and to get news. He wished to know who was winning.

He told himself that, despite his unprecedented suffering, he had never lost his greed for a victory, yet, he said, in a half-apologetic manner to his conscience, he could not but know that a defeat for the army this time might mean many favorable things for him. The blows of the enemy would splinter regiments into fragments. Thus, many men of courage, he considered, would be obliged to desert the colors and scurry like chickens. He would appear as one of them. They would be sullen brothers in distress, and he could then easily believe he had not run any farther or faster than they. And if he himself could believe in his virtuous perfection, he conceived that there would be small trouble in convincing all others.

He said, as if in excuse for this hope, that previously the army had encountered great defeats and in a few months had shaken off all blood and tradition of them, emerging as bright and valiant as a new one; thrusting out of sight the memory of disaster, and appearing with the valor and confidence of unconquered legions. The shrilling voices of the people at home would pipe dismally for a time, but various generals were usually compelled to listen to these ditties. He of course felt no compunctions for proposing a general as a sacrifice. He could not tell who the chosen for the barbs might be, so he could center no direct sympathy upon him. The people were afar and he did not conceive public opinion to be accurate at long range. It was quite probable they would hit the wrong man who, after he

---

* Cowardly lout or rogue.

had recovered from his amazement would perhaps spend the rest of his days in writing replies to the songs of his alleged failure. It would be very unfortunate, no doubt, but in this case a general was of no consequence to the youth.

In a defeat there would be a roundabout vindication of himself. He thought it would prove, in a manner, that he had fled early because of his superior powers of perception. A serious prophet upon predicting a flood should be the first man to climb a tree. This would demonstrate that he was indeed a seer.

A moral vindication was regarded by the youth as a very important thing. Without salve, he could not, he thought, wear the sore badge of his dishonor through life. With his heart continually assuring him that he was despicable, he could not exist without making it, through his actions, apparent to all men.

If the army had gone gloriously on he would be lost. If the din meant that now his army's flags were tilted forward he was a condemned wretch. He would be compelled to doom himself to isolation. If the men were advancing, their indifferent feet were trampling upon his chances for a successful life.

As these thoughts went rapidly through his mind, he turned upon them and tried to thrust them away. He denounced himself as a villain. He said that he was the most unutterably selfish man in existence. His mind pictured the soldiers who would place their defiant bodies before the spear of the yelling battle fiend, and as he saw their dripping corpses on an imagined field, he said that he was their murderer.

Again he thought that he wished he was dead. He believed that he envied a corpse. Thinking of the slain, he achieved a great contempt for some of them, as if they were guilty for thus becoming lifeless. They might have been killed by lucky chances, he said, before they had had opportunities to flee or before they had been really tested. Yet they would receive laurels from tradition. He cried out bitterly that their crowns were stolen and their robes of glorious memories were shams. However, he still said that it was a great pity he was not as they.

A defeat of the army had suggested itself to him as a means of escape from the consequences of his fall. He considered, now, however, that it was useless to think of such a possibility.

His education had been that success for that mighty blue machine was certain; that it would make victories as a contrivance turns out buttons. He presently discarded all his speculations in the other direction. He returned to the creed of soldiers.

When he perceived again that it was not possible for the army to be defeated, he tried to bethink him of a fine tale which he could take back to his regiment, and with it turn the expected shafts* of derision.

But, as he mortally feared these shafts, it became impossible for him to invent a tale he felt he could trust. He experimented with many schemes, but threw them aside one by one as flimsy. He was quick to see vulnerable places in them all.

Furthermore, he was much afraid that some arrow of scorn might lay him mentally low before he could raise his protecting tale.

He imagined the whole regiment saying: "Where's Henry Fleming? He run, didn't 'e? Oh, my!" He recalled various persons who would be quite sure to leave him no peace about it. They would doubtless question him with sneers, and laugh at his stammering hesitation. In the next engagement they would try to keep watch of him to discover when he would run.

Wherever he went in camp, he would encounter insolent and lingeringly cruel stares. As he imagined himself passing near a crowd of comrades, he could hear some one say, "There he goes!"

Then, as if the heads were moved by one muscle, all the faces were turned toward him with wide, derisive grins. He seemed to hear some one make a humorous remark in a low tone. At it the others all crowed and cackled. He was a slang phrase.[30]

---

* *Shaft* is slang for harsh and unfair usage; two paragraphs down, Crane playfully returns to the word's original meaning with the phrase *arrow of scorn*.

CHAPTER XII

THE COLUMN THAT HAD butted stoutly at the obstacles in the road-way was barely out of the youth's sight before he saw dark waves of men come sweeping out of the woods and down through the fields. He knew at once that the steel fibers had been washed from their hearts. They were bursting from their coats and their equipments as from entanglements. They charged down upon him like terrified buffaloes.[31]

Behind them blue smoke curled and clouded above the tree-tops, and through the thickets he could sometimes see a distant pink glare. The voices of the cannon were clamoring in inter-minable chorus.

The youth was horrorstricken. He stared in agony and amazement. He forgot that he was engaged in combating the universe. He threw aside his mental pamphlets on the philoso-phy of the retreated and rules for the guidance of the damned.

The fight was lost. The dragons were coming with invincible strides. The army, helpless in the matted thickets and blinded by the over-hanging night, was going to be swallowed. War, the red animal, war, the blood-swollen god, would have bloated fill.

Within him something bade to cry out. He had the impulse to make a rallying speech, to sing a battle hymn, but he could only get his tongue to call into the air: "Why—why—what—what's th' matter?"

Soon he was in the midst of them. They were leaping and scampering all about him. Their blanched faces shone in the dusk. They seemed, for the most part, to be very burly men. The youth turned from one to another of them as they galloped along. His incoherent questions were lost. They were heedless of his appeals. They did not seem to see him.

They sometimes gabbled insanely. One huge man was asking of the sky: "Say, where de plank road? Where de plank road!"[32] It was as if he had lost a child. He wept in his pain and dismay.

Presently, men were running hither and thither in all ways. The artillery booming, forward, rearward, and on the flanks made jumble of ideas of direction. Landmarks had vanished into the gathered gloom. The youth began to imagine that he had got into the center of the tremendous quarrel, and he could perceive no way out of it. From the mouths of the fleeing men came a thousand wild questions, but no one made answers.

The youth, after rushing about and throwing interrogations at the heedless bands of retreating infantry, finally clutched a man by the arm. They swung around face to face.

"Why—why——" stammered the youth struggling with his balking tongue.

The man screamed: "Let go me! Let go me!" His face was livid and his eyes were rolling uncontrolled. He was heaving and panting. He still grasped his rifle, perhaps having forgotten to release his hold upon it. He tugged frantically, and the youth being compelled to lean forward was dragged several paces.

"Let go me! Let go me!"

"Why—why——" stuttered the youth.

"Well, then!" bawled the man in a lurid rage. He adroitly and fiercely swung his rifle. It crushed upon the youth's head.[33] The man ran on.

The youth's fingers had turned to paste upon the other's arm. The energy was smitten from his muscles. He saw the flaming wings of lightning flash before his vision. There was a deafening rumble of thunder within his head.

Suddenly his legs seemed to die. He sank writhing to the ground. He tried to arise. In his efforts against the numbing pain he was like a man wrestling with a creature of the air.

There was a sinister struggle.

Sometimes he would achieve a position half erect, battle with the air for a moment, and then fall again, grabbing at the grass. His face was of a clammy pallor. Deep groans were wrenched from him.

At last, with a twisting movement, he got upon his hands and knees, and from thence, like a babe trying to walk, to his feet. Pressing his hands to his temples he went lurching over the grass.

He fought an intense battle with his body. His dulled senses wished him to swoon and he opposed them stubbornly, his mind portraying unknown dangers and mutilations if he should fall upon the field. He went tall soldier fashion. He imagined secluded spots where he could fall and be unmolested. To search for one he strove against the tide of his pain.

Once he put his hand to the top of his head and timidly touched the wound. The scratching pain of the contact made him draw a long breath through his clinched teeth. His fingers were dabbled with blood. He regarded them with a fixed stare.

Around him he could hear the grumble of jolted cannon as the scurrying horses were lashed toward the front. Once, a young officer on a besplashed charger nearly ran him down. He turned and watched the mass of guns, men, and horses sweeping in a wide curve toward a gap in a fence. The officer was making excited motions with a gauntleted hand. The guns followed the teams with an air of unwillingness, of being dragged by the heels.

Some officers of the scattered infantry were cursing and railing like fishwives.* Their scolding voices could be heard above the din. Into the unspeakable jumble in the roadway rode a squadron of cavalry. The faded yellow of their facings shone bravely. There was a mighty altercation.

The artillery were assembling as if for a conference.

The blue haze of evening was upon the field. The lines of forest were long purple shadows. One cloud lay along the western sky partly smothering the red.

As the youth left the scene behind him, he heard the guns suddenly roar out. He imagined them shaking in black rage. They belched and howled like brass devils guarding a gate. The soft air was filled with the tremendous remonstrance. With it came the shattering peal of opposing infantry. Turning to look behind him, he could see sheets of orange light illumine the shadowy distance. There were subtle and sudden lightnings in the far air. At times he thought he could see heaving masses of men.

He hurried on in the dusk. The day had faded until he could barely distinguish place for his feet. The purple darkness was

---

* Disparaging slang for "coarse, nagging, scolding women."

filled with men who lectured and jabbered. Sometimes he could see them gesticulating against the blue and somber sky. There seemed to be a great ruck of men and munitions spread about in the forest and in the fields.

The little narrow roadway now lay lifeless. There were overturned wagons like sun-dried bowlders. The bed of the former torrent was choked with the bodies of horses and splintered parts of war machines.

It had come to pass that his wound pained him but little. He was afraid to move rapidly, however, for a dread of disturbing it. He held his head very still and took many precautions against stumbling. He was filled with anxiety, and his face was pinched and drawn in anticipation of the pain of any sudden mistake of his feet in the gloom.

His thoughts, as he walked, fixed intently upon his hurt. There was a cool, liquid feeling about it and he imagined blood moving slowly down under his hair. His head seemed swollen to a size that made him think his neck to be inadequate.

The new silence of his wound made much worriment. The little blistering voices of pain that had called out from his scalp were, he thought, definite in their expression of danger. By them he believed that he could measure his plight. But when they remained ominously silent he became frightened and imagined terrible fingers that clutched into his brain.

Amid it he began to reflect upon various incidents and conditions of the past. He bethought him of certain meals his mother had cooked at home, in which those dishes of which he was particularly fond had occupied prominent positions. He saw the spread table. The pine walls of the kitchen were glowing in the warm light from the stove. Too, he remembered how he and his companions used to go from the schoolhouse to the bank of a shaded pool. He saw his clothes in disorderly array upon the grass of the bank. He felt the swash of the fragrant water upon his body. The leaves of the overhanging maple rustled with melody in the wind of youthful summer.

He was overcome presently by a dragging weariness. His head hung forward and his shoulders were stooped as if he were bearing a great bundle. His feet shuffled along the ground.

He held continuous arguments as to whether he should lie down and sleep at some near spot, or force himself on until he reached a certain haven. He often tried to dismiss the question, but his body persisted in rebellion and his senses nagged at him like pampered babies.

At last he heard a cheery voice near his shoulder: "Yeh seem t' be in a pretty bad way, boy?"[34]

The youth did not look up, but he assented with thick tongue. "Uh!"

The owner of the cheery voice took him firmly by the arm. "Well," he said, with a round laugh, "I'm goin' your way. Th' hull gang is goin' your way. An' I guess I kin give yeh a lift." They began to walk like a drunken man and his friend.

As they went along, the man questioned the youth and assisted him with the replies like one manipulating the mind of a child. Sometimes he interjected anecdotes. "What reg'ment do yeh b'long teh? Eh? What's that? Th' 304th N' York? Why, what corps is that in? Oh, it is? Why, I thought they wasn't engaged t'-day—they're 'way over in th' center. Oh, they was, eh? Well, pretty nearly everybody got their share 'a fightin' t'-day. By dad, I give myself up fer dead any number 'a times. There was shootin' here an' shootin' there, an' hollerin' here an' hollerin' there, in th' damn' darkness, until I couldn't tell t' save m' soul which side I was on. Sometimes I thought I was sure 'nough from Ohier, an' other times I could 'a swore I was from th' bitter end of Florida. It was th' most mixed up dern thing I ever see. An' these here hull woods is a reg'lar mess. It'll be a miracle if we find our reg'ments t'-night. Pretty soon, though, we'll meet a-plenty of guards an' provost-guards, an' one thing an' another. Ho! there they go with an off'cer, I guess. Look at his hand a-draggin'. He's got all th' war he wants, I bet. He won't be talkin' so big about his reputation an' all when they go t' sawin' off his leg. Poor feller! My brother's got whiskers jest like that. How did yeh git 'way over here, anyhow? Your reg'ment is a long way from here, ain't it? Well, I guess we can find it. Yeh know there was a boy killed in my comp'ny t'-day that I thought th' world an' all of. Jack was a nice feller. By ginger, it hurt like thunder t' see ol' Jack jest git knocked flat. We was a-standin' purty peaceable fer a spell, 'though there was men runnin' ev'ry way all 'round us, an' while we was a-standin' like that, 'long come a big fat feller. He began t' peck at Jack's elbow, an' he ses: 'Say, where's th' road t' th' river?' An' Jack, he never paid no attention, an' th' feller kept on a-peckin' at his elbow an' sayin': 'Say, where's th' road t' th' river?' Jack was a-lookin' ahead all th' time tryin' t' see th' Johnnies comin' through th' woods, an' he never paid no attention t' this big fat feller fer a long time, but at last he turned 'round an' he ses: 'Ah, go t' hell an' find th' road t' th' river!' An' jest then a shot slapped him bang on th' side th' head. He was a sergeant, too. Them was his last words. Thunder, I wish we was sure 'a findin' our reg'ments t'-night. It's goin' t' be long huntin'. But I guess we kin do it."

In the search which followed, the man of the cheery voice seemed to the youth to possess a wand of a magic kind. He threaded the mazes of the tangled forest with a strange fortune. In encounters with guards and patrols he displayed the keenness of a detective and the valor of a gamin.* Obstacles fell before him and became of assistance. The youth, with his chin still on his breast, stood woodenly by while his companion beat ways and means out of sullen things.

The forest seemed a vast hive of men buzzing about in frantic circles, but the cheery man conducted the youth without mistakes, until at last he began to chuckle with glee and self-satisfaction. "Ah, there yeh are! See that fire?"

The youth nodded stupidly.

"Well, there's where your reg'ment is. An' now, good-by, ol' boy, good luck t' yeh."

A warm and strong hand clasped the youth's languid fingers for an instant, and then he heard a cheerful and audacious whistling as the man strode away. As he who had so befriended him was thus passing out of his life, it suddenly occurred to the youth that he had not once seen his face.

---

* Neglected boy who lives primarily on city streets; Crane developed this metaphor from his experience in the Bowery district in New York City.

CHAPTER XIII

THE YOUTH WENT SLOWLY toward the fire indicated by his departed friend. As he reeled, he bethought him of the welcome his comrades would give him. He had a conviction that he would soon feel in his sore heart the barbed missiles of ridicule. He had no strength to invent a tale; he would be a soft target.

He made vague plans to go off into the deeper darkness and hide, but they were all destroyed by the voices of exhaustion and pain from his body. His ailments, clamoring, forced him to seek the place of food and rest, at whatever cost.

He swung unsteadily toward the fire. He could see the forms of men throwing black shadows in the red light, and as he went nearer it became known to him in some way that the ground was strewn with sleeping men.

Of a sudden he confronted a black and monstrous figure. A rifle barrel caught some glinting beams. "Halt! halt!" He was dismayed for a moment, but he presently thought that he recognized the nervous voice. As he stood tottering before the rifle barrel, he called out: "Why, hello, Wilson, you—you here?"

The rifle was lowered to a position of caution and the loud soldier came slowly forward. He peered into the youth's face. "That you, Henry?"

"Yes, it's—it's me."

"Well, well, ol' boy," said the other, "by ginger, I'm glad t' see yeh! I give yeh up fer a goner. I thought yeh was dead sure enough." There was husky emotion in his voice.

The youth found that now he could barely stand upon his feet. There was a sudden sinking of his forces. He thought he must hasten to produce his tale to protect him from the missiles already at the lips of his redoubtable comrades. So, staggering before the loud soldier, he began: "Yes, yes. I've—I've had an awful time. I've been all over. Way over on th' right. Ter'ble fightin' over there. I had an awful time. I got separated from th' reg'ment. Over on th' right, I got shot. In th' head. I never see

sech fightin'. Awful time. I don't see how I could a' got separated from th' reg'ment. I got shot, too."

His friend had stepped forward quickly.[35] "What? Got shot?
Why didn't yeh say so first? Poor ol' boy, we must—hol' on a
minnit; what am I doin'. I'll call Simpson."

Another figure at that moment loomed in the gloom. They
could see that it was the corporal. "Who yeh talkin' to, Wilson?"
he demanded. His voice was anger-toned. "Who yeh talkin' to?
Yeh th' derndest sentinel—why—hello, Henry, you here? Why, I
thought you was dead four hours ago! Great Jerusalem,* they
keep turnin' up every ten minutes or so! We thought we'd lost
forty-two men by straight count, but if they keep on a-comin'
this way, we'll git th' comp'ny all back by mornin' yit. Where
was yeh?"

"Over on th' right. I got separated"—began the youth with
considerable glibness.

But his friend had interrupted hastily. "Yes, an' he got shot in
th' head an' he's in a fix, an' we must see t' him right away." He
rested his rifle in the hollow of his left arm and his right around
the youth's shoulder.

"Gee, it must hurt like thunder!" he said.

The youth leaned heavily upon his friend. "Yes, it hurts—
hurts a good deal," he replied. There was a faltering in his voice.

"Oh," said the corporal. He linked his arm in the youth's and
drew him forward. "Come on, Henry. I'll take keer 'a yeh."

As they went on together the loud private called out after
them: "Put 'im t' sleep in my blanket, Simpson. An'—hol' on a
minnit—here's my canteen. It's full 'a coffee. Look at his head
by th' fire an' see how it looks. Maybe it's a pretty bad un. When
I git relieved in a couple 'a minnits, I'll be over an' see t' him."

The youth's senses were so deadened that his friend's voice
sounded from afar and he could scarcely feel the pressure of the
corporal's arm. He submitted passively to the latter's directing
strength. His head was in the old manner hanging forward
upon his breast. His knees wobbled.

---

* Popular interjection to indicate surprise.

The corporal led him into the glare of the fire. "Now, Henry," he said, "let's have look at yer ol' head."

The youth sat down obediently and the corporal, laying aside his rifle, began to fumble in the bushy hair of his comrade. He was obliged to turn the other's head so that the full flush of the fire light would beam upon it. He puckered his mouth with a critical air. He draw back his lips and whistled through his teeth when his fingers came in contact with the splashed blood and the rare wound.

"Ah, here we are!" he said. He awkwardly made further investigations. "Jest as I thought," he added, presently. "Yeh've been grazed by a ball.[36] It's raised a queer lump jest as if some feller had lammed yeh on th' head with a club. It stopped a-bleedin' long time ago. Th' most about it is that in th' mornin' yeh'll feel that a number ten hat wouldn't fit yeh. An' your head'll be all het up an' feel as dry as burnt pork. An' yeh may git a lot 'a other sicknesses, too, by mornin'. Yeh can't never tell. Still, I don't much think so. It's jest a damn' good belt on th' head, an' nothin' more. Now, you jest sit here an' don't move, while I go rout out th' relief. Then I'll send Wilson t' take keer 'a yeh."

The corporal went away. The youth remained on the ground like a parcel. He stared with a vacant look into the fire.

After a time he aroused, for some part, and the things about him began to take form. He saw that the ground in the deep shadows was cluttered with men, sprawling in every conceivable posture. Glancing narrowly into the more distant darkness, he caught occasional glimpses of visages that loomed pallid and ghostly, lit with a phosphorescent glow. These faces expressed in their lines the deep stupor of the tired soldiers. They made them appear like men drunk with wine. This bit of forest might have appeared to an ethereal wanderer as a scene of the result of some frightful debauch.

On the other side of the fire the youth observed an officer asleep, seated bolt upright, with his back against a tree. There was something perilous in his position. Badgered by dreams, perhaps, he swayed with little bounces and starts, like an old, toddy-stricken* grandfather in a chimney corner. Dust and stains were upon his face. His lower jaw hung down as if lacking strength to assume its normal position. He was the picture of an exhausted soldier after a feast of war.

He had evidently gone to sleep with his sword in his arms. These two had slumbered in an embrace, but the weapon had been allowed in time to fall unheeded to the ground. The brass-mounted hilt lay in contact with some parts of the fire.

Within the gleam of rose and orange light from the burning sticks were other soldiers, snoring and heaving, or lying death-like in slumber. A few pairs of legs were stuck forth, rigid and straight. The shoes displayed the mud or dust of marches and bits of rounded trousers, protruding from the blankets, showed rents and tears from hurried pitchings through the dense brambles.

The fire crackled musically. From it swelled light smoke. Overhead the foliage moved softly. The leaves, with their faces turned toward the blaze, were colored shifting hues of silver, often edged with red. Far off to the right, through a window in the forest could be seen a handful of stars lying, like glittering pebbles, on the black level of the night.

Occasionally, in this low-arched hall, a soldier would arouse and turn his body to a new position, the experience of his sleep having taught him of uneven and objectionable places upon the ground under him. Or, perhaps, he would lift himself to a sitting posture, blink at the fire for an unintelligent moment, throw a swift glance at his prostrate companion, and then cuddle down again with a grunt of sleepy content.

The youth sat in a forlorn heap until his friend the loud young soldier came, swinging two canteens by their light strings. "Well, now, Henry, ol' boy," said the latter, "we'll have yeh fixed up in jest about a minnit."

He had the bustling ways of an amateur nurse. He fussed around the fire and stirred the sticks to brilliant exertions. He made his patient drink largely from the canteen that contained the coffee. It was to the youth a delicious draught. He tilted his

---

* A *toddy* is a drink usually made from brandy, water, sugar, and spices.

head afar back and held the canteen long to his lips. The cool mixture went caressingly down his blistered throat. Having finished, he sighed with comfortable delight.

The loud young soldier watched his comrade with an air of satisfaction. He later produced an extensive handkerchief from his pocket. He folded it into a manner of bandage and soused water from the other canteen upon the middle of it. This crude arrangement he bound over the youth's head, tying the ends in a queer knot at the back of the neck.

"There," he said, moving off and surveying his deed, "yeh look like th' devil, but I bet yeh feel better."

The youth contemplated his friend with grateful eyes. Upon his aching and swelling head the cold cloth was like a tender woman's hand.

"Yeh don't holler ner say nothin'," remarked his friend approvingly. "I know I'm a blacksmith at takin' keer 'a sick folks, an' yeh never squeaked. Yer a good un, Henry. Most 'a men would a' been in th' hospital long ago. A shot in th' head ain't foolin' business."

The youth made no reply, but began to fumble with the buttons of his jacket.

"Well, come, now," continued his friend, "come on. I must put yeh t' bed an' see that yeh git a good night's rest."

The other got carefully erect, and the loud young soldier led him among the sleeping forms lying in groups and rows. Presently he stooped and picked up his blankets. He spread the rubber one upon the ground and placed the woolen one about the youth's shoulders.

"There now," he said, "lie down an' git some sleep."

The youth, with his manner of doglike obedience, got carefully down like a crone stooping. He stretched out with a murmur of relief and comfort. The ground felt like the softest couch.

But of a sudden he ejaculated: "Hol' on a minnit! Where you goin' t' sleep?"

His friend waved his hand impatiently. "Right down there by yeh."

"Well, but hol' on a minnit," continued the youth. "What yeh goin' t' sleep in? I've got your——"

The loud young soldier snarled: "Shet up an' go on t' sleep. Don't be makin' a damn' fool 'a yerself," he said severely.

After the reproof the youth said no more. An exquisite drowsiness had spread through him. The warm comfort of the blanket enveloped him and made a gentle languor. His head fell forward on his crooked arm and his weighted lids went softly down over his eyes. Hearing a splatter of musketry from the distance, he wondered indifferently if those men sometimes slept. He gave a long sigh, snuggled down into his blanket, and in a moment was like his comrades.

CHAPTER XIV

WHEN THE YOUTH AWOKE it seemed to him that he had been asleep for a thousand years, and he felt sure that he opened his eyes upon an unexpected world. Gray mists were slowly shifting before the first efforts of the sun rays. An impending splendor could be seen in the eastern sky. An icy dew had chilled his face, and immediately upon arousing he curled farther down into his blanket. He stared for a while at the leaves overhead, moving in a heraldic wind of the day.

The distance was splintering and blaring with the noise of fighting. There was in the sound an expression of a deadly persistency, as if it had not begun and was not to cease.

About him were the rows and groups of men that he had dimly seen the previous night. They were getting a last draught of sleep before the awakening. The gaunt, careworn features and dusty figures were made plain by this quaint light at the dawning, but it dressed the skin of the men in corpselike hues and made the tangled limbs appear pulseless and dead. The youth started up with a little cry when his eyes first swept over this motionless mass of men, thick-spread upon the ground, pallid, and in strange postures. His disordered mind interpreted the hall of the forest as a charnel place. He believed for an instant that he was in the house of the dead, and he did not dare to move lest these corpses start up, squalling and squawking. In a second, however, he achieved his proper mind. He swore a complicated oath at himself. He saw that this somber picture was not a fact of the present, but a mere prophecy.

He heard then the noise of a fire crackling briskly in the cold air, and, turning his head, he saw his friend pottering busily about a small blaze. A few other figures moved in the fog, and he heard the hard cracking of axe blows.

Suddenly there was a hollow rumble of drums. A distant bugle sang faintly. Similar sounds, varying in strength, came from near and far over the forest. The bugles called to each other like brazen gamecocks. The near thunder of the regimental drums rolled.

The body of men in the woods rustled. There was a general uplifting of heads. A murmuring of voices broke upon the air. In it there was much bass of grumbling oaths. Strange gods were addressed in condemnation of the early hours necessary to correct war. An officer's peremptory tenor rang out and quickened the stiffened movement of the men. The tangled limbs unraveled. The corpse-hued faces were hidden behind fists that twisted slowly in the eye sockets.

The youth sat up and gave vent to an enormous yawn. "Thunder!" he remarked petulantly. He rubbed his eyes, and then putting up his hand felt carefully of the bandage over his wound. His friend, perceiving him to be awake, came from the fire. "Well, Henry, ol' man, how do yeh feel this mornin'?" he demanded.

The youth yawned again. Then he puckered his mouth to a little pucker. His head, in truth, felt precisely like a melon, and there was an unpleasant sensation at his stomach.

"Oh, Lord, I feel pretty bad," he said.

"Thunder!" exclaimed the other. "I hoped ye'd feel all right this mornin'. Let's see th' bandage—I guess it's slipped." He began to tinker at the wound in rather a clumsy way until the youth exploded.

"Gosh-dern it!" he said in sharp irritation; "you're the hangdest* man I ever saw! You wear muffs on your hands. Why in good thunderation can't you be more easy? I'd rather you'd stand off an' throw guns at it. Now, go slow, an' don't act as if you was nailing down carpet."

He glared with insolent command at his friend, but the latter answered soothingly. "Well, well, come now, an' git some grub," he said. "Then, maybe, yeh'll feel better."

At the fireside the loud young soldier watched over his comrade's wants with tenderness and care. He was very busy marshaling the little black vagabonds of tin cups and pouring into them the streaming, iron colored mixture from a small and

---

* From the phrase "I'll be hanged"; suggests confoundedness.

sooty tin pail. He had some fresh meat, which he roasted hurriedly upon a stick. He sat down then and contemplated the youth's appetite with glee.

The youth took note of a remarkable change in his comrade since those days of camp life upon the river bank. He seemed no more to be continually regarding the proportions of his personal prowess. He was not furious at small words that pricked his conceits. He was no more a loud young soldier. There was about him now a fine reliance. He showed a quiet belief in his purposes and his abilities. And this inward confidence evidently enabled him to be indifferent to little words of other men aimed at him.

The youth reflected. He had been used to regarding his comrade as a blatant child with an audacity grown from his inexperience, thoughtless, headstrong, jealous, and filled with a tinsel courage. A swaggering babe accustomed to strut in his own dooryard. The youth wondered where had been born these new eyes; when his comrade had made the great discovery that there were many men who would refuse to be subjected by him. Apparently, the other had now climbed a peak of wisdom from which he could perceive himself as a very wee thing. And the youth saw that ever after it would be easier to live in his friend's neighborhood.

His comrade balanced his ebony coffee-cup on his knee. "Well, Henry," he said, "what d'yeh think th' chances are? D'yeh think we'll wallop 'em?"

The youth considered for a moment. "Day-b'fore-yesterday," he finally replied, with boldness, "you would 'a' bet you'd lick the hull kit-an'-boodle all by yourself."

His friend looked a trifle amazed. "Would I?" he asked. He pondered. "Well, perhaps I would," he decided at last. He stared humbly at the fire.

The youth was quite disconcerted at this surprising reception of his remarks. "Oh, no, you wouldn't either," he said, hastily trying to retrace.

But the other made a deprecating gesture. "Oh, yeh needn't mind, Henry," he said. "I believe I was a pretty big fool in those days." He spoke as after a lapse of years.

There was a little pause.

"All th' officers say we've got th' rebs in a pretty tight box," said the friend, clearing his throat in a commonplace way. "They all seem t' think we've got 'em jest where we want 'em."

"I don't know about that," the youth replied. "What I seen over on th' right makes me think it was th' other way about. From where I was, it looked as if we was gettin' a good poundin' yestirday."

"D'yeh think so?" inquired the friend. "I thought we handled 'em pretty rough yestirday."

"Not a bit," said the youth. "Why, lord, man, you didn't see nothing of the fight. Why!" Then a sudden thought came to him. "Oh! Jim Conklin's dead."

His friend started. "What? Is he? Jim Conklin?"

The youth spoke slowly. "Yes. He's dead. Shot in th' side."

"Yeh don't say so. Jim Conklin. . . . poor cuss!"

All about them were other small fires surrounded by men with their little black utensils. From one of these near came sudden sharp voices in a row. It appeared that two light-footed soldiers had been teasing a huge, bearded man, causing him to spill coffee upon his blue knees. The man had gone into a rage and had sworn comprehensively. Stung by his language, his tormentors had immediately bristled at him with a great show of resenting unjust oaths. Possibly there was going to be a fight.

The friend arose and went over to them, making pacific motions with his arms. "Oh, here, now, boys, what's th' use?" he said. "We'll be at th' rebs in less'n an hour. What's th' good fightin' 'mong ourselves?"

One of the light-footed soldiers turned upon him red-faced and violent. "Yeh needn't come around here with yer preachin'. I s'pose yeh don't approve 'a fightin' since Charley Morgan licked yeh; but I don't see what business this here is 'a yours or anybody else."

"Well, it ain't," said the friend mildly. "Still I hate t' see——"

There was a tangled argument.

"Well, he——," said the two, indicating their opponent with accusative forefingers.

The huge soldier was quite purple with rage. He pointed at

the two soldiers with his great hand, extended clawlike. "Well, they——"

But during this argumentative time the desire to deal blows seemed to pass, although they said much to each other. Finally the friend returned to his old seat. In a short while the three antagonists could be seen together in an amiable bunch.

"Jimmie Rogers ses I'll have t' fight him after th' battle t'-day," announced the friend as he again seated himself. "He ses he don't allow no interferin' in his business. I hate t' see th' boys fightin' 'mong themselves."

The youth laughed. "Yer changed a good bit. Yeh ain't at all like yeh was. I remember when you an' that Irish feller——" He stopped and laughed again.

"No, I didn't use t' be that way," said his friend thoughtfully. "That's true 'nough."

"Well, I didn't mean——" began the youth.

The friend made another deprecatory gesture. "Oh, yeh needn't mind, Henry."

There was another little pause.

"Th' reg'ment lost over half th' men yestirday," remarked the friend eventually. "I thought 'a course they was all dead, but, laws, they kep' a-comin' back last night until it seems, after all, we didn't lose but a few. They'd been scattered all over, wanderin' around in th' woods, fightin' with other reg'ments, an' everything. Jest like you done."[37]

"So?" said the youth.

CHAPTER XV

THE REGIMENT WAS STANDING at order arms* at the side of a lane, waiting for the command to march, when suddenly the youth remembered the little packet enwrapped in a faded yellow envelope which the loud young soldier with lugubrious words had intrusted to him. It made him start. He uttered an exclamation and turned toward his comrade.

"Wilson!"

"What?"

His friend, at his side in the ranks, was thoughtfully staring down the road. From some cause his expression was at that moment very meek. The youth, regarding him with sidelong glances, felt impelled to change his purpose. "Oh, nothing," he said.

His friend turned his head in some surprise, "Why, what was yeh goin' t' say?"

"Oh, nothing," repeated the youth.

He resolved not to deal the little blow. It was sufficient that the fact made him glad. It was not necessary to knock his friend on the head with the misguided packet.

He had been possessed of much fear of his friend, for he saw how easily questionings could make holes in his feelings. Lately, he had assured himself that the altered comrade would not tantalize him with a persistent curiosity, but he felt certain that during the first period of leisure his friend would ask him to relate his adventures of the previous day.

He now rejoiced in the possession of a small weapon with which he could prostrate his comrade at the first signs of a cross-examination. He was master. It would now be he who could laugh and shoot the shafts of derision.

The friend had, in a weak hour, spoken with sobs of his own death. He had delivered a melancholy oration previous to his

---

* In the manual of arms, a position in which a soldier holds his rifle vertically next to his right leg with the butt resting on the ground.

funeral, and had doubtless in the packet of letters, presented various keepsakes to relatives. But he had not died, and thus he had delivered himself into the hands of the youth.

The latter felt immensely superior to his friend, but he inclined to condescension. He adopted toward him an air of patronizing good humor.

His self-pride was now entirely restored. In the shade of its flourishing growth he stood with braced and self-confident legs, and since nothing could now be discovered he did not shrink from an encounter with the eyes of judges, and allowed no thoughts of his own to keep him from an attitude of manfulness. He had performed his mistakes in the dark, so he was still a man.

Indeed, when he remembered his fortunes of yesterday, and looked at them from a distance he began to see something fine there. He had license to be pompous and veteranlike.

His panting agonies of the past he put out of his sight.

In the present, he declared to himself that it was only the doomed and the damned who roared with sincerity at circumstances. Few but they ever did it. A man with a full stomach and the respect of his fellows had no business to scold about anything that he might think to be wrong in the ways of the universe, or even with the ways of society. Let the unfortunates rail; the others may play marbles.

He did not give a great deal of thought to these battles that lay directly before him. It was not essential that he should plan his ways in regard to them. He had been taught that many obligations of a life were easily avoided. The lessons of yesterday had been that retribution was a laggard and blind. With these facts before him he did not deem it necessary that he should become feverish over the possibilities of the ensuing twenty-four hours. He could leave much to chance. Besides, a faith in himself had secretly blossomed. There was a little flower of confidence growing within him. He was now a man of experience. He had been out among the dragons, he said, and he assured himself that they were not so hideous as he had imagined them. Also, they were inaccurate; they did not sting with precision. A stout heart often defied, and defying, escaped.

And, furthermore, how could they kill him who was the chosen of gods and doomed to greatness?

He remembered how some of the men had run from the battle. As he recalled their terror-struck faces he felt a scorn for them. They had surely been more fleet and more wild than was absolutely necessary. They were weak mortals. As for himself, he had fled with discretion and dignity.

He was aroused from this reverie by his friend, who, having hitched about nervously and blinked at the trees for a time, suddenly coughed in an introductory way, and spoke.

"Fleming!"

"What?"

The friend put his hand up to his mouth and coughed again. He fidgeted in his jacket.

"Well," he gulped, at last, "I guess yeh might as well give me back them letters." Dark, prickling blood had flushed into his cheeks and brow.

"All right, Wilson," said the youth. He loosened two buttons of his coat, thrust in his hand, and brought forth the packet. As he extended it to his friend the latter's face was turned from him.

He had been slow in the act of producing the packet because during it he had been trying to invent a remarkable comment upon the affair. He could conjure nothing of sufficient point. He was compelled to allow his friend to escape unmolested with his packet. And for this he took unto himself considerable credit. It was a generous thing.

His friend at his side seemed suffering great shame. As he contemplated him, the youth felt his heart grow more strong and stout. He had never been compelled to blush in such manner for his acts; he was an individual of extraordinary virtues.

He reflected, with condescending pity: "Too bad! Too bad! The poor devil, it makes him feel tough!"

After this incident, and as he reviewed the battle pictures he had seen, he felt quite competent to return home and make the hearts of the people glow with stories of war. He could see himself in a room of warm tints telling tales to listeners. He could exhibit laurels. They were insignificant; still, in a district where laurels were infrequent, they might shine.

He saw his gaping audience picturing him as the central figure in blazing scenes. And he imagined the consternation and the ejaculations of his mother and the young lady at the seminary as they drank his recitals. Their vague feminine formula for beloved ones doing brave deeds on the field of battle without risk of life would be destroyed.

CHAPTER XVI

A SPUTTERING OF MUSKETRY was always to be heard. Later, the cannon had entered the dispute. In the fog-filled air their voices made a thudding sound. The reverberations were continued. This part of the world led a strange, battleful existence.

The youth's regiment was marched to relieve a command that had lain long in some damp trenches.[38] The men took positions behind a curving line of rifle pits that had been turned up, like a large furrow, along the line of woods. Before them was a level stretch, peopled with short, deformed stumps. From the woods beyond came the dull popping of the skirmishers and pickets, firing in the fog. From the right came the noise of a terrific fracas.

The men cuddled behind the small embankment and sat in easy attitudes awaiting their turn. Many had their backs to the firing. The youth's friend lay down, buried his face in his arms, and almost instantly, it seemed, he was in a deep sleep.

The youth leaned his breast against the brown dirt and peered over at the woods and up and down the line. Curtains of trees interfered with his ways of vision. He could see the low line of trenches but for a short distance. A few idle flags were perched on the dirt hills. Behind them were rows of dark bodies with a few heads sticking curiously over the top.

Always the noise of skirmishers came from the woods on the front and left, and the din on the right had grown to frightful proportions. The guns were roaring without an instant's pause for breath. It seemed that the cannon had come from all parts and were engaged in a stupendous wrangle. It became impossible to make a sentence heard.

The youth wished to launch a joke—a quotation from newspapers. He desired to say, "All quiet on the Rappahannock," but the guns refused to permit even a comment upon their uproar. He never successfully concluded the sentence. But at last the guns stopped, and among the men in the rifle pits rumors again flew, like birds, but they were now for the most part black creatures who flapped their wings drearily near to the ground and refused to rise on any wings of hope. The men's faces grew doleful from the interpreting of omens. Tales of hesitation and uncertainty on the part of those high in place and responsibility came to their ears. Stories of disaster were borne into their minds with many proofs. This din of musketry on the right, growing like a released genie of sound, expressed and emphasized the army's plight.

The men were disheartened and began to mutter. They made gestures expressive of the sentence: "Ah, what more can we do?" And it could always be seen that they were bewildered by the alleged news and could not fully comprehend a defeat.

Before the gray mists had been totally obliterated by the sun rays, the regiment was marching in a spread column that was retiring carefully through the woods. The disordered, hurrying lines of the enemy could sometimes be seen down through the groves and little fields. They were yelling, shrill and exultant.

At this sight the youth forgot many personal matters and became greatly enraged. He exploded in loud sentences. "B'jiminey, we're generaled by a lot 'a lunkheads."*

"More than one feller has said that t'-day," observed a man.[39]

His friend, recently aroused, was still very drowsy. He looked behind him until his mind took in the meaning of the movement. Then he sighed. "Oh, well, I s'pose we got licked," he remarked sadly.

The youth had a thought that it would not be handsome for him to freely condemn other men. He made an attempt to restrain himself, but the words upon his tongue were too bitter. He presently began a long and intricate denunciation of the commander of the forces.

"Mebbe, it wa'n't all his fault—not all together. He did th' best he knowed. It's our luck t' git licked often," said his friend in a weary tone. He was trudging along with stooped shoulders and shifting eyes like a man who has been caned and kicked.

---

* Here meaning a stupid person; from a word once used to describe an ill-bred, ugly horse.

"Well, don't we fight like the devil? Don't we do all that men can?" demanded the youth loudly.

He was secretly dumfounded at this sentiment when it came from his lips. For a moment his face lost its valor and he looked guiltily about him. But no one questioned his right to deal in such words, and presently he recovered his air of courage. He went on to repeat a statement he had heard going from group to group at the camp that morning. "The brigadier said he never saw a new reg'ment fight the way we fought yestirday, didn't he?[40] And we didn't do better than many another reg'ment, did we? Well, then, you can't say it's th' army's fault, can you?"

In his reply, the friend's voice was stern. " 'A course not," he said. "No man dare say we don't fight like th' devil. No man will ever dare say it. Th' boys fight like hell-roosters.* But still—still, we don't have no luck."

"Well, then, if we fight like the devil an' don't ever whip, it must be the general's fault," said the youth grandly and decisively. "And I don't see any sense in fighting and fighting and fighting, yet always losing through some derned old lunkhead of a general."

A sarcastic man who was tramping at the youth's side, then spoke lazily. "Mebbe yeh think yeh fit th' hull battle yestirday, Fleming," he remarked.

The speech pierced the youth. Inwardly he was reduced to an abject pulp by these chance words. His legs quaked privately. He cast a frightened glance at the sarcastic man.

"Why, no," he hastened to say in a conciliating voice, "I don't think I fought the whole battle yesterday."

But the other seemed innocent of any deeper meaning. Apparently, he had no information. It was merely his habit. "Oh!" he replied in the same tone of calm derision.

The youth, nevertheless, felt a threat. His mind shrank from going near to the danger, and thereafter he was silent. The significance of the sarcastic man's words took from him all loud moods that would make him appear prominent. He became suddenly a modest person.

---

* Roughnecks, street brawlers.

There was low-toned talk among the troops. The officers were impatient and snappy, their countenances clouded with the tales of misfortune. The troops, sifting through the forest, were sullen. In the youth's company once a man's laugh rang out. A dozen soldiers turned their faces quickly toward him and frowned with vague displeasure.

The noise of firing dogged their footsteps. Sometimes, it seemed to be driven a little way, but it always returned again with increased insolence. The men muttered and cursed, throwing black looks in its direction.

In a clear space the troops were at last halted. Regiments and brigades, broken and detached through their encounters with thickets, grew together again and lines were faced toward the pursuing bark of the enemy's infantry.

This noise, following like the yellings of eager, metallic hounds, increased to a loud and joyous burst, and then, as the sun went serenely up the sky, throwing illuminating rays into the gloomy thickets, it broke forth into prolonged pealings. The woods began to crackle as if afire.

"Whoop-a-dadee," said a man, "here we are! Everybody fightin'. Blood an' destruction."

"I was willin' t' bet they'd attack as soon as th' sun got fairly up," savagely asserted the lieutenant who commanded the youth's company. He jerked without mercy at his little mustache. He strode to and fro with dark dignity in the rear of his men, who were lying down behind whatever protection they had collected.

A battery had trundled into position in the rear and was thoughtfully shelling the distance. The regiment, unmolested as yet, awaited the moment when the gray shadows of the woods before them should be slashed by the lines of flame. There was much growling and swearing.

"Good Gawd," the youth grumbled, "we're always being chased around like rats! It makes me sick. Nobody seems to know where we go or why we go. We just get fired around from pillar to post and get licked here and get licked there, and nobody knows what it's done for. It makes a man feel like a damn' kitten in a bag. Now, I'd like to know what the eternal thunders we was marched into these woods for anyhow, unless it was to give the rebs a regular pot shot at us. We came in here and got our legs all tangled up in these cussed briers, and then we begin to fight and the rebs had an easy time of it. Don't tell me it's just luck! I know better. It's this derned old———"

The friend seemed jaded, but he interrupted his comrade with a voice of calm confidence. "It'll turn out all right in th' end," he said.

"Oh, the devil it will! You always talk like a dog-hanged parson. Don't tell me! I know———"

At this time there was an interposition by the savage-minded lieutenant, who was obliged to vent some of his inward dissatisfaction upon his men. "You boys shut right up! There no need 'a your wastin' your breath in long-winded arguments about this an' that an' th' other. You've been jawin' like a lot 'a old hens. All you've got t' do is to fight, an' you'll get plenty 'a that t' do in about ten minutes. Less talkin' an' more fightin' is what's best for you boys. I never saw sech gabbling jackasses."

He paused, ready to pounce upon any man who might have the temerity to reply. No words being said, he resumed his dignified pacing.

"There's too much chin music* an' too little fightin' in this war, anyhow," he said to them, turning his head for a final remark.

The day had grown more white, until the sun shed his full radiance upon the thronged forest. A sort of a gust of battle came sweeping toward that part of the line where lay the youth's regiment. The front shifted a trifle to meet it squarely. There was a wait. In this part of the field there passed slowly the intense moments that precede the tempest.

A single rifle flashed in a thicket before the regiment. In an instant it was joined by many others. There was a mighty song of clashes and crashes that went sweeping through the woods. The guns in the rear, aroused and enraged by shells that had been thrown burr-like at them, suddenly involved themselves in a hideous altercation with another band of guns. The battle

—————————————————
* Purposeless chatter.

roar settled to a rolling thunder, which was a single, long explosion.

In the regiment there was a peculiar kind of hesitation denoted in the attitudes of the men. They were worn, exhausted, having slept but little and labored much. They rolled their eyes toward the advancing battle as they stood awaiting the shock. Some shrank and flinched. They stood as men tied to stakes.

CHAPTER XVII

THIS ADVANCE OF THE enemy had seemed to the youth like a ruthless hunting. He began to fume with rage and exasperation. He beat his foot upon the ground, and scowled with hate at the swirling smoke that was approaching like a phantom flood. There was a maddening quality in this seeming resolution of the foe to give him no rest, to give him no time to sit down and think. Yesterday he had fought and had fled rapidly. There had been many adventures. For to-day he felt that he had earned opportunities for contemplative repose. He could have enjoyed portraying to uninitiated listeners various scenes at which he had been a witness or ably discussing the processes of war with other proved men. Too it was important that he should have time for physical recuperation. He was sore and stiff from his experiences. He had received his fill of all exertions, and he wished to rest.

But those other men seemed never to grow weary; they were fighting with their old speed. He had a wild hate for the relentless foe. Yesterday, when he had imagined the universe to be against him, he had hated it, little gods and big gods; to-day he hated the army of the foe with the same great hatred. He was not going to be badgered of his life, like a kitten chased by boys, he said. It was not well to drive men into final corners; at those moments they could all develop teeth and claws.

He leaned and spoke into his friend's ear. He menaced the woods with a gesture. "If they keep on chasing us, by Gawd, they'd better watch out. Can't stand too much."

The friend twisted his head and made a calm reply. "If they keep on a-chasin' us they'll drive us all inteh th' river."

The youth cried out savagely at this statement. He crouched behind a little tree, with his eyes burning hatefully and his teeth set in a cur-like snarl. The awkward bandage was still about his head, and upon it, over his wound, there was a spot of dry blood. His hair was wondrously tousled, and some straggling, moving locks hung over the cloth of the bandage down toward his forehead. His jacket and shirt were open at the throat, and exposed his young bronzed neck. There could be seen spasmodic gulpings at his throat.

His fingers twined nervously about his rifle. He wished that it was an engine of annihilating power. He felt that he and his companions were being taunted and derided from sincere convictions that they were poor and puny. His knowledge of his inability to take vengeance for it made his rage into a dark and stormy specter, that possessed him and made him dream of abominable cruelties. The tormentors were flies sucking insolently at his blood, and he thought that he would have given his life for a revenge of seeing their faces in pitiful plights.

The winds of battle had swept all about the regiment, until the one rifle, instantly followed by others, flashed in its front. A moment later the regiment roared forth its sudden and valiant retort. A dense wall of smoke settled slowly down. It was furiously slit and slashed by the knifelike fire from the rifles.

To the youth the fighters resembled animals tossed for a death struggle into a dark pit. There was a sensation that he and his fellows, at bay, were pushing back, always pushing fierce onslaughts of creatures who were slippery. Their beams of crimson seemed to get no purchase upon the bodies of their foes; the latter seemed to evade them with ease, and come through, between, around, and about with unopposed skill.

When, in a dream, it occurred to the youth that his rifle was an impotent stick, he lost sense of everything but his hate, his desire to smash into pulp the glittering smile of victory which he could feel upon the faces of his enemies.

The blue smoke-swallowed line curled and writhed like a snake stepped upon. It swung its ends to and fro in an agony of fear and rage.

The youth was not conscious that he was erect upon his feet. He did not know the direction of the ground. Indeed, once he even lost the habit of balance and fell heavily. He was up again immediately. One thought went through the chaos of his brain at the time. He wondered if he had fallen because he had been shot. But the suspicion flew away at once. He did not think more of it.

He had taken up a first position behind the little tree, with a direct determination to hold it against the world. He had not deemed it possible that his army could that day succeed, and from this he felt the ability to fight harder. But the throng had surged in all ways, until he lost directions and locations, save that he knew where lay the enemy.

The flames bit him, and the hot smoke broiled his skin. His rifle barrel grew so hot that ordinarily he could not have borne it upon his palms; but he kept on stuffing cartridges into it, and pounding them with his clanking, bending ramrod. If he aimed at some changing form through the smoke, he pulled his trigger with a fierce grunt, as if he were dealing a blow of the fist with all his strength.

When the enemy seemed falling back before him and his fellows, he went instantly forward, like a dog who, seeing his foes lagging, turns and insists upon being pursued. And when he was compelled to retire again, he did it slowly, sullenly, taking steps of wrathful despair.

Once he, in his intent hate, was almost alone, and was firing, when all those near him had ceased. He was so engrossed in his occupation that he was not aware of a lull.

He was recalled by a hoarse laugh and a sentence that came to his ears in a voice of contempt and amazement. "Yeh infernal fool, don't yeh know enough t' quit when there ain't anything t' shoot at? Good Gawd!"

He turned then and, pausing with his rifle thrown half into position, looked at the blue line of his comrades. During this moment of leisure they seemed all to be engaged in staring with astonishment at him. They had become spectators. Turning to the front again he saw, under the lifted smoke, a deserted ground.

He looked bewildered for a moment. Then there appeared upon the glazed vacancy of his eyes a diamond point of intelligence. "Oh," he said, comprehending.[41]

He returned to his comrades and threw himself upon the ground. He sprawled like a man who had been thrashed. His flesh seemed strangely on fire, and the sounds of the battle continued in his ears. He groped blindly for his canteen.

The lieutenant was crowing. He seemed drunk with fighting. He called out to the youth: "By heavens, if I had ten thousand wild cats like you I could tear th' stomach outa this war in less'n a week!" He puffed out his chest with large dignity as he said it.

Some of the men muttered and looked at the youth in awe-struck ways. It was plain that as he had gone on loading and firing and cursing without the proper intermission, they had found time to regard him. And they now looked upon him as a war devil.

The friend came staggering to him. There was some fright and dismay in his voice. "Are yeh all right, Fleming? Do yeh feel all right? There ain't nothin' th' matter with yeh, Henry, is there?"

"No," said the youth with difficulty. His throat seemed full of knobs and burs.

These incidents made the youth ponder. It was revealed to him that he had been a barbarian, a beast. He had fought like a pagan who defends his religion. Regarding it, he saw that it was fine, wild, and, in some ways, easy. He had been a tremendous figure, no doubt. By this struggle he had overcome obstacles which he had admitted to be mountains. They had fallen like paper peaks, and he was now what he called a hero. And he had not been aware of the process. He had slept and, awakening, found himself a knight.

He lay and basked in the occasional stares of his comrades. Their faces were varied in degrees of blackness from the burned powder. Some were utterly smudged. They were reeking with perspiration, and their breaths came hard and wheezing. And from these soiled expanses they peered at him.

"Hot work! Hot work!" cried the lieutenant deliriously. He walked up and down, restless and eager. Sometimes his voice could be heard in a wild, incomprehensible laugh.

When he had a particularly profound thought upon the science of war he always unconsciously addressed himself to the youth.

There was some grim rejoicing by the men. "By thunder, I bet this army'll never see another new reg'ment like us!"

"You bet!"

"A dog, a woman, an' a walnut tree,
Th' more yeh beat 'em, th' better they be!*

That's like us."

"Lost a piler men, they did. If an' ol' woman swep' up th' woods she'd git a dustpanful."

"Yes, an' if she'll come around ag'in in 'bout an' hour she'll git a pile more."

The forest still bore its burden of clamor. From off under the trees came the rolling clatter of the musketry. Each distant thicket seemed a strange porcupine with quills of flame. A cloud of dark smoke, as from smoldering ruins, went up toward the sun now bright and gay in the blue, enameled sky.

---

* An English proverb that dates back to the Renaissance.

CHAPTER XVIII

THE RAGGED LINE HAD respite for some minutes, but during its pause the struggle in the forest became magnified until the trees seemed to quiver from the firing and the ground to shake from the rushing of the men. The voices of the cannon were mingled in a long and interminable row. It seemed difficult to live in such an atmosphere. The chests of the men strained for a bit of freshness, and their throats craved water.

There was one shot through the body, who raised a cry of bitter lamentation when came this lull. Perhaps he had been calling out during the fighting also, but at that time no one had heard him. But now the men turned at the woeful complaints of him upon the ground.

"Who is it? Who is it?"

"It's Jimmie Rogers. Jimmie Rogers."

When their eyes first encountered him there was a sudden halt, as if they feared to go near. He was thrashing about in the grass, twisting his shuddering body into many strange postures. He was screaming loudly. This instant's hesitation seemed to fill him with a tremendous, fantastic contempt, and he damned them in shrieked sentences.

The youth's friend had a geographical illusion concerning a stream, and he obtained permission to go for some water. Immediately canteens were showered upon him. "Fill mine, will yeh?" "Bring me some, too." "And me, too." He departed, ladened. The youth went with his friend, feeling a desire to throw his heated body onto the stream and, soaking there, drink quarts.

They made a hurried search for the supposed stream, but did not find it. "No water here," said the youth. They turned without delay and began to retrace their steps.

From their position as they again faced toward the place of the fighting, they could of course comprehend a greater amount of the battle than when their visions had been blurred by the hurling smoke of the line. They could see dark stretches winding along the land, and on one cleared space there was a row of guns making gray clouds, which were filled with large flashes of orange-colored flame. Over some foliage they could see the roof of a house. One window, glowing a deep murder red, shone squarely through the leaves. From the edifice a tall leaning tower of smoke went far into the sky.

Looking over their own troops, they saw mixed masses slowly getting into regular form. The sunlight made twinkling points of the bright steel. To the rear there was a glimpse of a distant roadway as it curved over a slope. It was crowded with retreating infantry. From all the interwoven forest arose the smoke and bluster of the battle. The air was always occupied by a blaring.

Near where they stood shells were flip-flapping and hooting. Occasional bullets buzzed in the air and spanged into tree trunks. Wounded men and other stragglers were slinking through the woods.

Looking down an aisle of the grove, the youth and his companion saw a jangling general and his staff almost ride upon a wounded man, who was crawling on his hands and knees. The general reined strongly at his charger's opened and foamy mouth and guided it with dexterous horsemanship past the man. The latter scrambled in wild and torturing haste. His strength evidently failed him as he reached a place of safety. One of his arms suddenly weakened, and he fell, sliding over upon his back. He lay stretched out, breathing gently.

A moment later the small, creaking cavalcade was directly in front of the two soldiers. Another officer, riding with the skillful abandon of a cowboy, galloped his horse to a position directly before the general. The two unnoticed foot soldiers made a little show of going on, but they lingered near in the desire to overhear the conversation. Perhaps, they thought, some great inner historical things would be said.

The general, whom the boys knew as the commander of their division, looked at the other officer and spoke coolly, as if he were criticising his clothes. "Th' enemy's formin' over there for another charge," he said. "It'll be directed against Whiterside, an' I fear they'll break through there unless we work like thunder t' stop them."

The other swore at his restive horse, and then cleared his throat. He made a gesture toward his cap. "It'll be hell t' pay stoppin' them," he said shortly.

"I presume so," remarked the general. Then he began to talk rapidly and in a lower tone. He frequently illustrated his words with a pointing finger. The two infantrymen could hear nothing until finally he asked: "What troops can you spare?"

The officer who rode like a cowboy reflected for an instant. "Well," he said, "I had to order in th' 12th to help th' 76th, an' I haven't really got any. But there's th' 304th.[42] They fight like a lot 'a mule drivers.* I can spare them best of any."

The youth and his friend exchanged glances of astonishment.

The general spoke sharply. "Get 'em ready, then. I'll watch developments from here, an' send you word when t' start them. It'll happen in five minutes."

As the other officer tossed his fingers toward his cap and wheeling his horse, started away, the general called out to him in a sober voice: "I don't believe many of your mule drivers will get back."

The other shouted something in reply. He smiled.

With scared faces, the youth and his companion hurried back to the line.

These happenings had occupied an incredibly short time, yet the youth felt that in them he had been made aged. New eyes were given to him. And the most startling thing was to learn suddenly that he was very insignificant. The officer spoke of the regiment as if he referred to a broom. Some part of the woods needed sweeping, perhaps, and he merely indicated a broom in a tone properly indifferent to its fate. It was war, no doubt, but it appeared strange.

---

* Literally, a teamster; here, a disparaging term used by military officers to describe troops not proven under fire. The term calls attention to noncombat activity, ironic here because several of Fleming's New York peers had likely been teamsters prior to their military service.

As the two boys approached the line, the lieutenant perceived them and swelled with wrath. "Fleming—Wilson—how long does it take yeh to git water, anyhow—where yeh been to."

But his oration ceased as he saw their eyes, which were large with great tales. "We're goin' t' charge—we're goin' t' charge!" cried the youth's friend, hastening with his news.

"Charge?" said the lieutenant. "Charge? Well, b'Gawd! Now, this is real fightin'." Over his soiled countenance there went a boastful smile. "Charge? Well, b'Gawd!"

A little group of soldiers surrounded the two youths. "Are we, sure 'nough? Well, I'll be derned! Charge? What fer? What at? Wilson, you're lyin'."

"I hope to die," said the youth, pitching his tones to the key of angry remonstrance. "Sure as shooting, I tell you."

And his friend spoke in re-enforcement. "Not by a blame sight, he ain't lyin'. We heard 'em talkin'."

They caught sight of two mounted figures a short distance from them. One was the colonel of the regiment and the other was the officer who had received orders from the commander of the division. They were gesticulating at each other. The soldier, pointing at them, interpreted the scene.

One man had a final objection: "How could yeh hear 'em talkin'?" But the men, for a large part, nodded, admitting that previously the two friends had spoken truth.

They settled back into reposeful attitudes with airs of having accepted the matter. And they mused upon it, with a hundred varieties of expression. It was an engrossing thing to think about. Many tightened their belts carefully and hitched at their trousers.

A moment later the officers began to bustle among the men, pushing them into a more compact mass and into a better alignment. They chased those that straggled and fumed at a few men who seemed to show by their attitudes that they had decided to remain at that spot. They were like critical shepherds struggling with sheep.

Presently, the regiment seemed to draw itself up and heave a deep breath. None of the men's faces were mirrors of large thoughts. The soldiers were bended and stooped like sprinters before a signal. Many pairs of glinting eyes peered from the grimy faces toward the curtains of the deeper woods. They seemed to be engaged in deep calculations of time and distance.

They were surrounded by the noises of the monstrous altercation between the two armies. The world was fully interested in other matters. Apparently, the regiment had its small affair to itself.

The youth, turning, shot a quick, inquiring glance at his friend. The latter returned to him the same manner of look. They were the only ones who possessed an inner knowledge. "Mule drivers—hell t' pay—don't believe many will get back." It was an ironical secret. Still, they saw no hesitation in each other's faces, and they nodded a mute and unprotesting assent when a shaggy man near them said in a meek voice: "We'll git swallowed."

CHAPTER XIX

THE YOUTH STARED AT the land in front of him. Its foliages now seemed to veil powers and horrors. He was unaware of the machinery of orders that started the charge, although from the corners of his eyes he saw an officer, who looked like a boy a-horseback, come galloping, waving his hat. Suddenly he felt a straining and heaving among the men. The line fell slowly forward like a toppling wall, and, with a convulsive gasp that was intended for a cheer, the regiment began its journey. The youth was pushed and jostled for a moment before he understood the movement at all, but directly he lunged ahead and began to run.

He fixed his eye upon a distant and prominent clump of trees where he had concluded the enemy were to be met, and he ran toward it as toward a goal. He had believed throughout that it was a mere question of getting over an unpleasant matter as quickly as possible, and he ran desperately, as if pursued for a murder. His face was drawn hard and tight with the stress of his endeavor. His eyes were fixed in a lurid glare. And with his soiled and disordered dress, his red and inflamed features surmounted by the dingy rag with its spot of blood, his wildly swinging rifle and banging accounterments, he looked to be an insane soldier.

As the regiment swung from its position out into a cleared space the woods and thickets before it awakened. Yellow flames leaped toward it from many directions. The forest made a tremendous objection.

The line lurched straight for a moment. Then the right wing swung forward; it in turn was surpassed by the left. Afterward the center careered to the front until the regiment was a wedge-shaped mass, but an instant later the opposition of the bushes, trees, and uneven places on the ground split the command and scattered it into detached clusters.

The youth, light-footed, was unconsciously in advance. His eyes still kept note of the clump of trees. From all places near it the clannish yell of the enemy could be heard. The little flames of rifles leaped from it. The song of the bullets was in the air and shells snarled among the treetops. One tumbled directly into the middle of a hurrying group and exploded in crimson fury. There was an instant's spectacle of a man, almost over it, throwing up his hands to shield his eyes.

Other men, punched by bullets, fell in grotesque agonies. The regiment left a coherent trail of bodies.

They had passed into a clearer atmosphere. There was an effect like a revelation in the new appearance of the landscape. Some men working madly at a battery were plain to them, and the opposing infantry's lines were defined by the gray walls and fringes of smoke.

It seemed to the youth that he saw everything. Each blade of the green grass was bold and clear. He thought that he was aware of every change in the thin, transparent vapor that floated idly in sheets. The brown or gray trunks of the trees showed each roughness of their surfaces. And the men of the regiment, with their starting eyes and sweating faces, running madly, or falling, as if thrown headlong, to queer, heaped-up corpses—all were comprehended. His mind took a mechanical but firm impression, so that afterward everything was pictured and explained to him, save why he himself was there.

But there was a frenzy made from this furious rush. The men, pitching forward insanely, had burst into cheerings, moblike and barbaric, but tuned in strange keys that can arouse the dullard and the stoic. It made a mad enthusiasm that, it seemed, would be incapable of checking itself before granite and brass. There was the delirium that encounters despair and death, and is heedless and blind to the odds. It is a temporary but sublime absence of selfishness. And because it was of this order was the reason, perhaps, why the youth wondered, afterward, what reasons he could have had for being there.

Presently the straining pace ate up the energies of the men. As if by agreement, the leaders began to slacken their speed. The volleys directed against them had had a seeming windlike effect. The regiment snorted and blew. Among some stolid trees it began to falter and hesitate. The men, staring intently, began to wait for some of the distant walls of smoke to move and

disclose to them the scene. Since much of their strength and
their breath had vanished, they returned to caution. They were
become men again.

The youth had a vague belief that he had run miles, and he
thought, in a way, that he was now in some new and unknown
land.

The moment the regiment ceased its advance the protesting
splutter of musketry became a steadied roar. Long and accurate
fringes of smoke spread out. From the top of a small hill came
level belchings of yellow flame that caused an inhuman
whistling in the air.

The men, halted, had opportunity to see some of their comrades dropping with moans and shrieks. A few lay under foot,
still or wailing. And now for an instant the men stood, their rifles slack in their hands, and watched the regiment dwindle.
They appeared dazed and stupid. This spectacle seemed to para-
lyze them, overcome them with a fatal fascination. They stared
woodenly at the sights, and, lowering their eyes, looked from
face to face. It was a strange pause, and a strange silence.

Then, above the sounds of the outside commotion, arose the
roar of the lieutenant. He strode suddenly forth, his infantile
features black with rage.

"Come on, yeh fools!" he bellowed. "Come on! Yeh can't stay
here. Yeh must come on." He said more, but much of it could
not be understood.

He started rapidly forward, with his head turned toward the
men. "Come on," he was shouting. The men stared with blank
and yokel-like eyes at him. He was obliged to halt and retrace
his steps. He stood then with his back to the enemy and delivered gigantic curses into the faces of the men. His body vibrated
from the weight and force of his imprecations. And he could
string oaths with the facility of a maiden who strings beads.

The friend of the youth aroused. Lurching suddenly forward
and dropping to his knees, he fired an angry shot at the persistent woods. This action awakened the men. They huddled no
more like sheep. They seemed suddenly to bethink them of their
weapons, and at once commenced firing. Belabored by their officers, they began to move forward. The regiment, involved like

a cart involved in mud and muddle, started unevenly with many jolts and jerks. The men stopped now every few paces to fire and load, and in this manner moved slowly on from trees to trees.

The flaming opposition in their front grew with their advance until it seemed that all forward ways were barred by the thin leaping tongues, and off to the right an ominous demonstration could sometimes be dimly discerned. The smoke lately generated was in confusing clouds that made it difficult for the regiment to proceed with intelligence. As he passed through each curling mass the youth wondered what would confront him on the farther side.

The command went painfully forward until an open space interposed between them and the lurid lines. Here, crouching and cowering behind some trees, the men clung with desperation, as if threatened by a wave. They looked wild-eyed, and as if amazed at this furious disturbance they had stirred. In the storm there was an ironical expression of their importance. The faces of the men, too, showed a lack of a certain feeling of responsibility for being there. It was as if they had been driven. It was the dominant animal failing to remember in the supreme moments the forceful causes of various superficial qualities. The whole affair seemed incomprehensible to many of them.

As they halted thus the lieutenant again began to bellow profanely. Regardless of the vindictive threats of the bullets, he went about coaxing, berating, and bedamning. His lips, that were habitually in a soft and childlike curve, were now writhed into unholy contortions. He swore by all possible deities.

Once he grabbed the youth by the arm. "Come on, yeh lunkhead!" he roared. "Come on! We'll all git killed if we stay here. We've on'y got t' go across that lot. An' then"—the remainder of his idea disappeared in a blue haze of curses.

The youth stretched forth his arm. "Cross there?" His mouth was puckered in doubt and awe.

"Certainly. Jest 'cross th' lot! We can't stay here," screamed the lieutenant. He poked his face close to the youth and waved his bandaged hand. "Come on!" Presently he grappled with him as if for a wrestling bout. It was as if he planned to drag the youth by the ear on to the assault.

The private felt a sudden unspeakable indignation against his officer. He wrenched fiercely and shook him off.

"Come on yerself, then," he yelled. There was a bitter challenge in his voice.

They galloped together down the regimental front. The friend scrambled after them. In front of the colors the three men began to bawl: "Come on! come on!" They danced and gyrated like tortured savages.

The flag, obedient to these appeals, bended its glittering form and swept toward them. The men wavered in indecision for a moment, and then with a long, wailful cry the dilapidated regiment surged forward and began its new journey.

Over the field went the scurrying mass. It was a handful of men splattered into the faces of the enemy. Toward it instantly sprang the yellow tongues. A vast quantity of blue smoke hung before them. A mighty banging made ears valueless.

The youth ran like a madman to reach the woods before a bullet could discover him. He ducked his head low, like a football player. In his haste his eyes almost closed, and the scene was a wild blur. Pulsating saliva stood at the corners of his mouth.

Within him, as he hurled himself forward, was born a love, a despairing fondness for this flag which was near him. It was a creation of beauty and invulnerability. It was a goddess, radiant, that bended its form with an imperious gesture to him. It was a woman, red and white, hating and loving, that called him with the voice of his hopes. Because no harm could come to it he endowed it with power. He kept near, as if it could be a saver of lives, and an imploring cry went from his mind.

In the mad scramble he was aware that the color sergeant flinched suddenly, as if struck by a bludgeon. He faltered, and then became motionless, save for his quivering knees.

He made a spring and a clutch at the pole. At the same instant his friend grabbed it from the other side. They jerked at it, stout and furious, but the color sergeant was dead, and the corpse would not relinquish its trust. For a moment there was a grim encounter. The dead man, swinging with bended back, seemed to be obstinately tugging, in ludicrous and awful ways, for the possession of the flag.

It was past in an instant of time. They wrenched the flag furiously from the dead man, and, as they turned again, the corpse swayed forward with bowed head. One arm swung high, and the curved hand fell with heavy protest on the friend's unheeding shoulder.

CHAPTER XX

WHEN THE TWO YOUTHS turned with the flag they saw that much of the regiment had crumbled away, and the dejected remnant was coming slowly back. The men, having hurled themselves in projectile fashion, had presently expended their forces. They slowly retreated, with their faces still toward the spluttering woods, and their hot rifles still replying to the din. Several officers were giving orders, their voices keyed to screams.

"Where in hell yeh goin'?" the lieutenant was asking in a sarcastic howl. And a red-bearded officer, whose voice of triple brass could plainly be heard, was commanding: "Shoot into 'em! Shoot into 'em, Gawd damn their souls!" There was a *mêlée* of screeches, in which the men were ordered to do conflicting and impossible things.

The youth and his friend had a small scuffle over the flag. "Give it t' me!" "No, let me keep it!" Each felt satisfied with the other's possession of it, but each felt bound to declare, by an offer to carry the emblem, his willingness to further risk himself. The youth roughly pushed his friend away.

The regiment fell back to the stolid trees. There it halted for a moment to blaze at some dark forms that had begun to steal upon its track. Presently it resumed its march again, curving among the tree trunks. By the time the depleted regiment had again reached the first open space they were receiving a fast and merciless fire. There seemed to be mobs all about them.

The greater part of the men, discouraged, their spirits worn by the turmoil, acted as if stunned. They accepted the pelting of the bullets with bowed and weary heads. It was of no purpose to strive against walls. It was of no use to batter themselves against granite. And from this consciousness that they had attempted to conquer an unconquerable thing there seemed to arise a feeling that they had been betrayed. They glowered with bent brows, but dangerously, upon some of the officers, more particularly upon the red-bearded one with the voice of triple brass.

However, the rear of the regiment was fringed with men, who continued to shoot irritably at the advancing foes. They seemed resolved to make every trouble. The youthful lieutenant was perhaps the last man in the disordered mass. His forgotten back was toward the enemy. He had been shot in the arm. It hung straight and rigid. Occasionally he would cease to remember it, and be about to emphasize an oath with a sweeping gesture. The multiplied pain caused him to swear with incredible power.

The youth went along with slipping, uncertain feet. He kept watchful eyes rearward. A scowl of mortification and rage was upon his face. He had thought of a fine revenge upon the officer who had referred to him and his fellows as mule drivers. But he saw that it could not come to pass. His dreams had collapsed when the mule drivers, dwindling rapidly, had wavered and hesitated on the little clearing, and then had recoiled. And now the retreat of the mule drivers was a march of shame to him.

A dagger-pointed gaze from without his blackened face was held toward the enemy, but his greater hatred was riveted upon the man, who, not knowing him, had called him a mule driver.

When he knew that he and his comrades had failed to do anything in successful ways that might bring the little pangs of a kind of remorse upon the officer, the youth allowed the rage of the baffled to possess him. This cold officer upon a monument, who dropped epithets unconcernedly down, would be finer as a dead man, he thought. So grievous did he think it that he could never possess the secret right to taunt truly in answer.

He had pictured red letters of curious revenge. "We *are* mule drivers, are we?" And now he was compelled to throw them away.

He presently wrapped his heart in the cloak of his pride and kept the flag erect. He harangued his fellows, pushing against their chests with his free hand. To those he knew well he made frantic appeals, beseeching them by name. Between him and the lieutenant, scolding and near to losing his mind with rage, there was felt a subtle fellowship and equality. They supported each other in all manner of hoarse, howling protests.

But the regiment was a machine run down. The two men babbled at a forceless thing. The soldiers who had heart to go slowly were continually shaken in their resolves by a knowledge that comrades were slipping with speed back to the lines. It was difficult to think of reputation when others were thinking of skins. Wounded men were left crying on this black journey.

The smoke fringes and flames blustered always. The youth, peering once through a sudden rift in a cloud, saw a brown mass of troops, interwoven and magnified until they appeared to be thousands. A fierce-hued flag flashed before his vision.

Immediately, as if the uplifting of the smoke had been pre-arranged, the discovered troops burst into a rasping yell, and a hundred flames jetted toward the retreating band. A rolling gray cloud again interposed as the regiment doggedly replied. The youth had to depend again upon his misused ears, which were trembling and buzzing from the *mêlée* of musketry and yells.

The way seemed eternal. In the clouded haze men became panic-stricken with the thought that the regiment had lost its path, and was proceeding in a perilous direction. Once the men who headed the wild procession turned and came pushing back against their comrades, screaming that they were being fired upon from points which they had considered to be toward their own lines. At this cry a hysterical fear and dismay beset the troops. A soldier, who heretofore had been ambitious to make the regiment into a wise little band that would proceed calmly amid the huge-appearing difficulties, suddenly sank down and buried his face in his arms with an air of bowing to a doom. From another a shrill lamentation rang out filled with profane allusions to a general. Men ran hither and thither, seeking with their eyes roads of escape. With serene regularity, as if controlled by a schedule, bullets buffed into men.

The youth walked stolidly into the midst of the mob, and with his flag in his hands took a stand as if he expected an attempt to push him to the ground. He unconsciously assumed the attitude of the color bearer in the fight of the preceding day. He passed over his brow a hand that trembled. His breath did not come freely. He was choking during this small wait for the crisis.

His friend came to him. "Well, Henry, I guess this is good-by—John."*

"Oh, shut up, you damned fool!" replied the youth, and he would not look at the other.

The officers labored like politicians to beat the mass into a proper circle to face the menaces. The ground was uneven and torn. The men curled into depressions and fitted themselves snugly behind whatever would frustrate a bullet.

The youth noted with vague surprise that the lieutenant was standing mutely with his legs far apart and his sword held in the manner of a cane. The youth wondered what had happened to his vocal organs that he no more cursed.

There was something curious in this little intent pause of the lieutenant. He was like a babe which, having wept its fill, raises its eyes and fixes them upon a distant toy. He was engrossed in this contemplation, and the soft under lip quivered from self-whispered words.

Some lazy and ignorant smoke curled slowly. The men, hiding from the bullets, waited anxiously for it to lift and disclose the plight of the regiment.

The silent ranks were suddenly thrilled by the eager voice of the youthful lieutenant bawling out: "Here they come! Right onto us, b'Gawd!" His further words were lost in a roar of wicked thunder from the men's rifles.

The youth's eyes had instantly turned in the direction indicated by the awakened and agitated lieutenant, and he had seen the haze of treachery disclosing a body of soldiers of the enemy. They were so near that he could see their features. There was a recognition as he looked at the types of faces. Also he perceived with dim amazement that their uniforms were rather gay in effect, being light gray, accented with a brilliant-hued facing. Moreover, the clothes seemed new.

These troops had apparently been going forward with caution, their rifles held in readiness, when the youthful lieutenant had discovered them and their movement had been interrupted

---

* "Good-by, John" was a popular American phrase indicating a hopeless situation.

by the volley from the blue regiment. From the moment's glimpse, it was derived that they had been unaware of the proximity of their dark-suited foes or had mistaken the direction. Almost instantly they were shut utterly from the youth's sight by the smoke from the energetic rifles of his companions. He strained his vision to learn the accomplishment of the volley, but the smoke hung before him.

The two bodies of troops exchanged blows in the manner of a pair of boxers. The fast angry firings went back and forth. The men in blue were intent with the despair of their circumstances and they seized upon the revenge to be had at close range. Their thunder swelled loud and valiant. Their curving front bristled with flashes and the place resounded with the clangor of their ramrods. The youth ducked and dodged for a time and achieved a few unsatisfactory views of the enemy. There appeared to be many of them and they were replying swiftly. They seemed moving toward the blue regiment, step by step. He seated himself gloomily on the ground with his flag between his knees.

As he noted the vicious, wolflike temper of his comrades he had a sweet thought that if the enemy was about to swallow the regimental broom as a large prisoner, it could at least have the consolation of going down with bristles forward.*

But the blows of the antagonist began to grow more weak. Fewer bullets ripped the air, and finally, when the men slackened to learn of the fight, they could see only dark, floating smoke. The regiment lay still and gazed. Presently some chance whim came to the pestering blur, and it began to coil heavily away. The men saw a ground vacant of fighters. It would have been an empty stage if it were not for a few corpses that lay thrown and twisted into fantastic shapes upon the sward.†

At sight of this tableau, many of the men in blue sprang from behind their covers and made an ungainly dance of joy. Their

---

* In chapter XVIII, an officer "spoke of the regiment as if he referred to a broom" that must clean the woods of Confederates. Crane perhaps developed this simile from the adage "a new broom sweeps clean."

† Meadow, which here does not provide cover from musket fire.

eyes burned and a hoarse cheer of elation broke from their dry lips.

It had begun to seem to them that events were trying to prove that they were impotent. These little battles had evidently endeavored to demonstrate that the men could not fight well. When on the verge of submission to these opinions, the small duel had showed them that the proportions were not impossible, and by it they had revenged themselves upon their misgivings and upon the foe.

The impetus of enthusiasm was theirs again. They gazed about them with looks of uplifted pride, feeling new trust in the grim, always confident weapons in their hands. And they were men.

CHAPTER XXI

PRESENTLY THEY KNEW THAT no firing threatened them. All ways seemed once more opened to them. The dusty blue lines of their friends were disclosed a short distance away. In the distance there were many colossal noises, but in all this part of the field there was a sudden stillness.

They perceived that they were free. The depleted band drew a long breath of relief and gathered itself into a bunch to complete its trip.

In this last length of journey the men began to show strange emotions. They hurried with nervous fear. Some who had been dark and unfaltering in the grimmest moments now could not conceal an anxiety that made them frantic. It was perhaps that they dreaded to be killed in insignificant ways after the times for proper military deaths had passed. Or, perhaps, they thought it would be too ironical to get killed at the portals of safety. With backward looks of perturbation, they hastened.

As they approached their own lines there was some sarcasm exhibited on the part of a gaunt and bronzed regiment that lay resting in the shade of trees. Questions were wafted to them.

"Where th' hell yeh been?"

"What yeh comin' back fer?"

"Why didn't yeh stay there?"

"Was it warm out there, sonny?"

"Goin' home now, boys?"

One shouted in taunting mimicry: "Oh, mother, come quick an' look at th' sojers!"

There was no reply from the bruised and battered regiment, save that one man made broadcast challenges to fist fights and the red-bearded officer walked rather near and glared in great swashbuckler style at a tall captain in the other regiment. But the lieutenant suppressed the man who wished to fist fight, and the tall captain, flushing at the little fanfare of the red-bearded one, was obliged to look intently at some trees.

The youth's tender flesh was deeply stung by these remarks.

From under his creased brows he glowered with hate at the mockers. He meditated upon a few revenges. Still, many in the regiment hung their heads in criminal fashion, so that it came to pass that the men trudged with sudden heaviness, as if they bore upon their bended shoulders the coffin of their honor. And the youthful lieutenant, recollecting himself, began to mutter softly in black curses.

They turned when they arrived at their old position to regard the ground over which they had charged.

The youth in this contemplation was smitten with a large astonishment. He discovered that the distances, as compared with the brilliant measurings of his mind, were trivial and ridiculous. The stolid trees, where much had taken place, seemed incredibly near. The time, too, now that he reflected, he saw to have been short. He wondered at the number of emotions and events that had been crowded into such little spaces. Elfin thoughts must have exaggerated and enlarged everything, he said.

It seemed, then, that there was bitter justice in the speeches of the gaunt and bronzed veterans. He veiled a glance of disdain at his fellows who strewed the ground, choking with dust, red from perspiration, misty-eyed, disheveled.

They were gulping at their canteens, fierce to wring every mite of water from them, and they polished at their swollen and watery features with coat sleeves and bunches of grass.

However, to the youth there was a considerable joy in musing upon his performances during the charge. He had had very little time previously in which to appreciate himself, so that there was now much satisfaction in quietly thinking of his actions. He recalled bits of color that in the flurry had stamped themselves unawares upon his engaged senses.

As the regiment lay heaving from its hot exertions the officer who had named them as mule drivers came galloping along the line. He had lost his cap. His tousled hair streamed wildly, and his face was dark with vexation and wrath. His temper was displayed with more clearness by the way in which he managed his horse. He jerked and wrenched savagely at his bridle, stopping the hard-breathing animal with a furious pull near the colonel of the regiment. He immediately exploded in reproaches which came unbidden to the ears of the men. They were suddenly alert, being always curious about black words between officers.

"Oh, thunder, MacChesnay, what an awful bull you made of this thing!" began the officer. He attempted low tones, but his indignation caused certain of the men to learn the sense of his words. "What an awful mess you made! Good Lord, man, you stopped about a hundred feet this side of a very pretty success! If your men had gone a hundred feet farther you would have made a great charge, but as it is—what a lot of mud diggers* you've got anyway!"

The men, listening with bated breath, now turned their curious eyes upon the colonel. They had a ragamuffin† interest in this affair.

The colonel was seen to straighten his form and put one hand forth in oratorical fashion. He wore an injured air; it was as if a deacon had been accused of stealing. The men were wiggling in an ecstasy of excitement.

But of a sudden the colonel's manner changed from that of a deacon to that of a Frenchman. He shrugged his shoulders. "Oh, well, general, we went as far as we could," he said calmly.

"As far as you could? Did you, b'Gawd?" snorted the other. "Well, that wasn't very far, was it?" he added, with a glance of cold contempt into the other's eyes. "Not very far, I think. You were intended to make a diversion in favor of Whiterside.[43] How well you succeeded your own ears can now tell you." He wheeled his horse and rode stiffly away.

The colonel, bidden to hear the jarring noises of an engagement in the woods to the left, broke out in vague damnations.

The lieutenant, who had listened with an air of impotent rage to the interview, spoke suddenly in firm and undaunted tones. "I don't care what a man is—whether he is a general or

---

* Military slang for infantrymen is mud crushers, which envisions men trudging through mud toward the front. Mud diggers thus is a disparaging term for infantrymen who refuse to move.

† Beggarly.

what—if he says th' boys didn't put up a good fight out there he's a damned fool."

"Lieutenant," began the colonel, severely, "this is my own affair, and I'll trouble you——"

The lieutenant made an obedient gesture. "All right, colonel, all right," he said. He sat down with an air of being content with himself.

The news that the regiment had been reproached went along the line. For a time the men were bewildered by it. "Good thunder!" they ejaculated, staring at the vanishing form of the general. They conceived it to be a huge mistake.

Presently, however, they began to believe that in truth their efforts had been called light. The youth could see this conviction weigh upon the entire regiment until the men were like cuffed and cursed animals, but withal rebellious.

The friend, with a grievance in his eye, went to the youth. "I wonder what he does want," he said. "He must think we went out there an' played marbles! I never see sech a man!"

The youth developed a tranquil philosophy for these moments of irritation. "Oh, well," he rejoined, "he probably didn't see nothing of it at all and got mad as blazes, and concluded we were a lot of sheep, just because we didn't do what he wanted done. It's a pity old Grandpa Henderson got killed yestirday—he'd have known that we did our best and fought good. It's just our awful luck, that's what."

"I should say so," replied the friend. He seemed to be deeply wounded at an injustice. "I should say we did have awful luck! There's no fun in fightin' fer people when everything yeh do—no matter what—ain't done right. I have a notion t' stay behind next time an' let 'em take their ol' charge an' go t' th' devil with it."

The youth spoke soothingly to his comrade. "Well, we both did good. I'd like to see the fool what'd say we both didn't do as good as we could!"

"Of course we did," declared the friend stoutly. "An' I'd break th' feller's neck if he was as big as a church. But we're all right, anyhow, for I heard one feller say that we two fit th' best in th' reg'ment, an' they had a great argument 'bout it. Another

feller, 'a course, he had t' up an' say it was a lie—he seen all
what was goin' on an' he never seen us from th' beginnin' t' th'
end. An' a lot more struck in an' ses it wasn't a lie—we did fight
like thunder, an' they give us quite a send-off. But this is what I
can't stand—these everlastin' ol' soldiers, titterin' an' laughin',
an' then that general, he's crazy."

The youth exclaimed with sudden exasperation: "He's a
lunkhead! He makes me mad. I wish he'd come along next time.
We'd show 'im what——"

He ceased because several men had come hurrying up. Their
faces expressed a bringing of great news.

"O Flem, yeh jest oughta heard!" cried one, eagerly.

"Heard what?" said the youth.

"Yeh jest oughta heard!" repeated the other, and he arranged
himself to tell his tidings. The others made an excited circle.
"Well, sir, th' colonel met your lieutenant right by us—it was
damnedest thing I ever heard—an' he ses: 'Ahem! ahem!' he ses.
'Mr. Hasbrouck!' he ses, 'by th' way, who was that lad what carried th' flag?' he ses. There, Flemin', what d' yeh think 'a that?
'Who was th' lad what carried th' flag?' he ses, an' th' lieutenant, he speaks up right away: 'That's Flemin', an' he's a
jimhickey,'* he ses, right away. What? I say he did. 'A jimhickey,'
he ses—those 'r his words. He did, too. I say he did. If you kin
tell this story better than I kin, go ahead an' tell it. Well, then,
keep yer mouth shet. Th' lieutenant, he ses: 'He's a jimhickey,'
an' th' colonel, he ses: 'Ahem! ahem! he is, indeed, a very good
man t' have, ahem! He kep' th' flag 'way t' th' front. I saw 'im.
He's a good un,' ses th' colonel. 'You bet,' ses th' lieutenant, 'he
an' a feller named Wilson was at th' head 'a th' charge, an'
howlin' like Indians all th' time,' he ses. 'Head 'a th' charge all
th' time,' he ses. 'A feller named Wilson,' he ses. There, Wilson,
m'boy, put that in a letter an' send it hum t' yer mother, hay? 'A
feller named Wilson,' he ses. An' th' colonel, he ses: 'Were they,
indeed? Ahem! ahem! My sakes!' he ses. 'At th' head 'a th'

---

* Similar to jim-dandy, jimhickey means exceptional; since "hick" suggests
an unsophisticated person, however, Fleming's comrade suggests that
fineness originates in one's ordinariness rather than in affected airs.

reg'ment?' he ses. 'They were,' ses th' lieutenant. 'My sakes!' ses th' colonel. He ses: 'Well, well, well,' he ses, 'those two babies?' 'They were,' ses th' lieutenant. 'Well, well,' ses th' colonel, 'they deserve t' be major generals,' he ses. 'They deserve t' be major-generals.'

The youth and his friend had said: "Huh!" "Yer lyin', Thompson." "Oh, go t' blazes!" "He never sed it." "Oh, what a lie!" "Huh!" But despite these youthful scoffings and embarrassments, they knew that their faces were deeply flushing from thrills of pleasure. They exchanged a secret glance of joy and congratulation.

They speedily forgot many things. The past held no pictures of error and disappointment. They were very happy, and their hearts swelled with grateful affection for the colonel and the youthful lieutenant.

CHAPTER XXII

WHEN THE WOODS AGAIN began to pour forth the dark-hued masses of the enemy the youth felt serene self-confidence. He smiled briefly when he saw men dodge and duck at the long screechings of shells that were thrown in giant handfuls over them. He stood, erect and tranquil, watching the attack begin against a part of the line that made a blue curve along the side of an adjacent hill. His vision being unmolested by smoke from the rifles of his companions, he had opportunities to see parts of the hard fight. It was a relief to perceive at last from whence came some of these noises which had been roared into his ears.

Off a short way he saw two regiments fighting a little separate battle with two other regiments. It was in a cleared space, wearing a set-apart look. They were blazing as if upon a wager, giving and taking tremendous blows. The firings were incredibly fierce and rapid. These intent regiments apparently were oblivious of all larger purposes of war, and were slugging each other as if at a matched game.

In another direction he saw a magnificent brigade going with the evident intention of driving the enemy from a wood. They passed in out of sight and presently there was a most awe-inspiring racket in the wood. The noise was unspeakable. Having stirred this prodigious uproar, and, apparently, finding it too prodigious, the brigade, after a little time, came marching airily out again with its fine formation in nowise disturbed. There were no traces of speed in its movements. The brigade was jaunty and seemed to point a proud thumb at the yelling wood.

On a slope to the left there was a long row of guns, gruff and maddened, denouncing the enemy, who, down through the woods, were forming for another attack in the pitiless monotony of conflicts. The round red discharges from the guns made a crimson flare and a high, thick smoke. Occasional glimpses could be caught of groups of the toiling artillerymen. In the rear of this row of guns stood a house, calm and white, amid bursting shells.[44] A congregation of horses, tied to a long railing, were tugging frenziedly at their bridles. Men were running hither and thither.

The detached battle between the four regiments lasted for some time. There chanced to be no interference, and they settled their dispute by themselves. They struck savagely and powerfully at each other for a period of minutes, and then the lighter-hued regiments faltered and drew back, leaving the dark-blue lines shouting. The youth could see the two flags shaking with laughter amid the smoke remnants.

Presently there was a stillness, pregnant with meaning. The blue lines shifted and changed a trifle and stared expectantly at the silent woods and fields before them. The hush was solemn and churchlike, save for a distant battery that, evidently unable to remain quiet, sent a faint rolling thunder over the ground. It irritated, like the noises of unimpressed boys. The men imagined that it would prevent their perched ears from hearing the first words of the new battle.

Of a sudden the guns on the slope roared out a message of warning. A spluttering sound had begun in the woods. It swelled with amazing speed to a profound clamor that involved the earth in noises. The splitting crashes swept along the lines until an interminable roar was developed. To those in the midst of it it became a din fitted to the universe. It was the whirring and thumping of gigantic machinery, complications among the smaller stars. The youth's ears were filled up. They were incapable of hearing more.

On an incline over which a road wound he saw wild and desperate rushes of men perpetually backward and forward in riotous surges. These parts of the opposing armies were two long waves that pitched upon each other madly at dictated points. To and fro they swelled. Sometimes, one side by its yells and cheers would proclaim decisive blows, but a moment later the other side would be all yells and cheers. Once the youth saw a spray of light forms go in houndlike leaps toward the waving blue lines. There was much howling, and presently it went away with a vast mouthful of prisoners. Again, he saw a blue wave dash with such thunderous force against a gray obstruction that it seemed to clear the earth of it and leave nothing but trampled sod. And always in their swift and deadly rushes to and fro the men screamed and yelled like maniacs.

Particular pieces of fence or secure positions behind collections of trees were wrangled over, as gold thrones or pearl bedsteads. There were desperate lunges at these chosen spots seemingly every instant, and most of them were bandied like light toys between the contending forces. The youth could not tell from the battle flags flying like crimson foam in many directions which color of cloth was winning.

His emaciated regiment bustled forth with undiminished fierceness when its time came. When assaulted again by bullets, the men burst out in a barbaric cry of rage and pain. They bent their heads in aims of intent hatred behind the projected hammers of their guns. Their ramrods clanged loud with fury as their eager arms pounded the cartridges into the rifle barrels. The front of the regiment was a smoke-wall penetrated by the flashing points of yellow and red.

Wallowing in the fight, they were in an astonishingly short time resmudged. They surpassed in stain and dirt all their previous appearances. Moving to and fro with strained exertion, jabbering the while, they were, with their swaying bodies, black faces, and glowing eyes, like strange and ugly friends jigging heavily in the smoke.

The lieutenant, returning from a tour after a bandage, produced from a hidden receptacle of his mind new and portentous oaths suited to the emergency. Strings of expletives he swung lashlike over the backs of his men, and it was evident that his previous efforts had in nowise impaired his resources.

The youth, still the bearer of the colors, did not feel his idleness. He was deeply absorbed as a spectator. The crash and swing of the great drama made him lean forward, intent-eyed, his face working in small contortions. Sometimes he prattled, words coming unconsciously from him in grotesque exclamations. He did not know that he breathed; that the flag hung silently over him, so absorbed was he.

A formidable line of the enemy came within dangerous range. They could be seen plainly—tall, gaunt men with excited faces running with long strides toward a wandering fence.

At sight of this danger the men suddenly ceased their cursing monotone. There was an instant of strained silence before they threw up their rifles and fired a plumping volley at the foes. There had been no order given; the men, upon recognizing the menace, had immediately let drive their flock of bullets without waiting for word of command.

But the enemy were quick to gain the protection of the wandering line of fence. They slid down behind it with remarkable celerity, and from this position they began briskly to slice up the blue men.

These latter braced their energies for a great struggle. Often, white clinched teeth shone from the dusky faces. Many heads surged to and fro, floating upon a pale sea of smoke. Those behind the fence frequently shouted and yelped in taunts and gibelike cries, but the regiment maintained a stressed silence. Perhaps, at this new assault the men recalled the fact that they had been named mud diggers, and it made their situation thrice bitter. They were breathlessly intent upon keeping the ground and thrusting away the rejoicing body of the enemy. They fought swiftly and with a despairing savageness denoted in their expressions.

The youth had resolved not to budge whatever should happen. Some arrows of scorn that had buried themselves in his heart had generated strange and unspeakable hatred. It was clear to him that his final and absolute revenge was to be achieved by his dead body lying, torn and gluttering, upon the field. This was to be a poignant retaliation upon the officer who had said "mule drivers," and later "mud diggers," for in all the wild graspings of his mind for a unit responsible for his sufferings and commotions he always seized upon the man who had dubbed him wrongly. And it was his idea, vaguely formulated, that his corpse would be for those eyes a great and salt reproach.

The regiment bled extravagantly. Grunting bundles of blue began to drop. The orderly sergeant* of the youth's company was shot through the cheeks. Its supports being injured, his jaw

---

* Sergeant who attends the company captain and performs messenger duties.

hung afar down, disclosing in the wide cavern of his mouth a pulsing mass of blood and teeth. And with it all he made attempts to cry out. In his endeavor there was a dreadful earnestness, as if he conceived that one great shriek would make him well.

The youth saw him presently go rearward. His strength seemed in nowise impaired. He ran swiftly, casting wild glances for succor.

Others fell down about the feet of their companions. Some of the wounded crawled out and away, but many lay still, their bodies twisted into impossible shapes.

The youth looked once for his friend. He saw a vehement young man, powder-smeared and frowzled, whom he knew to be him. The lieutenant, also, was unscathed in his position at the rear. He had continued to curse, but it was now with the air of a man who was using his last box of oaths.

For the fire of the regiment had begun to wane and drip. The robust voice, that had come strangely from the thin ranks, was growing rapidly weak.

CHAPTER XXIII

THE COLONEL CAME RUNNING along back of the line. There were other officers following him. "We must charge'm!" they shouted. "We must charge'm!" they cried with resentful voices, as if anticipating a rebellion against this plan by the men.[45]

The youth, upon hearing the shouts, began to study the distance between him and the enemy. He made vague calculations. He saw that to be firm soldiers they must go forward. It would be death to stay in the present place, and with all the circumstances to go backward would exalt too many others. Their hope was to push the galling foes away from the fence.

He expected that his companions, weary and stiffened, would have to be driven to this assault, but as he turned toward them he perceived with a certain surprise that they were giving quick and unqualified expressions of assent. There was an ominous, clanging overture to the charge when the shafts of the bayonets rattled upon the rifle barrels. At the yelled words of command the soldiers sprang forward in eager leaps. There was new and unexpected force in the movement of the regiment. A knowledge of its faded and jaded condition made the charge appear like a paroxysm, a display of the strength that comes before a final feebleness. The men scampered in insane fever of haste, racing as if to achieve a sudden success before an exhilarating fluid should leave them. It was a blind and despairing rush by the collection of men in dusty and tattered blue, over a green sward and under a sapphire sky, toward a fence, dimly outlined in smoke, from behind which spluttered the fierce rifles of enemies.

The youth kept the bright colors to the front. He was waving his free arm in furious circles, the while shrieking mad calls and appeals, urging on those that did not need to be urged, for it seemed that the mob of blue men hurling themselves on the dangerous group of rifles were again grown suddenly wild with an enthusiasm of unselfishness. From the many firings starting toward them, it looked as if they would merely succeed in mak-

133

ing a great sprinkling of corpses on the grass between their former position and the fence. But they were in a state of frenzy, perhaps because of forgotten vanities, and it made an exhibition of sublime recklessness. There was no obvious questioning, nor figurings, nor diagrams. There was, apparently, no considered loopholes. It appeared that the swift wings of their desires would have shattered against the iron gates of the impossible.

He himself felt the daring spirit of a savage religion-mad. He was capable of profound sacrifices, a tremendous death. He had no time for dissections, but he knew that he thought of the bullets only as things that could prevent him from reaching the place of his endeavor. There were subtle flashings of joy within him that thus should be his mind.

He strained all his strength. His eyesight was shaken and dazzled by the tension of thought and muscle. He did not see anything excepting the mist of smoke gashed by the little knives of fire, but he knew that in it lay the aged fence of a vanished farmer protecting the snuggled bodies of the gray men.

As he ran a thought of the shock of contact gleamed in his mind. He expected a great concussion when the two bodies of troops crashed together. This became a part of his wild battle madness. He could feel the onward swing of the regiment about him and he conceived of a thunderous, crushing blow that would prostrate the resistance and spread consternation and amazement for miles. The flying regiment was going to have a catapultian effect. This dream made him run faster among his comrades, who were giving vent to hoarse and frantic cheers.

But presently he could see that many of the men in gray did not intend to abide the blow. The smoke, rolling, disclosed men who ran, their faces still turned. These grew to a crowd, who retired stubbornly. Individuals wheeled frequently to send a bullet at the blue wave.

But at one part of the line there was a grim and obdurate group that made no movement. They were settled firmly down behind posts and rails. A flag, ruffled and fierce, waved over them and their rifles dinned fiercely.

The blue whirl of men got very near, until it seemed that in truth there would be a close and frightful scuffle. There was an expressed disdain in the opposition of the little group, that changed the meaning of the cheers of the men in blue. They became yells of wrath, directed, personal. The cries of the two parties were now in sound an interchange of scathing insults.

They in blue showed their teeth; their eyes shone all white. They launched themselves as at the throats of those who stood resisting. The space between dwindled to an insignificant distance.

The youth had centered the gaze of his soul upon that other flag. Its possession would be high pride. It would express bloody minglings, near blows. He had a gigantic hatred for those who made great difficulties and complications. They caused it to be as a craved treasure of mythology, hung amid tasks and contrivances of danger.

He plunged like a mad horse at it. He was resolved it should not escape if wild blows and darings of blows could seize it. His own emblem, quivering and aflare, was winging toward the other. It seemed there would shortly be an encounter of strange beaks and claws, as of eagles.

The swirling body of blue men came to a sudden halt at close and disastrous range and roared a swift volley. The group in gray was split and broken by this fire, but its riddled body still fought. The men in blue yelled again and rushed in upon it.

The youth, in his leapings, saw, as through a mist, a picture of four or five men stretched upon the ground or writhing upon their knees with bowed heads as if they had been stricken by bolts from the sky. Tottering among them was the rival color bearer, whom the youth saw had been bitten vitally by the bullets of the last formidable volley. He perceived this man fighting a last struggle, the struggle of one whose legs are grasped by demons. It was a ghastly battle. Over his face was the bleach of death, but set upon it was the dark and hard lines of desperate purpose. With this terrible grin of resolution he hugged his precious flag to him and was stumbling and staggering in his design to go the way that led to safety for it.

But his wounds always made it seem that his feet were retarded, held, and he fought a grim fight, as with invisible ghouls fastened greedily upon his limbs. Those in advance of the scampering blue men, howling cheers, leaped at the fence. The despair of the lost was in his eyes as he glanced back at them.

The youth's friend went over the obstruction in a tumbling heap and sprang at the flag as a panther at prey. He pulled at it and, wrenching it free, swung up its red brilliancy with a mad cry of exultation even as the color bearer, gasping, lurched over in a final throe and, stiffening convulsively, turned his dead face to the ground. There was much blood upon the grass blades.

At the place of success there began more wild clamorings of cheers. The men gesticulated and bellowed in an ecstasy. When they spoke it was as if they considered their listener to be a mile away. What hats and caps were left to them they often slung high in the air.

At one part of the line four men had been swooped upon, and they now sat as prisoners. Some blue men were about them in an eager and curious circle. The soldiers had trapped strange birds, and there was an examination. A flurry of fast questions was in the air.

One of the prisoners was nursing a superficial wound in the foot. He cuddled it, baby-wise, but he looked up from it often to curse with an astonishing utter abandon straight at the noses of his captors. He consigned them to red regions; he called upon the pestilential wrath of strange gods. And with it all he was singularly free from recognition of the finer points of the conduct of prisoners of war. It was as if a clumsy clod had trod upon his toe and he conceived it to be his privilege, his duty, to use deep, resentful oaths.

Another, who was a boy in years, took his plight with great calmness and apparent good nature. He conversed with the men in blue, studying their faces with his bright and keen eyes. They spoke of battles and conditions. There was an acute interest in all their faces during this exchange of view points. It seemed a great satisfaction to hear voices from where all had been darkness and speculation.

The third captive sat with a morose countenance. He preserved a stoical and cold attitude. To all advances he made one reply without variation, "Ah, go t' hell!"

The last of the four was always silent and, for the most part, kept his face turned in unmolested directions. From the views the youth received he seemed to be in a state of absolute dejection. Shame was upon him, and with it profound regret that he was, perhaps, no more to be counted in the ranks of his fellows. The youth could detect no expression that would allow him to believe that the other was giving a thought to his narrowed future, the pictured dungeons, perhaps, and starvations and brutalities, liable to the imagination. All to be seen was shame for captivity and regret for the right to antagonize.

After the men had celebrated sufficiently they settled down behind the old rail fence, on the opposite side to the one from which their foes had been driven. A few shot perfunctorily at distant marks.

There was some long grass. The youth nestled in it and rested, making a convenient rail support the flag. His friend, jubilant and glorified, holding his treasure with vanity, came to him there. They sat side by side and congratulated each other.

CHAPTER XXIV

THE ROARINGS THAT HAD stretched in a long line of sound across the face of the forest began to grow intermittent and weaker. The stentorian speeches of the artillery continued in some distant encounter, but the crashes of the musketry had almost ceased. The youth and his friend of a sudden looked up, feeling a deadened form of distress at the waning of these noises, which had become a part of life. They could see changes going on among the troops. There were marchings this way and that way. A battery wheeled leisurely. On the crest of a small hill was the thick gleam of many departing muskets.

The youth arose. "Well, what now, I wonder?" he said. By his tone he seemed to be preparing to resent some new monstrosity in the way of dins and smashes. He shaded his eyes with his grimy hand and gazed over the field.

His friend also arose and stared. "I bet we're goin' t' git along out of this an' back over th' river," said he.

"Well, I swan!"* said the youth.

They waited, watching. Within a little while the regiment received orders to retrace its way. The men got up grunting from the grass, regretting the soft repose. They jerked their stiffened legs, and stretched their arms over their heads. One man swore as he rubbed his eyes. They all groaned "O Lord!" They had as many objections to this change as they would have had to a proposal for a new battle.

They trampled slowly back over the field across which they had run in a mad scamper.

The regiment marched until it had joined its fellows. The reformed brigade, in column, aimed through a wood at the road. Directly they were in a mass of dust-covered troops, and were trudging along in a way parallel to the enemy's lines as these had been defined by the previous turmoil.

They passed within view of a stolid white house, and saw in

---

* American colloquialism for "I swear."

front of it groups of their comrades lying in wait behind a neat breastwork. A row of guns were booming at a distant enemy. Shells thrown in reply were raising clouds of dust and splinters. Horsemen dashed along the line of intrenchments.

At this point of its march the division curved away from the field and went winding off in the direction of the river. When the significance of this movement had impressed itself upon the youth he turned his head and looked over his shoulder toward the trampled and débris-strewed ground. He breathed a breath of new satisfaction. He finally nudged his friend. "Well, it's all over," he said to him.

His friend gazed backward. "B'Gawd, it is," he assented. They mused.

For a time the youth was obliged to reflect in a puzzled and uncertain way. His mind was undergoing a subtle change. It took moments for it to cast off its battleful ways and resume its accustomed course of thought. Gradually his brain emerged from the clogged clouds, and at last he was enabled to more closely comprehend himself and circumstance.

He understood then that the existence of shot and counter-shot was in the past. He had dwelt in a land of strange, squalling upheavals and had come forth. He had been where there was red of blood and black of passion, and he was escaped. His first thoughts were given to rejoicings at this fact.

Later he began to study his deeds, his failures, and his achievements. Thus, fresh from scenes where many of his usual machines of reflection had been idle, from where he had proceeded sheeplike, he struggled to marshal all his acts.

At last they marched before him clearly. From this present view point he was enabled to look upon them in spectator fashion and to criticise them with some correctness, for his new condition had already defeated certain sympathies.

Regarding his procession of memory he felt gleeful and unregretting, for in it his public deeds were paraded in great and shining prominence. Those performances which had been witnessed by his fellows marched now in wide purple and gold, having various deflections. They went gayly with music. It was pleasure to watch these things. He spent delightful minutes viewing the gilded images of memory.

He saw that he was good. He recalled with a thrill of joy the respectful comments of his fellows upon his conduct.

Nevertheless, the ghost of his flight from the first engagement appeared to him and danced. There were small shoutings in his brain about these matters. For a moment he blushed, and the light of his soul flickered with shame.

A specter of reproach came to him. There loomed the dogging memory of the tattered soldier—he who, gored by bullets and faint for blood, had fretted concerning an imagined wound in another; he who had loaned his last of strength and intellect for the tall soldier; he who, blind with weariness and pain, had been deserted in the field.

For an instant a wretched chill of sweat was upon him at the thought that he might be detected in the thing. As he stood persistently before his vision, he gave vent to a cry of sharp irritation and agony.

His friend turned. "What's the matter, Henry?" he demanded. The youth's reply was an outburst of crimson oaths.

As he marched along the little branch-hung roadway among his prattling companions this vision of cruelty brooded over him. It clung near him always and darkened his view of these deeds in purple and gold. Whichever way his thoughts turned they were followed by the somber phantom of the desertion in the fields. He looked stealthily at his companions, feeling sure that they must discern in his face evidences of this pursuit. But they were plodding in ragged array, discussing with quick tongues the accomplishments of the late battle.

"Oh, if a man should come up an' ask me, I'd say we got a dum good lickin'."[46]

"Lickin'—in yer eye! We ain't licked, sonny. We're goin' down here aways, swing aroun', an' come in behint 'em."

"Oh, hush, with your comin' in behint 'em. I've seen all 'a that I wanta. Don't tell me about comin' in behint——"

"Bill Smithers, he ses he'd rather been in ten hundred battles than been in that heluva hospital. He ses they got shootin' in th'

night-time, an' shells dropped plum among 'em in th' hospital.
He ses sech hollerin' he never see."

"Hasbrouck? He's th' best off'cer in this here reg'ment. He's
a whale."*

"Didn't I tell yeh we'd come aroun' in behint 'em? Didn't I
tell yeh so? We——"

"Oh, shet yeh mouth!"

For a time this pursuing recollection of the tattered man
took all elation from the youth's veins. He saw his vivid error,
and he was afraid that it would stand before him all his life. He
took no share in the chatter of his comrades, nor did he look at
them or know them, save when he felt sudden suspicion that
they were seeing his thoughts and scrutinizing each detail of
the scene with the tattered soldier.

Yet gradually he mustered force to put the sin at a distance.
And at last his eyes seemed to open to some new ways. He
found that he could look back upon the brass and bombast of
his earlier gospels and see them truly. He was gleeful when he
discovered that he now despised them.

With this conviction came a store of assurance. He felt a
quiet manhood, nonassertive but of sturdy and strong blood.
He knew that he would no more quail before his guides wherever they should point. He had been to touch the great death,
and found that, after all, it was but the great death. He was a
man.

So it came to pass that as he trudged from the place of blood
and wrath his soul changed. He came from hot plowshares to
prospects of clover tranquilly, and it was as if hot plowshares
were not.[47] Scars faded as flowers.

It rained. The procession of weary soldiers became a bedrag-
gled train, despondent and muttering, marching with churning
effort in a trough of liquid brown mud under a low, wretched
sky. Yet the youth smiled, for he saw that the world was a world
for him, though many discovered it to be made of oaths and
walking sticks. He had rid himself of the red sickness of battle.

---

* A superior, excellent, or large example; a phrase popular in Crane's
time was *to go ahead like a whale*, which meant "to forge ahead."

The sultry nightmare was in the past. He had been an animal blistered and sweating in the heat and pain of war. He turned now with a lover's thirst to images of tranquil skies, fresh meadows, cool brooks—an existence of soft and eternal peace.

Over the river a golden ray of sun came through the hosts of leaden rain clouds.

THE OPEN BOAT[1]

A TALE INTENDED TO BE AFTER THE FACT: BEING THE EXPERIENCE OF FOUR MEN FROM THE SUNK STEAMER COMMODORE

I

NONE OF THEM KNEW the color of the sky. Their eyes glanced level, and were fastened upon the waves that swept toward them. These waves were of the hue of slate, save for the tops, which were of foaming white, and all of the men knew the colors of the sea. The horizon narrowed and widened, and dipped and rose, and at all times its edge was jagged with waves that seemed thrust up in points like rocks.

Many a man ought to have a bathtub larger than the boat which here rode upon the sea. These waves were most wrongfully and barbarously abrupt and tall, and each froth-top was a problem in small-boat navigation.

The cook squatted in the bottom, and looked with both eyes at the six inches of gunwale* which separated him from the ocean. His sleeves were rolled over his fat forearms, and the two flaps of his unbuttoned vest dangled as he bent to bail out the boat. Often he said, "Gawd! that was a narrow clip."† As he remarked it he invariably gazed eastward over the broken sea.

The oiler, steering with one of the two oars in the boat, sometimes raised himself suddenly to keep clear of water that

---

* The upper edge of the dinghy's side.

† Slang for "a hurried escape"; variation of the more popular phrase *a close shave*; here refers to abandoning the sinking *Commodore*.

swirled in over the stern. It was a thin little oar, and it seemed often ready to snap.

The correspondent, pulling at the other oar, watched the waves and wondered why he was there.

The injured captain, lying in the bow, was at this time buried in that profound dejection and indifference which comes, temporarily at least, to even the bravest and most enduring when, willy-nilly,* the firm fails, the army loses, the ship goes down.[2] The mind of the master of a vessel is rooted deep in the timbers of her, though he command for a day or a decade; and this captain had on him the stern impression of a scene in the grays of dawn of seven turned faces, and later a stump of a topmast with a white ball on it, that slashed to and fro at the waves, went low and lower, and down. Thereafter there was something strange in his voice. Although steady, it was deep with mourning, and of a quality beyond oration or tears.

"Keep 'er a little more south, Billie," said he.

"A little more south, sir," said the oiler in the stern.

A seat in this boat was not unlike a seat upon a bucking broncho, and by the same token a broncho is not much smaller. The craft pranced and reared and plunged like an animal. As each wave came, and she rose for it, she seemed like a horse making at a fence outrageously high. The manner of her scramble over these walls of water is a mystic thing, and, moreover, at the top of them were ordinarily these problems in white water, the foam racing down from the summit of each wave requiring a new leap, and a leap from the air. Then, after scornfully bumping a crest, she would slide and race and splash down a long incline, and arrive bobbing and nodding in front of the next menace.

A singular disadvantage of the sea lies in the fact that after successfully surmounting one wave you discover that there is another behind it just as important and just as nervously anxious to do something effective in the way of swamping boats. In a ten-foot dinghy one can get an idea of the resources of the sea in the line of waves that is not probable to the average experience, which is never at sea in a dinghy. As each slaty wall of wa-

---

* Popular phrase that means "occurring regardless of human volition."

ter approached, it shut all else from the view of the men in the boat, and it was not difficult to imagine that this particular wave was the final outburst of the ocean, the last effort of the grim water. There was a terrible grace in the move of the waves, and they came in silence, save for the snarling of the crests.

In the wan light the faces of the men must have been gray. Their eyes must have glinted in strange ways as they gazed steadily astern. Viewed from a balcony, the whole thing would doubtless have been weirdly picturesque. But the men in the boat had no time to see it, and if they had had leisure, there were other things to occupy their minds. The sun swung steadily up the sky, and they knew it was broad day because the color of the sea changed from slate to emerald-green streaked with amber lights, and the foam was like tumbling snow. The process of the breaking day was unknown to them. They were aware only of this effect upon the color of the waves that rolled toward them.

In disjointed sentences the cook and the correspondent argued as to the difference between a life-saving station and a house of refuge. The cook had said: "There's a house of refuge just north of the Mosquito Inlet Light, and as soon as they see us they'll come off in their boat and pick us up."[3]

"As soon as who see us?" said the correspondent.

"The crew," said the cook.

"Houses of refuge don't have crews," said the correspondent. "As I understand them, they are only places where clothes and grub are stored for the benefit of shipwrecked people. They don't carry crews."

"Oh, yes, they do," said the cook.

"No, they don't," said the correspondent.

"Well, we're not there yet, anyhow," said the oiler, in the stern.

"Well," said the cook, "perhaps it's not a house of refuge that I'm thinking of as being near Mosquito Inlet Light; perhaps it's a lifesaving station."

"We're not there yet," said the oiler in the stern.

II

As the boat bounced from the top of each wave the wind tore through the hair of the hatless men, and as the craft plopped her stern down again the spray slashed past them. The crest of each of these waves was a hill, from the top of which the men surveyed for a moment a broad tumultuous expanse, shining and wind-riven. It was probably splendid, it was probably glorious, this play of the free sea, wild with lights of emerald and white and amber.

"Bully good thing it's an onshore wind," said the cook. "If not, where would we be? Wouldn't have a show."

"That's right," said the correspondent.

The busy oiler nodded his assent.

Then the captain, in the bow, chuckled in a way that expressed humor, contempt, tragedy, all in one. "Do you think we've got much of a show now, boys?" said he.

Whereupon the three were silent, save for a trifle of hemming and hawing. To express any particular optimism at this time they felt to be childish and stupid, but they all doubtless possessed this sense of the situation in their minds. A young man thinks doggedly at such times. On the other hand, the ethics of their condition was decidedly against any open suggestion of hopelessness. So they were silent.

"Oh, well," said the captain, soothing his children, "we'll get ashore all right."

But there was that in his tone which made them think; so the oiler quoth, "Yes! if this wind holds."

The cook was bailing. "Yes! if we don't catch hell in the surf."

Canton-flannel* gulls flew near and far. Sometimes they sat down on the sea, near patches of brown seaweed that rolled over the waves with a movement like carpets on a line in a gale. The birds sat comfortably in groups, and they were envied by some in the dinghy, for the wrath of the sea was no more to them than it was to a covey of prairie chickens a thousand miles

---

* Cotton fabric with a fleecy nap on one side only; here Crane refers to the storm-disheveled plumage of the bird.

inland. Often they came very close and stared at the men with black bead-like eyes. At these times they were uncanny and sinister in their unblinking scrutiny, and the men hooted angrily at them, telling them to be gone. One came, and evidently decided to alight on the top of the captain's head. The bird flew parallel to the boat and did not circle, but made short sidelong jumps in the air in chicken fashion. His black eyes were wistfully fixed upon the captain's head. "Ugly brute," said the oiler to the bird. "You look as if you were made with a jackknife." The cook and the correspondent swore darkly at the creature. The captain naturally wished to knock it away with the end of the heavy painter,* but he did not dare do it, because anything resembling an emphatic gesture would have capsized this freighted boat; and so, with his open hand, the captain gently and carefully waved the gull away. After it had been discouraged from the pursuit the captain breathed easier on account of his hair, and others breathed easier because the bird struck their minds at this time as being somehow gruesome and ominous.

In the meantime the oiler and the correspondent rowed. And also they rowed. They sat together in the same seat, and each rowed an oar. Then the oiler took both oars; then the correspondent took both oars; then the oiler; then the correspondent. They rowed and they rowed. The very ticklish part of the business was when the time came for the reclining one in the stern to take his turn at the oars. By the very last star of truth, it is easier to steal eggs from under a hen than it was to change seats in the dinghy. First the man in the stern slid his hand along the thwart† and moved with care, as if he were of Sèvres.‡ Then the man in the rowing-seat slid his hand along the other thwart. It was all done with the most extraordinary care. As the two sidled past each other, the whole party kept watchful eyes on the coming wave, and the captain cried: "Look out, now! Steady, there!"

The brown mats of seaweed that appeared from time to time

---

* Rope fastened to the bow of a boat, usually for tying it up to a dock or another vessel.

† The oarsman's seat on the dinghy.

‡ City on the Seine River southwest of Paris.

were like islands, bits of earth. They were traveling, apparently, neither one way nor the other. They were, to all intents, stationary. They informed the men in the boat that it was making progress slowly toward the land.

The captain, rearing cautiously in the bow after the dinghy soared on a great swell, said that he had seen the lighthouse at Mosquito Inlet. Presently the cook remarked that he had seen it. The correspondent was at the oars then, and for some reason he too wished to look at the lighthouse; but his back was toward the far shore, and the waves were important, and for some time he could not seize an opportunity to turn his head. But at last there came a wave more gentle than the others, and when at the crest of it he swiftly scoured the western horizon.

"See it?" said the captain.

"No," said the correspondent, slowly; "I didn't see anything."

"Look again," said the captain. He pointed. "It's exactly in that direction."

At the top of another wave the correspondent did as he was bid, and this time his eyes chanced on a small, still thing on the edge of the swaying horizon. It was precisely like the point of a pin. It took an anxious eye to find a lighthouse so tiny.

"Think we'll make it, Captain?"

"If this wind holds and the boat don't swamp, we can't do much else," said the captain.

The little boat, lifted by each towering sea and splashed viciously by the crests, made progress that in the absence of seaweed was not apparent to those in her. She seemed just a wee thing wallowing, miraculously top up, at the mercy of five oceans. Occasionally a great spread of water, like white flames, swarmed into her.

"Bail her, cook," said the captain, serenely.

"All right, Captain," said the cheerful cook.

III

It would be difficult to describe the subtle brotherhood of men that was here established on the seas. No one said that it was so. No one mentioned it. But it dwelt in the boat, and each man felt it warm him. They were a captain, an oiler, a cook, and a correspondent, and they were friends—friends in a more curiously ironbound degree than may be common. The hurt captain, lying against the water jar in the bow, spoke always in a low voice and calmly; but he could never command a more ready and swiftly obedient crew than the motley three of the dinghy. It was more than a mere recognition of what was best for the common safety. There was surely in it a quality that was personal and heartfelt. And after this devotion to the commander of the boat, there was this comradeship, that the correspondent, for instance, who had been taught to be cynical of men, knew even at the time was the best experience of his life. But no one said that it was so. No one mentioned it.

"I wish we had a sail," remarked the captain. "We might try my overcoat on the end of an oar, and give you two boys a chance to rest." So the cook and the correspondent held the mast and spread wide the overcoat; the oiler steered; and the little boat made good way with her new rig. Sometimes the oiler had to scull sharply to keep a sea from breaking into the boat, but otherwise sailing was a success.

Meanwhile the lighthouse had been growing slowly larger. It had now almost assumed color, and appeared like a little gray shadow on the sky. The man at the oars could not be prevented from turning his head rather often to try for a glimpse of this little gray shadow.

At last, from the top of each wave, the men in the tossing boat could see land. Even as the lighthouse was an upright shadow on the sky, this land seemed but a long black shadow on the sea. It certainly was thinner than paper. "We must be about opposite New Smyrna,"* said the cook, who had coasted this

---

* Florida beach located about 4 miles south-southwest of the Mosquito Inlet Lighthouse.

shore often in schooners. "Captain, by the way, I believe they abandoned that lifesaving station there about a year ago."

"Did they?" said the captain.

The wind slowly died away. The cook and the correspondent were not now obliged to slave in order to hold high the oar. But the waves continued their old impetuous swooping at the dinghy, and the little craft, no longer under way, struggled woundily over them. The oiler or the correspondent took the oars again.

Shipwrecks are *apropos* of nothing. If men could only train for them and have them occur when the men had reached pink condition, there would be less drowning at sea. Of the four in the dinghy none had slept any time worth mentioning for two days and two nights previous to embarking in the dinghy, and in the excitement of clambering about the deck of a foundering ship they had also forgotten to eat heartily.

For these reasons, and for others, neither the oiler nor the correspondent was fond of rowing at this time. The correspondent wondered ingenuously how in the name of all that was sane could there be people who thought it amusing to row a boat. It was not an amusement; it was a diabolical punishment, and even a genius of mental aberrations could never conclude that it was anything but a horror to the muscles and a crime against the back. He mentioned to the boat in general how the amusement of rowing struck him, and the weary-faced oiler smiled in full sympathy. Previously to the foundering, by the way, the oiler had worked a double watch in the engine room of the ship.

"Take her easy now, boys," said the captain. "Don't spend yourselves. If we have to run a surf you'll need all your strength, because we'll sure have to swim for it. Take your time."

Slowly the land arose from the sea. From a black line it became a line of black and a line of white—trees and sand. Finally the captain said that he could make out a house on the shore. "That's the house of refuge, sure," said the cook. "They'll see us before long, and come out after us."

The distant lighthouse reared high. "The keeper ought to be

able to make us out now, if he's looking through a glass," said the captain. "He'll notify the lifesaving people."

"None of those other boats could have got ashore to give word of this wreck," said the oiler, in a low voice, "else the lifeboat would be out hunting us."

Slowly and beautifully the land loomed out of the sea. The wind came again. It had veered from the northeast to the southeast. Finally a new sound struck the ears of the men in the boat. It was the low thunder of the surf on the shore. "We'll never be able to make the lighthouse now," said the captain. "Swing her head a little more north, Billie."

"A little more north, sir," said the oiler.

Whereupon the little boat turned her nose once more down the wind, and all but the oarsman watched the shore grow. Under the influence of this expansion doubt and direful apprehension were leaving the minds of the men. The management of the boat was still most absorbing, but it could not prevent a quiet cheerfulness. In an hour, perhaps, they would be ashore.

Their backbones had become thoroughly used to balancing in the boat, and they now rode this wild colt of a dinghy like circus men. The correspondent thought that he had been drenched to the skin, but happening to feel in the top pocket of his coat, he found therein eight cigars. Four of them were soaked with seawater; four were perfectly scatheless. After a search, somebody produced three dry matches; and thereupon the four waifs rode impudently in their little boat and, with an assurance of an impending rescue shining in their eyes, puffed at the big cigars, and judged well and ill of all men. Everybody took a drink of water.

IV

"Cook," remarked the captain, "there don't seem to be any signs of life about your house of refuge."

"No," replied the cook. "Funny they don't see us!"

A broad stretch of lowly coast lay before the eyes of the men.

It was of low dunes topped with dark vegetation. The roar of the surf was plain, and sometimes they could see the white lip of a wave as it spun up the beach. A tiny house was blocked out black upon the sky. Southward, the slim lighthouse lifted its little gray length.

Tide, wind, and waves were swinging the dinghy northward. "Funny they don't see us," said the men.

The surf's roar was here dulled, but its tone was nevertheless thunderous and mighty. As the boat swam over the great rollers the men sat listening to this roar. "We'll swamp sure," said everybody.

It is fair to say here that there was not a lifesaving station within twenty miles in either direction; but the men did not know this fact, and in consequence they made dark and opprobrious remarks concerning the eyesight of the nation's lifesavers. Four scowling men sat in the dinghy and surpassed records in the invention of epithets.

"Funny they don't see us."

The light-heartedness of a former time had completely faded. To their sharpened minds it was easy to conjure pictures of all kinds of incompetency and blindness and, indeed, cowardice. There was the shore of the populous land, and it was bitter and bitter to them that from it came no sign.

"Well," said the captain, ultimately, "I suppose we'll have to make a try for ourselves. If we stay out here too long, we'll none of us have strength left to swim after the boat swamps."

And so the oiler, who was at the oars, turned the boat straight for the shore. There was a sudden tightening of muscles. There was some thinking.

"If we don't all get ashore," said the captain—"if we don't all get ashore, I suppose you fellows know where to send news of my finish?"

They then briefly exchanged some addresses and admonitions. As for the reflections of the men, there was a great deal of rage in them. Perchance they might be formulated thus: "If I am going to be drowned—if I am going to be drowned—if I am going to be drowned, why, in the name of the seven mad gods who rule the sea, was I allowed to come thus far and contemplate sand and trees?⁴ Was I brought here merely to have my nose dragged away as I was about to nibble the sacred cheese* of life? It is preposterous. If this old ninny-woman,† Fate, cannot do better than this, she should be deprived of the management of men's fortunes. She is an old hen who knows not her intention. If she has decided to drown me, why did she not do it in the beginning and save me all this trouble? The whole affair is absurd . . . But no; she cannot mean to drown me. She dare not drown me. She cannot drown me. Not after all this work." Afterward the man might have had an impulse to shake his fist at the clouds. "Just you drown me now and then hear what I call you!"

The billows that came at this time were more formidable. They seemed always just about to break and roll over the little boat in a turmoil of foam. There was a preparatory and long growl in the speech of them. No mind unused to the sea would have concluded that the dinghy could ascend these sheer heights in time. The shore was still afar. The oiler was a wily surfman. "Boys," he said swiftly, "she won't live three minutes more, and we're too far out to swim. Shall I take her to sea again, Captain?"

"Yes; go ahead!" said the captain.

This oiler, by a series of quick miracles and fast and steady oarsmanship, turned the boat in the middle of the surf and took her safely to sea again.

There was a considerable silence as the boat bumped over the furrowed sea to deeper water. Then somebody in gloom spoke: "Well, anyhow, they must have seen us from the shore by now."

The gulls went in slanting flight up the wind toward the

---

* *Cheese* is slang here for the essential quality of an object; just as cheese is cultivated from milk, so is the sacred essence of being (here manifested in the arousal of each man's survival instinct) distilled from ordinary life.

† *Ninny* means "simpleton" or "fool"; linguists believe it was derived from *innocent*. Crane here stresses how the universe does not follow a well-considered plan.

gray, desolate east. A squall, marked by dingy clouds and clouds
brick-red, like smoke from a burning building, appeared from
the southeast.

"What do you think of those lifesaving people? Ain't they
peaches?"

"Funny they haven't seen us."

"Maybe they think we're out here for sport! Maybe they
think we're fishin'. Maybe they think we're damned fools."

It was a long afternoon. A changed tide tried to force them
southward, but wind and wave said northward. Far ahead,
where coastline, sea, and sky formed their mighty angle, there
were little dots which seemed to indicate a city on the shore.

"St. Augustine?"

The captain shook his head. "Too near Mosquito Inlet."

And the oiler rowed, and then the correspondent rowed;
then the oiler rowed. It was a weary business. The human back
can become the seat of more aches and pains than are registered
in books for the composite anatomy of a regiment. It is a limited
area, but it can become the theater of innumerable muscular
conflicts, tangles, wrenches, knots, and other comforts.

"Did you ever like to row, Billie?" asked the correspondent.

"No," said the oiler; "hang it!"

When one exchanged the rowing-seat for a place in the bottom of the boat, he suffered a bodily depression that caused him
to be careless of everything save an obligation to wiggle one finger. There was cold seawater swashing to and fro in the boat,
and he lay in it. His head, pillowed on a thwart, was within an
inch of the swirl of a wave-crest, and sometimes a particularly
obstreperous sea came inboard and drenched him once more.
But these matters did not annoy him. It is almost certain that if
the boat had capsized he would have tumbled comfortably out
upon the ocean as if he felt sure that it was a great soft mattress.

"Look! There's a man on the shore!"

"Where?"

"There! See 'im? See 'im?"

"Yes, sure! He's walking along."

"Now he's stopped. Look! He's facing us!"

"He's waving at us!"

"So he is! By thunder!"

"Ah, now we're all right! Now we're all right! There'll be a boat out here for us in half an hour."

"He's going on. He's running. He's going up to that house there."

The remote beach seemed lower than the sea, and it required a searching glance to discern the little black figure. The captain saw a floating stick, and they rowed to it. A bath towel was by some weird chance in the boat, and, tying this on the stick, the captain waved it. The oarsman did not dare turn his head, so he was obliged to ask questions.

"What's he doing now?"

"He's standing still again. He's looking, I think. . . . There he goes again—toward the house. . . . Now he's stopped again."

"Is he waving at us?"

"No, not now; he was, though."

"Look! There comes another man!"

"He's running."

"Look at him go, would you!"

"Why, he's on a bicycle. Now he's met the other man. They're both waving at us. Look!"

"There comes something up the beach."

"What the devil is that thing?"

"Why, it looks like a boat."

"Why, certainly, it's a boat."

"No; it's on wheels."

"Yes, so it is. Well, that must be the lifeboat. They drag them along shore on a wagon."

"That's the lifeboat, sure."

"No, by God, it's—it's an omnibus."*

"I tell you it's a lifeboat."

"It is not! It's an omnibus. I can see it plain. See? One of these big hotel omnibuses."

"By thunder, you're right. It's an omnibus, sure as fate. What do you suppose they are doing with an omnibus? Maybe they are going around collecting the life-crew, hey?"

---

* Large, horse-drawn covered wagon used for public transportation.

"That's it, likely. Look! There's a fellow waving a little black flag. He's standing on the steps of the omnibus. There come those other two fellows. Now they're all talking together. Look at the fellow with the flag. Maybe he ain't waving it!"

"That ain't a flag, is it? That's his coat. Why, certainly, that's his coat."

"So it is; it's his coat. He's taken it off and is waving it around his head. But would you look at him swing it!"

"Oh, say, there isn't any lifesaving station there. That's just a winter-resort hotel omnibus that has brought over some of the boarders to see us drown."

"What's that idiot with the coat mean? What's he signaling, anyhow?"

"It looks as if he were trying to tell us to go north. There must be a lifesaving station up there."

"No; he thinks we're fishing. Just giving us a merry hand. See? Ah, there, Willie!"

"Well, I wish I could make something out of those signals. What do you suppose he means?"

"He don't mean anything; he's just playing."

"Well, if he'd just signal us to try the surf again, or to go to sea and wait, or go north, or go south, or go to hell, there would be some reason in it. But look at him! He just stands there and keeps his coat revolving like a wheel. The ass!"

"There come more people."

"Now there's quite a mob. Look! Isn't that a boat?"

"Where? Oh, I see where you mean. No, that's no boat."

"That fellow is still waving his coat."

"He must think we like to see him do that. Why don't he quit it? It don't mean anything."

"I don't know. I think he is trying to make us go north. It must be that there's a lifesaving station there somewhere."

"Say, he ain't tired yet. Look at 'im wave!"

"Wonder how long he can keep that up. He's been revolving his coat ever since he caught sight of us. He's an idiot. Why aren't they getting men to bring a boat out? A fishing boat—one of those big yawls—could come out here all right. Why don't he do something?"

"Oh, it's all right now."

"They'll have a boat out here for us in less than no time, now that they've seen us."

A faint yellow tone came into the sky over the low land. The shadows on the sea slowly deepened. The wind bore coldness with it, and the men began to shiver.

"Holy smoke!" said one, allowing his voice to express his impious mood, "if we keep on monkeying out here! If we've got to flounder out here all night!"

"Oh, we'll never have to stay here all night! Don't you worry. They've seen us now, and it won't be long before they'll come chasing out after us."

The shore grew dusky. The man waving a coat blended gradually into this gloom, and it swallowed in the same manner the omnibus and the group of people. The spray, when it dashed uproariously over the side, made the voyagers shrink and swear like men who were being branded.

"I'd like to catch the chump who waved the coat. I feel like socking him one, just for luck."

"Why? What did he do?"

"Oh, nothing, but then he seemed so damned cheerful."

In the meantime the oiler rowed, and then the correspondent rowed, and then the oiler rowed. Gray-faced and bowed forward, they mechanically, turn by turn, plied the leaden oars. The form of the lighthouse had vanished from the southern horizon, but finally a pale star appeared, just lifting from the sea.[5] The streaked saffron in the west passed before the all-merging darkness, and the sea to the east was black. The land had vanished, and was expressed only by the low and drear thunder of the surf.

"If I am going to be drowned—if I am going to be drowned—if I am going to be drowned, why, in the name of the seven mad gods who rule the sea, was I allowed to come thus far and contemplate sand and trees? Was I brought here merely to have my nose dragged away as I was about to nibble the sacred cheese of life?"

The patient captain, drooped over the water jar, was sometimes obliged to speak to the oarsman.

"Keep her head up! Keep her head up!"

"Keep her head up, sir." The voices were weary and low.

This was surely a quiet evening. All save the oarsman lay heavily and listlessly in the boat's bottom. As for him, his eyes were just capable of noting the tall black waves that swept forward in a most sinister silence, save for an occasional subdued growl of a crest.

The cook's head was on a thwart, and he looked without interest at the water under his nose. He was deep in other scenes. Finally he spoke. "Billie," he murmured, dreamfully, "what kind of pie do you like best?"

V

"Pie!" said the oiler and the correspondent, agitatedly. "Don't talk about those things, blast you!"

"Well," said the cook, "I was just thinking about ham sandwiches, and—"

A night on the sea in an open boat is a long night. As darkness settled finally, the shine of the light, lifting from the sea in the south, changed to full gold. On the northern horizon a new light appeared, a small bluish gleam on the edge of the waters. These two lights were the furniture of the world. Otherwise there was nothing but waves.

Two men huddled in the stern, and distances were so magnificent in the dinghy that the rower was enabled to keep his feet partly warm by thrusting them under his companions. Their legs indeed extended far under the rowing-seat until they touched the feet of the captain forward. Sometimes, despite the efforts of the tired oarsman, a wave came piling into the boat, an icy wave of the night, and the chilling water soaked them anew. They would twist their bodies for a moment and groan, and sleep the dead sleep once more, while the water in the boat gurgled about them as the craft rocked.

The plan of the oiler and the correspondent was for one to row until he lost the ability, and then arouse the other from his sea-water couch in the bottom of the boat.

The oiler plied the oars until his head drooped forward and the overpowering sleep blinded him; and he rowed yet afterward. Then he touched a man in the bottom of the boat, and called his name. "Will you spell me for a little while?" he said meekly.

"Sure, Billie," said the correspondent, awaking and dragging himself to a sitting position. They exchanged places carefully, and the oiler, cuddling down in the seawater at the cook's side, seemed to go to sleep instantly.

The particular violence of the sea had ceased. The waves came without snarling. The obligation of the man at the oars was to keep the boat headed so that the tilt of the rollers would not capsize her, and to preserve her from filling when the crests rushed past. The black waves were silent and hard to be seen in the darkness. Often one was almost upon the boat before the oarsman was aware.

In a low voice the correspondent addressed the captain. He was not sure that the captain was awake, although this iron man seemed to be always awake. "Captain, shall I keep her making for that light north, sir?"

The same steady voice answered him. "Yes. Keep it about two points off the port bow."[6]

The cook had tied a lifebelt around himself in order to get even the warmth which this clumsy cork contrivance could donate, and he seemed almost stove-like when a rower, whose teeth invariably chattered wildly as soon as he ceased his labor, dropped down to sleep.

The correspondent, as he rowed, looked down at the two men sleeping underfoot. The cook's arm was around the oiler's shoulders, and, with their fragmentary clothing and haggard faces, they were the babes of the sea—a grotesque rendering of the old babes in the wood.

Later he must have grown stupid at his work, for suddenly there was a growling of water, and a crest came with a roar and a swash into the boat, and it was a wonder that it did not set the cook afloat in his lifebelt. The cook continued to sleep, but the oiler sat up, blinking his eyes and shaking with the new cold.

"Oh, I'm awful sorry, Billie," said the correspondent, contritely.

"That's all right, old boy," said the oiler, and lay down again and was asleep.

Presently it seemed that even the captain dozed, and the correspondent thought that he was the one man afloat on all the oceans. The wind had a voice as it came over the waves, and it was sadder than the end.

There was a long, loud swishing astern of the boat, and a gleaming trail of phosphorescence, like blue flame, was furrowed on the black waters. It might have been made by a monstrous knife.

Then there came a stillness, while the correspondent breathed with open mouth and looked at the sea.

Suddenly there was another swish and another long flash of bluish light, and this time it was alongside the boat, and might almost have been reached with an oar. The correspondent saw an enormous fin speed like a shadow through the water, hurling the crystalline spray and leaving the long glowing trail.

The correspondent looked over his shoulder at the captain. His face was hidden, and he seemed to be asleep. He looked at the babes of the sea. They certainly were asleep. So, being bereft of sympathy, he leaned a little way to one side and swore softly into the sea.

But the thing did not then leave the vicinity of the boat. Ahead or astern, on one side or the other, at intervals long or short, fled the long sparkling streak, and there was to be heard the whirroo* of the dark fin. The speed and power of the thing was greatly to be admired. It cut the water like a gigantic and keen projectile.

The presence of this biding thing did not affect the man with the same horror that it would if he had been a picnicker. He simply looked at the sea dully and swore in an undertone.

Nevertheless, it is true that he did not wish to be alone with the thing. He wished one of his companions to awake by chance and keep him company with it. But the captain hung motionless

---

* Variant of the Irish exclamation and lament wirra, which roughly translates as "O Mary."

over the water jar, and the oiler and the cook in the bottom of the boat were plunged in slumber.

VI

"If I am going to be drowned—if I am going to be drowned—if I am going to be drowned, why, in the name of the seven mad gods who rule the sea, was I allowed to come thus far and contemplate sand and trees?"

During this dismal night, it may be remarked that a man would conclude that it was really the intention of the seven mad gods to drown him, despite the abominable injustice of it. For it was certainly an abominable injustice to drown a man who had worked so hard, so hard. The man felt it would be a crime most unnatural. Other people had drowned at sea since galleys swarmed with painted sails, but still—

When it occurs to a man that nature does not regard him as important, and that she feels she would not maim the universe by disposing of him, he at first wishes to throw bricks at the temple, and he hates deeply the fact that there are no bricks and no temples. Any visible expression of nature would surely be pelleted with his jeers.

Then, if there be no tangible thing to hoot, he feels, perhaps, the desire to confront a personification and indulge in pleas, bowed to one knee, and with hands supplicant, saying, "Yes, but I love myself."

A high cold star on a winter's night is the word he feels that she says to him. Thereafter he knows the pathos of his situation.

The men in the dinghy had not discussed these matters, but each had, no doubt, reflected upon them in silence and according to his mind. There was seldom any expression upon their faces save the general one of complete weariness. Speech was devoted to the business of the boat.

To chime the notes of his emotion, a verse mysteriously entered the correspondent's head. He had even forgotten that he had forgotten this verse, but it suddenly was in his mind.

A soldier of the Legion lay dying in Algiers;
There was lack of woman's nursing, there was
    dearth of woman's tears;
But a comrade stood beside him, and he took
    that comrade's hand,
And he said, "I never more shall see my own, my
    native land."[7]

In his childhood the correspondent had been made acquainted with the fact that a soldier of the Legion lay dying in Algiers, but he had never regarded the fact as important. Myriads of his schoolfellows had informed him of the soldier's plight, but the dinning had naturally ended by making him perfectly indifferent. He had never considered it his affair that a soldier of the Legion lay dying in Algiers, nor had it appeared to him as a matter for sorrow. It was less to him than the breaking of a pencil's point.

Now, however, it quaintly came to him as a human, living thing. It was no longer merely a picture of a few throes in the breast of a poet, meanwhile drinking tea and warming his feet at the grate; it was an actuality—stern, mournful, and fine.

The correspondent plainly saw the soldier. He lay on the sand with his feet out straight and still. While his pale left hand was upon his chest in an attempt to thwart the going of his life, the blood came between his fingers. In the far Algerian distance, a city of low square forms was set against a sky that was faint with the last sunset hues. The correspondent, plying the oars and dreaming of the slow and slower movements of the lips of the soldier, was moved by a profound and perfectly impersonal comprehension. He was sorry for the soldier of the Legion who lay dying in Algiers.

The thing which had followed the boat and waited had evidently grown bored at the delay. There was no longer to be heard the slash of the cut-water, and there was no longer the flame of the long trail. The light in the north still glimmered, but it was apparently no nearer to the boat. Sometimes the boom of the surf rang in the correspondent's ears, and he turned the craft seaward then and rowed harder. Southward, some one had evidently built a watch fire on the beach. It was too low and too far to be seen, but it made a shimmering, roseate reflection upon the bluff in back of it, and this could be discerned from the boat. The wind came stronger, and sometimes a wave suddenly raged out like a mountain cat, and there was to be seen the sheen and sparkle of a broken crest.

The captain, in the bow, moved on his water jar and sat erect. "Pretty long night," he observed to the correspondent. He looked at the shore. "Those lifesaving people take their time."

"Did you see that shark playing around?"

"Yes, I saw him. He was a big fellow, all right."

"Wish I had known you were awake."

Later the correspondent spoke into the bottom of the boat. "Billie!" There was a slow and gradual disentanglement. "Billie, will you spell me?"

"Sure," said the oiler.

As soon as the correspondent touched the cold, comfortable seawater in the bottom of the boat and had huddled close to the cook's lifebelt he was deep in sleep, despite the fact that his teeth played all the popular airs. This sleep was so good to him that it was but a moment before he heard a voice call his name in a tone that demonstrated the last stages of exhaustion. "Will you spell me?"

"Sure, Billie."

The light in the north had mysteriously vanished, but the correspondent took his course from the wide-awake captain.

Later in the night they took the boat farther out to sea, and the captain directed the cook to take one oar at the stern and keep the boat facing the seas. He was to call out if he should hear the thunder of the surf. This plan enabled the oiler and the correspondent to get respite together. "We'll give those boys a chance to get into shape again," said the captain. They curled down and, after a few preliminary chatterings and trembles, slept once more the dead sleep. Neither knew they had bequeathed to the cook the company of another shark, or perhaps the same shark.

As the boat caroused on the waves, spray occasionally bumped over the side and gave them a fresh soaking, but this had no power to break their repose. The ominous slash of the wind and the water affected them as it would have affected mummies.

"Boys," said the cook, with the notes of every reluctance in his voice, "she's drifted in pretty close. I guess one of you had better take her to sea again." The correspondent, aroused, heard the crash of the toppled crests.

As he was rowing, the captain gave him some whisky-and-water, and this steadied the chills out of him. "If I ever get ashore, and anybody shows me even a photograph of an oar—"

At last there was a short conversation.

"Billie!—Billie, will you spell me?"

"Sure," said the oiler.

VII

When the correspondent again opened his eyes, the sea and the sky were each of the gray hue of the dawning. Later, carmine and gold was painted upon the waters. The morning appeared finally, in its splendor, with a sky of pure blue, and the sunlight flamed on the tips of the waves.

On the distant dunes were set many little black cottages, and a tall white windmill reared above them. No man, nor dog, nor bicycle appeared on the beach. The cottages might have formed a deserted village.

The voyagers scanned the shore. A conference was held in the boat. "Well," said the captain, "if no help is coming, we might better try a run through the surf right away. If we stay out here much longer we will be too weak to do anything for ourselves at all." The others silently acquiesced in this reasoning. The boat was headed for the beach. The correspondent wondered if none ever ascended the tall wind-tower, and if then they never looked seaward. This tower was a giant, standing with its back to the plight of the ants. It represented in a degree, to the correspondent, the serenity of nature amid the struggles of the individual—nature in the wind, and nature in the vision of men. She did not seem cruel to him then, nor beneficent, nor treacherous, nor wise. But she was indifferent, flatly indifferent. It is, perhaps, plausible that a man in this situation, impressed with the unconcern of the universe, should see the innumerable flaws of his life, and have them taste wickedly in his mind, and wish for another chance. A distinction between right and wrong seems absurdly clear to him, then, in this new ignorance of the grave-edge, and he understands that if he were given another opportunity he would mend his conduct and his words, and be better and brighter during an introduction or at a tea.

"Now, boys," said the captain, "she is going to swamp sure. All we can do is to work her in as far as possible, and then when she swamps, pile out and scramble for the beach. Keep cool now, and don't jump until she swamps sure."

The oiler took the oars. Over his shoulders he scanned the surf. "Captain," he said, "I think I'd better bring her about and keep her head-on to the seas and back her in."

"All right, Billie," said the captain. "Back her in." The oiler swung the boat then, and, seated in the stern, the cook and the correspondent were obliged to look over their shoulders to contemplate the lonely and indifferent shore.

The monstrous inshore rollers heaved the boat high until the men were again enabled to see the white sheets of water scudding up the slanted beach. "We won't get in very close," said the captain. Each time a man could wrest his attention from the rollers, he turned his glance toward the shore, and in the expression of the eyes during this contemplation there was a singular quality. The correspondent, observing the others, knew that they were not afraid, but the full meaning of their glances was shrouded.

As for himself, he was too tired to grapple fundamentally with the fact. He tried to coerce his mind into thinking of it, but the mind was dominated at this time by the muscles, and the muscles said they did not care. It merely occurred to him that if he should drown it would be a shame.

There were no hurried words, no pallor, no plain agitation. The men simply looked at the shore. "Now, remember to get well clear of the boat when you jump," said the captain.

Seaward the crest of a roller suddenly fell with a thunderous crash, and the long white comber came roaring down upon the boat.

"Steady now," said the captain. The men were silent. They turned their eyes from the shore to the comber and waited. The boat slid up the incline, leaped at the furious top, bounced over it, and swung down the long back of the wave. Some water had been shipped, and the cook bailed it out.

But the next crest crashed also. The tumbling, boiling flood of white water caught the boat and whirled it almost perpendicular. Water swarmed in from all sides. The correspondent had his hands on the gunwale at this time, and when the water entered at that place he swiftly withdrew his fingers, as if he objected to wetting them.

The little boat, drunken with this weight of water, reeled and snuggled deeper into the sea.

"Bail her out, cook! Bail her out!" said the captain.

"All right, Captain," said the cook.

"Now, boys, the next one will do for us sure," said the oiler. "Mind to jump clear of the boat."

The third wave moved forward, huge, furious, implacable. It fairly swallowed the dinghy, and almost simultaneously the men tumbled into the sea. A piece of lifebelt had lain in the bottom of the boat, and as the correspondent went overboard he held this to his chest with his left hand.

The January water was icy, and he reflected immediately that it was colder than he had expected to find it off the coast of Florida. This appeared to his dazed mind as a fact important enough to be noted at the time. The coldness of the water was sad; it was tragic. This fact was somehow mixed and confused with his opinion of his own situation, so that it seemed almost a proper reason for tears. The water was cold.

When he came to the surface he was conscious of little but the noisy water. Afterward he saw his companions in the sea. The oiler was ahead in the race. He was swimming strongly and rapidly. Off to the correspondent's left, the cook's great white and corked back bulged out of the water; and in the rear the captain was hanging with his one good hand to the keel of the overturned dinghy.[8]

There is a certain immovable quality to a shore, and the correspondent wondered at it amid the confusion of the sea.

It seemed also very attractive; but the correspondent knew that it was a long journey, and he paddled leisurely. The piece of life preserver lay under him, and sometimes he whirled down the incline of a wave as if he were on a hand-sled.

But finally he arrived at a place in the sea where travel was beset with difficulty. He did not pause swimming to inquire what manner of current had caught him, but there his progress ceased. The shore was set before him like a bit of scenery on a stage, and he looked at it and understood with his eyes each detail of it.

As the cook passed, much farther to the left, the captain was calling to him, "Turn over on your back, cook! Turn over on your back and use the oar."

"All right, sir." The cook turned on his back, and, paddling with an oar, went ahead as if he were a canoe.

Presently the boat also passed to the left of the correspondent, with the captain clinging with one hand to the keel. He would have appeared like a man raising himself to look over a board fence if it were not for the extraordinary gymnastics of the boat. The correspondent marveled that the captain could still hold to it.

They passed on nearer to shore—the oiler, the cook, the captain—and following them went the water jar, bouncing gaily over the seas.

The correspondent remained in the grip of this strange new enemy—a current. The shore, with its white slope of sand and its green bluff topped with little silent cottages, was spread like a picture before him. It was very near to him then, but he was impressed as one who, in a gallery, looks at a scene from Brittany or Algiers.[9]

He thought: "I am going to drown? Can it be possible? Can it be possible? Can it be possible?" Perhaps an individual must consider his own death to be the final phenomenon of nature.

But later a wave perhaps whirled him out of this small deadly current, for he found suddenly that he could again make progress toward the shore. Later still he was aware that the captain, clinging with one hand to the keel of the dinghy, had his face turned away from the shore and toward him, and was calling his name. "Come to the boat! Come to the boat!"

In his struggle to reach the captain and the boat, he reflected that when one gets properly wearied drowning must really be a comfortable arrangement—a cessation of hostilities accompanied by a large degree of relief; and he was glad of it, for the main thing in his mind for some moments had been horror of the temporary agony. He did not wish to be hurt.

Presently he saw a man running along the shore. He was undressing with most remarkable speed. Coat, trousers, shirt, everything flew magically off him.

"Come to the boat!" called the captain.

"All right, Captain." As the correspondent paddled, he saw the captain let himself down to bottom and leave the boat. Then the correspondent performed his one little marvel of the voyage. A large wave caught him and flung him with ease and supreme speed completely over the boat and far beyond it. It struck him even then as an event in gymnastics and a true miracle of the sea. An overturned boat in the surf is not a plaything to a swimming man.

The correspondent arrived in water that reached only to his waist, but his condition did not enable him to stand for more than a moment. Each wave knocked him into a heap, and the undertow pulled at him.

Then he saw the man who had been running and undressing, and undressing and running, come bounding into the water. He dragged ashore the cook, and then waded toward the captain; but the captain waved him away and sent him to the correspondent. He was naked—naked as a tree in winter; but a halo was about his head, and he shone like a saint. He gave a strong pull, and a long drag, and a bully heave at the correspondent's hand.[10] The correspondent, schooled in the minor formulae, said, "Thanks, old man." But suddenly the man cried, "What's that?" He pointed a swift finger. The correspondent said, "Go."

In the shallows, face downward, lay the oiler.[11] His forehead touched sand that was periodically, between each wave, clear of the sea.

The correspondent did not know all that transpired afterward. When he achieved safe ground he fell, striking the sand with each particular part of his body. It was as if he had dropped from a roof, but the thud was grateful to him.

It seems that instantly the beach was populated with men with blankets, clothes, and flasks, and women with coffeepots and all the remedies sacred to their minds. The welcome of the land to the men from the sea was warm and generous; but a still and dripping shape was carried slowly up the beach, and the land's welcome for it could only be the different and sinister hospitality of the grave.

When it came night, the white waves paced to and fro in the moonlight, and the wind brought the sound of the great sea's voice to the men on the shore, and they felt that they could then be interpreters.

THE VETERAN[1]

OUT OF THE LOW window could be seen three hickory trees placed irregularly in a meadow that was resplendent in springtime green. Farther away, the old, dismal belfry of the village church loomed over the pines. A horse meditating in the shade of one of the hickories lazily swished his tail. The warm sunshine made an oblong of vivid yellow on the floor of the grocery.

"Could you see the whites of their eyes?" said the man who was seated on a soapbox.

"Nothing of the kind," replied old Henry warmly. "Just a lot of flitting figures, and I let go at where they 'peared to be the thickest. Bang!"

"Mr. Fleming," said the grocer—his deferential voice expressed somehow the old man's exact social weight—"Mr. Fleming, you never was frightened much in them battles, was you?"

The veteran looked down and grinned. Observing his manner, the entire group tittered. "Well, I guess I was," he answered finally. "Pretty well scared, sometimes. Why, in my first battle I thought the sky was falling down. I thought the world was coming to an end. You bet I was scared."

Every one laughed. Perhaps it seemed strange and rather wonderful to them that a man should admit the thing, and in the tone of their laughter there was probably more admiration than if old Fleming had declared that he had always been a lion.[2] Moreover, they knew that he had ranked as an orderly sergeant, and so their opinion of his heroism was fixed. None, to be sure, knew how an orderly sergeant ranked, but then it was understood to be somewhere just shy of a major general's stars.[3] So when old Henry admitted that he had been frightened, there was a laugh.

"The trouble was," said the old man, "I thought they were all shooting at me. Yes, sir, I thought every man in the other army was aiming at me in particular, and only me. And it seemed so darned unreasonable, you know. I wanted to explain to 'em what an almighty good fellow I was, because I thought then they might quit all trying to hit me. But I couldn't explain, and they kept on being unreasonable—blim!—blam!—bang! So I run!"

Two little triangles of wrinkles appeared at the corners of his eyes. Evidently he appreciated some comedy in this recital. Down near his feet, however, little Jim, his grandson, was visibly horror-stricken.[4] His hands were clasped nervously, and his eyes were wide with astonishment at this terrible scandal, his most magnificent grandfather telling such a thing.

"That was at Chancellorsville. Of course, afterward I got kind of used to it. A man does. Lots of men, though, seem to feel all right from the start. I did, as soon as I 'got on to it,' as they say now; but at first I was pretty flustered. Now, there was young Jim Conklin, old Si Conklin's son—that used to keep the tannery—you none of you recollect him—well, he went into it from the start just as if he was born to it. But with me it was different. I had to get used to it."

When little Jim walked with his grandfather he was in the habit of skipping along on the stone pavement in front of the three stores and the hotel of the town and betting that he could avoid the cracks. But upon this day he walked soberly, with his hand gripping two of his grandfather's fingers. Sometimes he kicked abstractedly at dandelions that curved over the walk. Any one could see that he was much troubled.

"There's Sickles's colt over in the medder, Jimmie," said the old man.[5] "Don't you wish you owned one like him?"

"Um," said the boy, with a strange lack of interest. He continued his reflections. Then finally he ventured: "Grandpa—now—was that true what you was telling those men?"

"What?" asked the grandfather. "What was I telling them?"

"Oh, about your running."

"Why, yes, that was true enough, Jimmie. It was my first fight, and there was an awful lot of noise, you know."

Jimmie seemed dazed that this idol, of its own will, should so totter. His stout boyish idealism was injured.

Presently the grandfather said: "Sickles's colt is going for a drink. Don't you wish you owned Sickles's colt, Jimmie?"

The boy merely answered: "He ain't as nice as our'n." He lapsed then into another moody silence.

One of the hired men, a Swede, desired to drive to the county-seat for purposes of his own. The old man loaned a horse and an unwashed buggy. It appeared later that one of the purposes of the Swede was to get drunk.

After quelling some boisterous frolic of the farm hands and boys in the garret, the old man had that night gone peacefully to sleep, when he was aroused by clamoring at the kitchen door. He grabbed his trousers, and they waved out behind as he dashed forward. He could hear the voice of the Swede, screaming and blubbering. He pushed the wooden button, and, as the door flew open, the Swede, a maniac, stumbled inward, chattering, weeping, still screaming. "De barn fire! Fire! Fire! De barn fire! Fire! Fire! Fire!"

There was a swift and indescribable change in the old man. His face ceased instantly to be a face; it became a mask, a gray thing, with horror written about the mouth and eyes. He hoarsely shouted at the foot of the little rickety stairs, and, immediately, it seemed, there came down an avalanche of men. No one knew that during this time the old lady had been standing in her night clothes at the bedroom door, yelling: "What's th' matter? What's th' matter? What's th' matter?"

When they dashed toward the barn it presented to their eyes its usual appearance, solemn, rather mystic in the black night. The Swede's lantern was overturned at a point some yards in front of the barn doors. It contained a wild little conflagration of its own, and even in their excitement some of those who ran felt a gentle secondary vibration of the thrifty part of their minds at sight of this overturned lantern. Under ordinary circumstances it would have been a calamity.

But the cattle in the barn were trampling, trampling, trampling, and above this noise could be heard a humming like the song of innumerable bees. The old man hurled aside the great doors, and a yellow flame leaped out at one corner and sped and wavered frantically up the old gray wall. It was glad, terrible, this single flame, like the wild banner of deadly and triumphant foes.

The motley crowd from the garret had come with all the pails of the farm. They flung themselves upon the well. It was a leisurely old machine, long dwelling in indolence. It was in the habit of giving out water with a sort of reluctance. The men stormed at it, cursed it; but it continued to allow the buckets to be filled only after the wheezy windlass had howled many protests at the mad-handed men.

With his opened knife in his hand old Fleming himself had gone headlong into the barn, where the stifling smoke swirled with the air currents, and where could be heard in its fullness the terrible chorus of the flames, laden with tones of hate and death, a hymn of wonderful ferocity.

He flung a blanket over an old mare's head, cut the halter close to the manger, led the mare to the door, and fairly kicked her out to safety. He returned with the same blanket, and rescued one of the workhorses. He took five horses out, and then came out himself, with his clothes bravely on fire. He had no whiskers, and very little hair on his head. They soused five pailfuls of water on him. His eldest son made a clean miss with the sixth pailful, because the old man had turned and was running down the decline and around to the basement of the barn, where were the stanchions of the cows. Some one noticed at the time that he ran very lamely, as if one of the frenzied horses had smashed his hip.

The cows, with their heads held in the heavy stanchions, had thrown themselves, strangled themselves, tangled themselves: done everything which the ingenuity of their exuberant fear could suggest to them.

Here, as at the well, the same thing happened to every man save one. Their hands went mad. They became incapable of everything save the power to rush into dangerous situations.

The old man released the cow nearest the door, and she, blind drunk with terror, crashed into the Swede. The Swede had been running to and fro babbling. He carried an empty milk pail, to which he clung with an unconscious, fierce enthusiasm. He shrieked like one lost as he went under the cow's hoofs, and the milk pail, rolling across the floor, made a flash of silver in the gloom.

Old Fleming took a fork, beat off the cow, and dragged the paralyzed Swede to the open air. When they had rescued all the cows save one, which had so fastened herself that she could not be moved an inch, they returned to the front of the barn and stood sadly, breathing like men who had reached the final point of human effort.

Many people had come running. Someone had even gone to the church, and now, from the distance, rang the tocsin note of the old bell. There was a long flare of crimson on the sky, which made remote people speculate as to the whereabouts of the fire.

The long flames sang their drumming chorus in voices of the heaviest bass. The wind whirled clouds of smoke and cinders into the faces of the spectators. The form of the old barn was outlined in black amid these masses of orange-hued flames.

And then came this Swede again, crying as one who is the weapon of the sinister fates. "De colts! De colts! You have forgot de colts!"

Old Fleming staggered. It was true; they had forgotten the two colts in the box stalls at the back of the barn. "Boys," he said, "I must try to get 'em out." They clamored about him then, afraid for him, afraid of what they should see. Then they talked wildly each to each. "Why, it's sure death!" "He would never get out!" "Why, it's suicide for a man to go in there!" Old Fleming stared absent-mindedly at the open doors. "The poor little things," he said. He rushed into the barn.

When the roof fell in, a great funnel of smoke swarmed toward the sky, as if the old man's mighty spirit, released from its body—a little bottle—had swelled like the genie of fable.[6] The smoke was tinted rose-hue from the flames, and perhaps the unutterable midnights of the universe will have no power to daunt the color of this soul.

THE MEN IN THE STORM[1]

THE BLIZZARD BEGAN TO swirl great clouds of snow along the streets, sweeping it down from the roofs, and up from the pavements, until the faces of pedestrians tingled and burned as from a thousand needle-prickings. Those on the walks huddled their necks closely in the collars of their coats, and went along stooping like a race of aged people. The drivers of vehicles hurried their horses furiously on their way. They were made more cruel by the exposure of their position, aloft on high seats. The street cars, bound uptown, went slowly, the horses slipping and straining in the spongy brown mass that lay between the rails. The drivers, muffled to the eyes, stood erect, facing the wind, models of grim philosophy. Overhead trains rumbled and roared, and the dark structure of the elevated railroad, stretching over the avenue, dripped little streams and drops of water upon the mud and snow beneath.

All the clatter of the street was softened by the masses that lay upon the cobbles, until, even to one who looked from a window, it became important music, a melody of life made necessary to the ear by the dreariness of the pitiless beat and sweep of the storm. Occasionally one could see black figures of men busily shoveling the white drifts from the walks. The sounds from their labor created new recollections of rural experiences which every man manages to have in a measure. Later, the immense windows of the shops became aglow with light, throwing great beams of orange and yellow upon the pavement. They were infinitely cheerful, yet in a way they accentuated the force and discomfort of the storm, and gave a meaning to the pace of the people and the vehicles, scores of pedestrians and drivers, wretched with cold faces, necks, and feet, speeding for scores of unknown doors and entrances, scattering to an infinite variety of shelters, to places which the imagination made warm with the familiar colors of home.

There was an absolute expression of hot dinners in the pace of the people. If one dared to speculate upon the destination of those who came trooping, he lost himself in a maze of social calculation; he might fling a handful of sand and attempt to follow the flight of each particular grain. But as to the suggestion of hot dinners, he was in firm lines of thought, for it was upon every hurrying face. It is a matter of tradition; it is from the tales of childhood. It comes forth with every storm.

However, in a certain part of a dark west-side street, there was a collection of men to whom these things were as if they were not. In this street was located a charitable house where for five cents the homeless of the city could get a bed at night, and in the morning coffee and bread.

During the afternoon of the storm, the whirling snows acted as drivers, as men with whips, and at half-past three the walk before the closed doors of the house was covered with wanderers of the street, waiting. For some distance on either side of the place they could be seen lurking in the doorways and behind projecting parts of buildings, gathering in close bunches in an effort to get warm. A covered wagon drawn up near the curb sheltered a dozen of them. Under the stairs that led to the elevated railway station, there were six or eight, their hands stuffed deep in their pockets, their shoulders stooped, jiggling their feet. Others always could be seen coming, a strange procession, some slouching along with the characteristic hopeless gait of professional strays, some coming with hesitating steps, wearing the air of men to whom this sort of thing was new.

It was an afternoon of incredible length. The snow, blowing in twisting clouds, sought out the men in their meager hiding places, and skillfully beat in among them, drenching their persons with showers of fine stinging flakes. They crowded together, muttering, and fumbling in their pockets to get their red inflamed wrists covered by the cloth.

Newcomers usually halted at one end of the groups and addressed a question, perhaps much as a matter of form, "Is it open yet?"

Those who had been waiting inclined to take the questioner seriously and became contemptuous. "No; do yeh think we'd be standin' here?"

The gathering swelled in numbers steadily and persistently.

One could always see them coming, trudging slowly through the storm.

Finally, the little snow plains in the street began to assume a leaden hue from the shadows of evening. The buildings up-reared gloomily save where various windows became brilliant figures of light, that made shimmers and splashes of yellow on the snow. A street lamp on the curb struggled to illuminate, but it was reduced to impotent blindness by the swift gusts of sleet crusting its panes.

In this half-darkness, the men began to come from their shelter-places and mass in front of the doors of charity.[2] They were of all types, but the nationalities were mostly American, German, and Irish. Many were strong, healthy, clear-skinned fellows, with that stamp of countenance which is not frequently seen upon seekers after charity. There were men of undoubted patience, industry, and temperance, who, in time of ill-fortune, do not habitually turn to rail at the state of society, snarling at the arrogance of the rich, and bemoaning the cowardice of the poor, but who at these times are apt to wear a sudden and singular meekness, as if they saw the world's progress marching from them, and were trying to perceive where they had failed, what they had lacked, to be thus vanquished in the race.[3] Then there were others, of the shifting Bowery element, who were used to paying ten cents for a place to sleep, but who now came here because it was cheaper.

But they were all mixed in one mass so thoroughly that one could not have discerned the different elements, but for the fact that the laboring men, for the most part, remained silent and impassive in the blizzard, their eyes fixed on the windows of the house, statues of patience.

The sidewalk soon became completely blocked by the bodies of the men. They pressed close to one another like sheep in a winter's gale, keeping one another warm by the heat of their bodies. The snow came upon this compressed group of men until, directly from above, it might have appeared like a heap of snow-covered merchandise, if it were not for the fact that the crowd swayed gently with a unanimous rhythmical motion. It was wonderful to see how the snow lay upon the heads and shoulders of these men, in little ridges an inch thick perhaps in places, the flakes steadily adding drop and drop, precisely as they fall upon the unresisting grass of the fields. The feet of the men were all wet and cold, and the wish to warm them accounted for the slow, gentle rhythmical motion. Occasionally some man whose ear or nose tingled acutely from the cold winds would wriggle down until his head was protected by the shoulders of his companions.

There was a continuous murmuring discussion as to the probability of the doors being speedily opened. They persistently lifted their eyes toward the windows. One could hear little combats of opinion.

"There's a light in th' winder!"

"Naw; it's a reflection f'm across th' way."

"Well, didn't I see 'em light it?"

"You did?"

"I did!"

"Well, then, that settles it!"

As the time approached when they expected to be allowed to enter, the men crowded to the doors in an unspeakable crush, jamming and wedging in a way that it seemed would crack bones. They surged heavily against the building in a powerful wave of pushing shoulders. Once a rumor flitted among all the tossing heads.

"They can't open th' door! Th' fellers er smack up agin 'em."

Then a dull roar of rage came from the men on the outskirts; but all the time they strained and pushed until it appeared to be impossible for those that they cried out against to do anything but be crushed to pulp.

"Ah, git away f'm th' door!"

"Git outa that!"

"Throw 'em out!"

"Kill 'em!"

"Say, fellers, now, what th' 'ell? G've 'em a chance t' open th' door!"

"Yeh damn pigs, give 'em a chance t' open th' door!"

Men in the outskirts of the crowd occasionally yelled when a boot-heel of one of the trampling feet crushed on their freezing extremities.

"Git off me feet, yeh clumsy tarrier!"*

"Say, don't stand on me feet! Walk on th' ground!"

A man near the doors suddenly shouted: "O-o-oh! Le' me out—le' me out!" And another, a man of infinite valor, once twisted his head so as to half face those who were pushing behind him. "Quit yer shovin', yeh"—and he delivered a volley of the most powerful and singular invective, straight into the faces of the men behind him. It was as if he was hammering the noses of them with curses of triple brass. His face, red with rage, could be seen, upon it an expression of sublime disregard of consequences. But nobody cared to reply to his imprecations; it was too cold. Many of them snickered, and all continued to push.

In occasional pauses of the crowd's movement the men had opportunities to make jokes; usually grim things, and no doubt very uncouth. Nevertheless, they were notable—one does not expect to find the quality of humor in a heap of old clothes under a snowdrift.

The winds seemed to grow fiercer as time wore on. Some of the gusts of snow that came down on the close collection of heads cut like knives and needles, and the men huddled, and swore, not like dark assassins, but in a sort of American fashion, grimly and desperately, it is true, but yet with a wondrous under-effect, indefinable and mystic, as if there was some kind of humor in this catastrophe, in this situation in a night of snow-laden winds.

Once the window of the huge dry-goods shop across the street furnished material for a few moments of forgetfulness. In the brilliantly lighted space appeared the figure of a man. He was rather stout and very well clothed. His beard was fashioned charmingly after that of the Prince of Wales.[4] He stood in an attitude of magnificent reflection. He slowly stroked his mustache with a certain grandeur of manner, and looked down at the snow-encrusted mob. From below, there was denoted a

---

* Vulgar for *terrier*, an ethnic slur directed at Irishmen.

supreme complacence in him. It seemed that the sight operated inversely, and enabled him to more clearly regard his own delightful environment.

One of the mob chanced to turn his head, and perceived the figure in the window. "Hello, look-it 'is whiskers," he said genially.

Many of the men turned then, and a shout went up. They called to him in all strange keys. They addressed him in every manner, from familiar and cordial greetings to carefully-worded advice concerning changes in his personal appearance. The man presently fled, and the mob chuckled ferociously, like ogres who had just devoured something.

They turned then to serious business. Often they addressed the stolid front of the house.

"Oh, let us in fer Gawd's sake!"

"Let us in, or we'll all drop dead!"

"Say, what's th' use o' keepin' us poor Indians out in th' cold?"[5]

And always some one was saying, "Keep off my feet."

The crushing of the crowd grew terrific toward the last. The men, in keen pain from the blasts, began almost to fight. With the pitiless whirl of snow upon them, the battle for shelter was going to the strong. It became known that the basement door at the foot of a little steep flight of stairs was the one to be opened, and they jostled and heaved in this direction like laboring fiends. One could hear them panting and groaning in their fierce exertion.

Usually some one in the front ranks was protesting to those in the rear—"O-o-ow! Oh, say now, fellers, let up, will yeh? Do yeh wanta kill somebody?"

A policeman arrived and went into the midst of them, scolding and berating, occasionally threatening, but using no force but that of his hands and shoulders against these men who were only struggling to get in out of the storm. His decisive tones rang out sharply—"Stop that pushin' back there! Come, boys, don't push! Stop that! Here you, quit yer shovin'! Cheese that!"[*]

_____

[*] Variation of a slang phrase meaning "stop that."

When the door below was opened, a thick stream of men forced a way down the stairs, which were of an extraordinary narrowness, and seemed only wide enough for one at a time. Yet they somehow went down almost three abreast. It was a difficult and painful operation. The crowd was like a turbulent water forcing itself through one tiny outlet. The men in the rear, excited by the success of the others, made frantic exertions, for it seemed that this large band would more than fill the quarters, and that many would be left upon the pavements. It would be disastrous to be of the last, and accordingly men with the snow biting their faces writhed and twisted with their might. One expected that, from the tremendous pressure, the narrow passage to the basement door would be so choked and clogged with human limbs and bodies that movement would be impossible. Once indeed the crowd was forced to stop, and a cry went along that a man had been injured at the foot of the stairs. But presently the slow movement began again, and the policeman fought at the top of the flight to ease the pressure of those that were going down.

A reddish light from a window fell upon the faces of the men when they, in turn, arrived at the last three steps and were about to enter. One could then note a change of expression that had come over their features. As they stood thus upon the threshold of their hopes, they looked suddenly contented and complacent. The fire had passed from their eyes and the snarl had vanished from their lips. The very force of the crowd in the rear, which had previously vexed them, was regarded from another point of view, for it now made it inevitable that they should go through the little doors into the place that was cheery and warm with light.

The tossing crowd on the sidewalk grew smaller and smaller. The snow beat with merciless persistence upon the bowed heads of those who waited. The wind drove it up from the pavements in frantic forms of winding white, and it seethed in circles about the huddled forms passing in one by one, three by three, out of the storm.

ENDNOTES

The Red Badge of Courage

Chapter I

1. (p. 1) *The Red Badge of Courage:* The book was first published in 1894 in a greatly abridged version by a newspaper syndicate that included the Philadelphia *Press*, the New York *Press*, and hundreds of other dailies across the nation. D. Appleton and Company published the full version in book form in 1895.

2. (p. 3) *an army stretched out on the hills:* The time is late April 1863, on the eve of the Battle of Chancellorsville. The Army of the Potomac occupies the north bank of the Rappahannock River near Falmouth, Virginia, where it has been encamped since its defeat in the Battle of Fredericksburg the previous December. Abraham Lincoln has just placed Major General Joseph ("Fighting Joe") Hooker in command. The Union's opponent during the battle is the Army of Northern Virginia, under the command of Robert E. Lee. Hooker's forces total about 135,000; Lee's, about 59,000.

3. (p. 3) *tall soldier:* One of Crane's more significant manuscript revisions prior to publication involved replacing names of significant characters with epithets (characteristic words or phrases), a choice that reinforces the imagistic qualities of the novel and the universality of its characters. Here he substitutes "tall soldier" for Jim Conklin. Other significant epithets at the onset include "the youth" for Henry Fleming and "the loud soldier" for Wilson.

4. (p. 3) *division headquarters:* During the battle for Chancellorsville, the Union command structure was organized as follows: Hooker's Army of the Potomac consisted of seven infantry corps, each commanded by a major general, and one cavalry corps. Each infantry corps was subdivided into three divisions, usually commanded by a brigadier general. Each division had three or four brigades, commanded by a colonel or a brigadier general, along with artillery support. The brigade had from four to six regiments, each headed by a colonel or lieutenant colonel. At the beginning of the Civil War, each regiment was designed to have 1,000 men divided

into ten companies, each with a captain in charge; in later years, however, new recruits were formed into new regiments rather than sent to existing regiments as replacements for men lost in battle and for other reasons. Because of such organizational peculiarities, historians estimate that by May 1863 the average size of a Union regiment had fallen to 530. Nevertheless, since Fleming's regiment consists of recruits, it likely is manned at full strength, with approximately 100 men in his company, about 80 of them privates.

5. (p. 5) *a Greeklike struggle:* Fleming's initial misconceptions about war are formed in part from a romantic misreading of *The Iliad,* by Homer.

6. (p. 9) *conversed across the stream:* Because the Confederate Army had occupied positions just south of the Rappahannock since January, friendly exchanges between opposing sentries were common.

7. (p. 11) *the cavalry:* Two weeks prior to the battle, Hooker dispatched most of his cavalry corps on an independent mission to disrupt Confederate communication lines, a move that most historians agree was a tactical blunder.

Chapter II

8. (p. 14) *a blue demonstration:* Crane repeats this phrase several times in the novel, changing its implied meaning in each occurrence. Here it obviously represents Fleming's frustration with pointless parading. Later the phrase suggests more ominous symbolic consequences for the "mob" of men that he must move with.

9. (p. 16) *the colonel on a gigantic horse:* This officer is likely the commander of Fleming's regiment. The image Crane creates is reminiscent of an image Ambrose Bierce (1842–1914?) describes in "A Horseman in the Sky," a story in *Tales of Soldiers and Civilians* (1891).

10. (p. 17) *come around in behind the enemy:* Hooker's plan called for a "double envelopment," dividing his infantry forces into two wings that would attack Lee's army from different directions. The right wing was to cross the river 20 miles west of Falmouth and then head back east to flank the Confederates, a 40-mile forced march in all. The left wing crossed the Rappahannock near Fredericksburg. Both groups were to converge on Chancellorsville.

11. (p. 19) "*they've licked us*": The Confederacy had won the majority of battles up to this point, including the Union's humiliating defeat at Fredericksburg in December 1862. Lee, however, did not have the men or resources to exploit these victories.

12. (p. 21) *Napoleon Bonaparte*: In the middle of the nineteenth century, Napoleon Bonaparte represented to the average American soldier not only military genius but also complete mastery of the battlefield. Here Crane highlights how little an infantryman knows about the tactics and strategy of a campaign.

13. (p. 21) "*I'll bid five. . . . Seven goes*": The men are probably playing a version of the card game whist. Bidding "seven" means the speaker will try to take all thirteen tricks.

Chapter III

14. (p. 22) *very good shirts*: Remember the care Fleming's mother put into the making of his shirts. Their discarding here symbolically refutes her vision of what war demands of soldiers, which had previously helped to shape her son's erroneous conceptions. Crane imitates a long literary tradition of veterans confronting a civilian reader with his or her misconceptions about combat.

15. (p. 23) *not a brigade*: The length of the regiment's column not only indicates its inefficiency and inexperience but also symbolizes the disunity among the men, thus rendering the "blue demonstration" a mob.

16. (p. 24) *skirmishers*: Skirmishers moved in advance of the main body of troops to scout out enemy positions and strength.

17. (p. 26) "*No skulking'll do here*": Note how Fleming's psychological skulking here goes against his mother's admonitions about "shirking."

18. (p. 26) *cathedral light of a forest*: This is the initial image that reflects Crane's fusing of nature and spirituality in the novel. It anticipates the secluded grove that the deserting Fleming comes upon in chapter VII, "a place where the high, arching boughs made a chapel." Chapter VIII opens with trees as they "began . . . to sing a hymn of twilight."

Chapter IV

19. (p. 31) *'G' Company*: Companies in a normal regiment were designated by letters from A through K, skipping over the letter J.

20. (p. 31) *"Hannises' batt'ry is took"*: Each Union infantry division had from two to four artillery batteries in support.

21. (p. 31) *"when we go inteh action"*: The date for the 304th's first experience under enemy fire is May 2, 1863. The "304th New York" is Crane's invention. The highest-numbered regiment from New York that participated in the battle of Chancellorsville was the 157th. The 304th's battle episodes correspond to events experienced by several actual regiments, suggesting that Crane conflated a number of accounts into one cohesive narrative. We learn from the "cheery" soldier in chapter XII that Fleming's regiment is "in th' center," which suggests that it belonged to either the Third Corps under the command of Major General Daniel E. Sickles or the Twelfth Corps under Major General Henry W. Slocum. The 304th's forced march up to this point is consistent with Slocum's orders for his troops. Its redeployment in chapter XVI, however, corresponds with Sickles's attempt to shore up the right wing on May 3. In chapter V, Fleming hears a battle raging to his left; on May 2, Slocum's division was positioned to the left of Sickles's. In "The Veteran," a short story that chronicles Fleming as an old man, Crane uses the suggestive phrase "Sickles's colt." Crane would have been very familiar with the long, colorful career of the notorious New York politician and Civil War hero Dan Sickles.

In the Third Corps, the Second Brigade of the Second Division was composed of five New York veteran and new regiments. The Second Division's leader, Major General Hiram G. Berry, was killed, similar to what is reported about the fictional 304th's division commander in chapter XXI. Another interesting point that Crane knew about from articles in the *Century* was that Hooker had ordered that corps badges be worn on all uniforms. The badge worn by the First Division of the Third Corps was suggestively a red diamond. (The Second Division wore white diamond badges.) Given all this, it is possible that Crane came up with the number 304 by adding the numbers of four New York regiments in the Third Corps (the 40th, the 70th, the 74th, and the 120th; or the 40th, the 71st, the 73rd, and the 120th), which would nu-

merically symbolize the cumulation of the infantry's experience
during the battle. In chapter XXI, we learn that the name of the
colonel in charge of the 304th is MacChesnay.

For a different assessment of how occurrences in the novel
correspond to events at Chancellorsville, see Harold R. Hunger-
ford, " 'That Was at Chancellorsville': The Factual Framework of
The Red Badge of Courage," *American Literature* 34 (1963), pp. 520–531.

Chapter V

22. (p. 35) *"You've got to hold 'em back!"*: In a bold, calculated stratagem,
Lee had dispatched the bulk of his troops under the command of
Lieutenant General Thomas J. ("Stonewall") Jackson on a daring
maneuver to surprise Union forces from the west—in essence,
outflanking Hooker's flanking maneuver. To divert attention from
Jackson's clandestine deployment, the remaining Confederate
forces under Lee periodically engaged the Union center on May 2,
where the fictional 304th had been deployed. Thus, despite the
regimental commander's histrionics here, this initial confronta-
tion was only a diversionary action and was not where the brunt
of the battle was to be fought that day.

23. (p. 36) *the question of his piece being loaded*: Fleming and his regiment
were armed with muskets, probably either the Model 1861
Springfield (manufactured in the United States) or the Enfield
(imported from England). An experienced infantryman could reload and fire within thirty seconds.

Chapter VI

24. (p. 45) *a general of division*: Quite possibly "Grandpa Henderson," the
division general later reported killed in chapter XXI.

Chapter VIII

25. (p. 54) *imitative of some sublime drum major*: Each Union regiment was
allotted two musicians. Among other functions, a drummer
would beat a tattoo to set the pace for an advance. Here Crane emphasizes one of a drum major's noncombative roles—to strut before a band in parade.

26. (p. 54) *"Sing a song . . . pie"*: Crane rewords the Mother Goose

rhyme: "Sing a song of sixpence, a pocketful of rye; four and twenty blackbirds baked in a pie. . . ." The alteration of the number to "five an' twenty" may have been intended to correspond with the number of chapters in the original manuscript.

27. (p. 54) *the specter of a soldier:* Crane changes Conklin's epithet from "the tall soldier" to "the specter" and later the "spectral soldier." Fleming's initial inability to recognize Conklin resembles an incident in Ambrose Bierce's tale "One of the Missing" (published in *Tales of Soldiers and Civilians*), in which horror so disfigures an infantryman's face that his own brother does not recognize him.

28. (p. 55) *a tattered man:* This is perhaps the most interesting of Crane's epithets. Note how Crane avoids calling him a "soldier," a term that associates an individual with an organization. The word "man" sets him apart from the army that surrounds him and thus emphasizes how war has broken him physically and psychologically and sent him into isolation.

Chapter IX

29. (p. 62) *like a wafer:* Critics have long debated how much of a religious dimension Crane intended in this concluding image. Some maintain that the spectral soldier's death parallels Christ's crucifixion. Jim Conklin shares initials with Jesus Christ. Both had wounds in their sides. The "wafer" may symbolize a secular Eucharist, Crane's homage to the price ordinary men had to pay for the sins of their country. Biographer Robert Stallman traces the image to Rudyard Kipling's *The Light That Failed* (1890), a novel known to have had a significant impact upon Crane's self-image as an artist.

Chapter XI

30. (p. 72) *He was a slang phrase:* Many alterations and excisions of text occurred between the various manuscripts and the first printing of the book. At this point, for instance, Crane discarded his original chapter XII, reducing the novel from twenty-five to twenty-four chapters. As with many of the other passages he eliminated, the chapter explored Fleming's philosophical musings of the moment: "He was unfit, then. He did not come into the scheme of further life. His tiny part had been done and he must go. There was no room for him."

Chapter XII

31. (p. 73) *they charged down upon him*: We began to see the signs of the collapse of the Union right wing in the previous chapter. Stonewall Jackson's flanking maneuver succeeded spectacularly. The Union's Eleventh Corps, commanded by Major General Oliver O. Howard, panicked and fled in disarray, thus nullifying Hooker's strategy and threatening his army with immediate defeat. In chapter XII, Fleming confronts the most chaotic point in the battle. That night, after reconnoitering the Union position, Jackson was accidentally shot by his own troops; he died on May 10, 1863.

32. (p. 73) *"Where de plank road?"*: Built to transport tobacco to market, the strategically important plank road extended more than 11 miles from Wilderness Church in the west to Fredericksburg in the east. It had been constructed by abutting and fastening 2-inch-thick planks transversely laid across the road surface and was now in poor condition.

33. (p. 74) *It crushed upon the youth's head*: Many scholars agree that this incident marks the "turning point" in the novel. Ironically, Fleming's "red badge of courage" comes at the end of a Union rifle butt held by a psychological mirror image of the man he had been when he fled in chapter VI. As employed by Dante Alighieri in *The Inferno*, Edmund Spenser in *The Faerie Queene*, and many other major writers, such turning points are accompanied by a period of unconsciousness for the protagonist.

34. (p. 77) *a cheery voice near his shoulder*: Some scholars suggest that this scene parallels the parable about the Good Samaritan in the Bible, Luke 10:29–37.

Chapter XIII

35. (p. 80) *his friend*: Note how Wilson's epithet has changed from "loud soldier" to "friend."

36. (p. 81) *"Yeh've been grazed by a ball"*: This incident typifies Crane's contrasting the truth of perception with the fallacy of human reason-

ing. The corporal here dismisses what he sees despite the evidence. Remember that in a parallel situation the company lieutenant tried to stop Fleming from skedaddling in chapter VI, but the officer either does not remember or chooses not to do anything about the desertion in the second half of the novel.

Chapter XIV

37. (p. 89) *"Jest like you done"*: This is tacit evidence that the panic that had seized Fleming had been more common among his peers than he realizes.

Chapter XVI

38. (p. 94) *to relieve a command*: The 304th's movement parallels the redeployment of the Third Corps on May 3 to reinforce the right wing of the Union line.

39. (p. 95) *"More than one feller has said that t'-day"*: Fleming's attitude was common among Union soldiers. Most Union generals paled when compared to the tactical brilliance of Robert E. Lee. Abraham Lincoln's firing of ineffective generals probably reinforced the infantrymen's distrust of their military leadership.

40. (p. 96) *the brigadier*: This is probably the brigade commander.

Chapter XVII

41. (p. 102) *"Oh," he said, comprehending*: Fleming's unease when he realizes that others notice his actions under fire ironically anticipates an incident that occurred later when Crane was a war correspondent in Cuba during the Spanish-American War in 1898. In the company of the Rough Riders, who at one point were pinned down by enemy fire, Crane needlessly and nonchalantly strolled along a ridge in his white rain slicker, smoking his pipe and inviting a hail of Spanish bullets. He ignored the orders of an American colonel and others to regain cover until fellow correspondent and fiction writer Richard Harding Davis commented, "You're not impressing anyone by doing that, Crane," at which point a self-conscious, embarrassed Crane ended his show of bravado and rejoined the entrenched troops.

Chapter XVIII

42. (p. 107) *th' 12th . . . th' 76th . . . th' 304th:* The officer's omission of
state names before regimental numbers may be because all are
from New York, as was the case for the actual Second Brigade of
the Second Division in the Third Corps.

Chapter XXI

43. (p. 124) *Whiterside:* This is probably a commander of another
brigade in Fleming's division.

Chapter XXII

44. (p. 128) *a house:* This is possibly the Bullock house, a structure that
stood near a strategic crossroads just north of Chancellorsville.

Chapter XXIII

45. (p. 133) *"We must charge'm!":* A "charge" is among the more desperate of military tactics. It concedes that a sizable percentage of a
regiment will become casualties while traversing open ground,
yet presumes that the size of the advancing force will not be depleted by gunfire before overrunning the enemy's position and
that its survivors will overwhelm the defending force and take the
position. History is replete with examples of commanders who
miscalculated the strength of their own and opposing forces.

Chapter XXIV

46. (p. 140) *"we got a dum good lickin'":* Although some historians argue
that Hooker still had enough forces in reserve to win the battle,
his decision to withdraw iced the cake of the Confederate victory.
Union casualties for the battle totaled 17,304 killed, wounded,
and missing; Confederate casualties totaled 13,460 killed,
wounded, and missing. The next major battle in the East would
come two months later at Gettysburg, Pennsylvania.

47. (p. 141) *as if hot plowshares:* The metaphor comes from the popular
religious symbol taken from the Bible, Isaiah 2:4: "and they shall
beat their swords into plowshares."

The Open Boat

1. (p. 143) *The Open Boat*: In November 1896, Crane traveled to
   Jacksonville, Florida, employed as a correspondent by a newspaper
   syndicate. He had been assigned to cover the Cuban insurrection
   against Spanish authority and so tried to secure passage on any available "filibuster" vessel, one that would run the blockade of the island to transport supplies and personnel. This was the only way an
   American reporter could make his way to the fighting. After a
   month of intrigue and frustration, on January 1, 1897, he embarked on the steamer *Commodore*, which was to convey weapons,
   supplies, and rebel troops to Cuba. Under mysterious circumstances, the vessel sank rapidly in the open ocean on January 2,
   drowning many crew members and passengers. Crane and three
   others escaped certain death in a small, precarious dinghy and
   rowed their way back to Florida's east coast, where they landed near
   Daytona Beach on the morning of January 3. William Higgins, an
   oilman, was killed after the boat capsized in the surf. On January 7
   Crane published in the New York *Press* a news account of his experience that focuses on events involving the sinking and almost entirely ignores the thirty hours spent in the dinghy. During the
   following months, while recuperating in Jacksonville, he composed
   "The Open Boat," which reverses the focus in the newspaper arti-
   cle. He first published the story in the June 1897 issue of *Scribner's
   Magazine* and later collected it in *The Open Boat and Other Stories* (1898).

2. (pp. 145–46) *the cook . . . the oiler . . . the correspondent . . . the captain*:
   The captain's name was Edward Murphy, the oilman's William
   Higgins, and the cook's Charles Montgomery; the correspondent
   represents Crane himself. As he did in *The Red Badge of Courage*, Crane
   transforms names in the short story to occupational epithets, suggesting the characters' symbolic significance and enhancing the
   universal aspect of their collective plight.

3. (p. 147) *the Mosquito Inlet Light*: The name Mosquito Coast Inlet was
   changed to Ponce Inlet in 1927. Located approximately 11 miles
   south-southeast from the center of Daytona Beach, Florida, this
   lighthouse went into service in 1887. Located in a region known
   for shipwrecks since the sixteenth century, it radiated a beam of
   light visible 20 miles out at sea.

4. (p. 154) *the seven mad gods*: Critics have advanced several possibilities

about the gods Crane had in mind. Most believe that one of the seven was the Olympian god Poseidon (Neptune in Roman mythology) and that the other six were compilations of the many sea deities from Greek myth. Crane may have considered Pontos, the most ancient of Greek sea gods, and his children Phorkos, Thaumas, Nereus, Eurybia, Keto, and Aigaion. Robert Stallman suggests that Crane chose their number to correspond to the seven men stranded on the deck of the sinking *Commodore*.

5. (p. 159) *a pale star appeared*: Given that Crane saw this celestial object near the eastern horizon, it was most likely Betelgeuse. Less likely possibilities include Aldebaran and the planet Mars.

6. (p. 161) *two points off the port bow*: There are thirty-two points on a mariner's compass; here the captain orders the oiler to angle the boat 22.5 degrees off the port bow to compensate for the current.

7. (p. 164) *"I never more shall see my own, my native land"*: This line is from the opening stanza of British poet Caroline Norton's "Bingen on the Rhine," which was often included in poetry anthologies of the period.

8. (p. 168) *hanging with his one good hand*: The captain's calculation causes him to violate his own advice. His broken arm compels him to hang on to the surf-tossed boat in order to increase his chances for survival.

9. (p. 169) *a scene from Brittany or Algiers*: Brittany is a former province in northwestern France; Algiers is the capital of Algeria, which France had occupied in 1830 and annexed in 1848. Many nineteenth-century French artists, especially Impressionists and proto-Impressionists, painted landscapes and portraits from these regions.

10. (p. 170) *he gave a strong pull*: In his dispatch, Crane identifies his rescuer as John Kitchell, a boatyard manager and ferryman from Daytona Beach.

11. (p. 170) *face downward, lay the oiler*: Although he was likely struck by the dinghy as the surf thrashed it about, the cause for Billy Higgins's death was never ascertained.

The Veteran

1. (p. 173) *The Veteran*: This story was first published in *McClure's Magazine* in June 1896 and was collected later that year in *The Little Regiment and Other Episodes of the American Civil War*.

2. (p. 175) *old Fleming:* Crane employs this phrase in contrast with the epithet "youth" in *The Red Badge of Courage.*

3. (p. 175) *how an orderly sergeant ranked:* An orderly sergeant was a position of great trust in a regiment. Toward the end of *The Red Badge of Courage* Fleming had just begun to earn such recognition—he was praised by his superiors for being a "jimhickey."

4. (p. 176) *little Jim:* Another interesting Crane contrast: In *The Red Badge of Courage* Jim Conklin was called the "tall soldier," while here his namesake is "little Jim."

5. (p. 176) *Sickles's colt:* This is perhaps an allusion to Daniel Sickles; see note 21 to *The Red Badge of Courage* regarding Fleming's possible Corps commander.

6. (p. 179) *the genie of fable:* This is an allusion to Arabian myths, such as the story of Aladdin.

The Men in the Storm

1. (p. 181) *The Men in the Storm:* Prior to his success with *The Red Badge of Courage,* Crane had been making a study of tenement life in New York City while enduring the hardships of poverty himself. In late February 1894, the city was experiencing an intense cold snap, with temperatures in the single digits intensified by strong winds. On February 25, as a major snow storm brewed, Crane and a friend dressed in rags and went to the Bowery district. Over the next day, they mingled with homeless men as they waited for free day-old bread from a bakery and then spent the night with them in a flophouse. New York newspapers reported that 14 inches of wind-driven snow had fallen on the city by February 26. Crane's experiences that night inspired him to compose this story and "An Experiment in Misery" (1894). "The Men in the Storm" was first published in an October 1894 issue of *The Arena* and later collected in *The Open Boat and Other Stories* (1898).

2. (p. 185) *the men began to come:* Given this subject, one of Crane's literary influences could have been Bierce's tale "The Applicant," collected in *Tales of Soldiers and Civilians* (1891).

3. (p. 185) *at these times:* The economic event that underlies the story is the Panic of 1893, a crisis of confidence, monetary policy, and unemployment that led to 14,000 commercial failures and 4,000 bank collapses. The rate of unemployment peaked during the summer of 1894, a period marked by violent strikes and strike busting. This economic depression did not end until America's trade position improved in 1897.

4. (p. 187) *the Prince of Wales:* In 1894 Albert Edward, the Prince of Wales, son of Queen Victoria and Prince Albert, was widely known for his distinctive whiskers. He acceded to the British throne as Edward VII in 1901.

5. (p. 188) *us poor Indians:* This metaphorical allusion may be the product of Crane's friendship with author Hamlin Garland (1860–1940), who at the turn of the century sympathetically depicted the plight of Native Americans in his fiction and elsewhere.

INSPIRED BY THE RED BADGE
OF COURAGE

I get a little tired of saying, "Is this true?"
— Stephen Crane, to his biographer Thomas Beer

RARELY HAS THE MARRIAGE of literature and the subject of war been more successful than in *The Red Badge of Courage*, and perhaps that is because Stephen Crane regarded himself first and foremost as a realist. Explaining the blurred line between fiction and nonfiction in his writing, he stated, "I decided that the nearer a writer gets to life the greater he becomes as an artist, and most of my prose writings have been toward the goal partially described by that misunderstood and abused word, realism."

Ernest Hemingway greatly admired Stephen Crane, and Hemingway's direct, concise style and steely-eyed attention to the elemental challenges of human life is consistent with the literary precepts Crane lived by. In his introduction to his anthology *Men at War: The Best War Stories of All Time* (1942), which presents selections from the chosen works, Hemingway addresses the difficulty of excerpting *The Red Badge of Courage*. He writes, "I am sure [Crane] cut it all himself as he wrote it to the exact measure of the poem it is." By this time, Hemingway had established himself as the most important war writer since Stephen Crane.

Hemingway's war experiences and literary career occurred in a sequence opposite to Crane's. Born several years after the end of the Civil War, Stephen Crane was not personally acquainted with the battlefield; he relied on secondary sources for his facts and lore; he landed a job as a war correspondent because of his convincingly real *Red Badge of Courage*. Hemingway wrote his war masterpieces based on his own wartime experiences. Though he started out as a reporter for the Kansas City *Star*, he volunteered for service in World War I and drove an ambulance for the American Red Cross, an experience that led to his seminal novel *A Farewell to Arms* (1929). It tells the story of an American lieutenant who is wounded while serving as an ambulance driver on the Italian front line, and tragically juxtaposes a doomed love affair with the war effort. So accurate was Hemingway's account of the Italian retreat that the book was immediately banned in Italy.

Later Hemingway covered the Spanish Civil War and gained an intimate knowledge of the landscape he would describe in *For Whom the Bell Tolls* (1940), his most popular novel. This somber book encompasses three days during which an American dynamite expert fighting for the loyalists makes a failed attempt to destroy a bridge and is left behind to die. In World War II, Hemingway worked again as a war reporter; *Across the River and into the Trees* (1950) came out of this experience. This novel, lambasted by most critics, chronicles a war-ravaged American colonel whose failing health mirrors Hemingway's own physical decline.

In more recent times, Tim O'Brien's memoir *If I Die in a Combat Zone: Box Me Up and Ship Me Home* (1973) takes war writing to an even more realistic level. (The title is the first two lines of a song soldiers sing during Army training; the second couplet is "Pin my medals to my chest/Tell my mom I did my best.") Whereas Hemingway based the plots, characters, and descriptions in his fiction on his experiences in wartime, O'Brien directly chronicles, with stark realism, the personal trauma he suffered fighting the "wrong war": the American intervention in the civil war in Vietnam. Like Stephen Crane, O'Brien is concerned with the meaning of human courage and valor. Unlike the youth Henry Fleming, O'Brien is unable to flee; he is drawn, incomprehensibly, toward the horror, toward a war he had always opposed. *If I Die in a Combat Zone* painfully details events and images from the war in Vietnam—the mismanagement of American forces, the accidental shellings of villages, the red flesh and white bone of maimed soldiers and children, the invisibility of the enemy, unseen mines that render bodies unrecognizable, and the impossibility of communication. Tim O'Brien has also written of Vietnam with raw clarity in several short stories and novels, among them the fictional *Going After Cacciato* (1978), which won the National Book Award in 1979.

COMMENTS & QUESTIONS

In this section, we aim to provide the reader with an array of perspectives on the text, as well as questions that challenge those perspectives. The commentary has been culled from sources as diverse as reviews contemporaneous with the work, letters written by the author, literary criticism of later generations, and appreciations written throughout the history of the book. Following the commentary, a series of questions seeks to filter Stephen Crane's The Red Badge of Courage *through a variety of points of view and bring about a richer understanding of this enduring work.*

Comments

GEORGE WYNDHAM

Mr. Stephen Crane, the author of *The Red Badge of Courage* (London: Heinemann), is a great artist, with something new to say, and consequently, with a new way of saying it. His theme, indeed, is an old one, but old themes re-handled anew in the light of novel experience are the stuff out of which masterpieces are made, and in *The Red Badge of Courage* Mr. Crane has surely contrived a masterpiece. He writes of war—the ominous and alluring possibility for every man, since the heir of all the ages has won and must keep his inheritance by secular combat. The conditions of the age-long contention have changed and will change, but its certainty is coeval with progress: so long as there are things worth fighting for fighting will last, and the fashion of fighting will change under the reciprocal stresses of rival inventions. Hence its double interest of abiding necessity and ceaseless variation. Of all these variations the most marked has followed, within the memory of most of us, upon the adoption of long-range weapons of precision, and continues to develop, under our eyes, with the development of rapidity in firing. And yet, with the exception of Zola's *la Débâcle*, no considerable attempt has been made to portray war under its new conditions.

Mr. Crane, for his distinction, has hit on a new device, or at least on one which has never been used before with such consistency and effect. In order to show the features of modern war, he takes a subject—a youth with a peculiar temperament, capable of exaltation and yet morbidly sensitive. Then he traces the successive impressions made on such a temperament, from minute to minute, during two days of heavy fighting. He stages the drama of war, so to speak, within the mind of one man, and then admits you as to a theatre. You may, if you please, object that his youth is unlike most other young men who serve in the ranks, and that the same events would have impressed the average man differently; but you are convinced that this man's soul is truly drawn, and that the impressions made in it are faithfully rendered. The youth's temperament is merely the medium which the artist has chosen: that it is exceptionally plastic makes but for the deeper incision of his work. It follows from Mr. Crane's method that he creates by his art even such a first-hand report of war as we seek in vain among the journals and letters of soldiers. But the book is not written in the form of an autobiography: the author narrates. He is therefore at liberty to give scenery and action, down to the slightest gestures and outward signs of inward elation or suffering, and he does this with the vigour and terseness of a master. Had he put his descriptions of scenery and his atmospheric effects, or his reports of overheard conversations, into the mouth of his youth, their very excellence would have belied all likelihood. Yet in all his descriptions and all his reports he confines himself only to such things as that youth heard and saw, and, of these, only to such as influenced his emotions. By this compromise he combines the strength and truth of a monodrama with the directness and colour of the best narrative prose.

—from *New Review* (January 1896)

NEW YORK TIMES

If there were in existence any books of a similar character, one could start confidently by saying that [*The Red Badge of Courage*] was the best of its kind. But it has no fellows. It is a book outside of all classification. So unlike anything else is it, that the temptation rises to deny that it is a book at all. When one searches for comparisons, they can only be found by culling out selected portions from the trunks of masterpieces, and considering these detached fragments one by one, with reference to the "Red Badge of Courage," which is itself a fragment, and yet is complete. Thus one lifts the best battle pictures from Tolstoi's great "War and Peace," from Balzac's "Chouans," from Hugo's "Les Misérables," and the forest flight in " '93," from Prosper Merimée's assault of the redoubt, from Zola's "La Débâcle" and "Attack of the Mill," (it is strange enough that equivalents in the literature of our own language do not suggest themselves,) and studies them side by side with this tremendously effective battle painting by the unknown youngster. Positively they are cold and ineffectual beside it. The praise may sound exaggerated, but really it is inadequate. These renowned battle descriptions of the big men are made to seem all wrong. The "Red Badge of Courage" impels the feeling that the actual truth about a battle has never been guessed before.

—January 26, 1896

THE NATION

Mr. Stephen Crane is said never to have seen a battle; but his first book, "The Red Badge of Courage," is made up of the account of one. The success of the story, however, is due, not merely to what Mr. Crane knows of battle-fields, but to what he knows of the human heart. He describes the adventures of a private—a raw recruit—in one of those long engagements, so common in our civil war, and indeed in all modern wars, in which the field of battle is too extensive for those in one part of it to know what is going on elsewhere, and where often a regiment remains in ignorance for some time whether it is victorious or defeated, where the nature of the country prevents hand-to-hand fighting, and a *coup d'oeil* of the whole scene is out of the question. In such an action Mr. Crane's hero plays an active part. It is what goes on in his mind that we hear of, and his experience is in part so exactly what old soldiers tell young soldiers that Mr. Crane might easily have got it at second-hand. The hero is at first mortally afraid that he is going to be afraid, he then does his duty well enough, but later is seized with a panic and runs away, only to come out a hero again in the end. His panic and flight are managed well; the accidental wound which he luckily gets in running, helps him to a reputation for bravery before he has earned it. When he fights in the end, he fights like a devil, he saves the regimental flag, he is insane with the passion of the battle; he is baptized into the brotherhood of those who have been to hell and returned alive. The book is undeniably clever; its vice is over-emphasis. Mr. Crane has not learnt the secret that carnage itself is eloquent, and does not need epithets to make it so. What is a "crimson roar"? Do soldiers hear crimson roars, or do they hear simply roars? If this way of getting expression out of language is allowable, why not extend it to the other senses, and have not only crimson sounds, but purple smells, prehensile views, adhesive music? Color in language is just now a fashionable affectation; Mr. Crane's originality does not lie in falling into it.

—July 2, 1896

H. G. WELLS

It was a new thing, in a new school. When one looked for sources, one thought at once of Tolstoy; but, though it was clear that Tolstoy had exerted a powerful influence upon the conception, if not the actual writing, of [The Red Badge of Courage], there still remained something entirely original and novel. To a certain extent, of course, that was the new man as an individual; but, to at least an equal extent, it was the new man as a typical young American, free at last, as no generation of Americans have been free before, of any regard for English criticism, comment, or tradition, and applying to literary work the conception and theories of the cosmopolitan studio with a quite American directness and vigor.

—from The North American Review (August 1900)

STEPHEN CRANE

Tolstoy ranks as the supreme living writer of our time to me. But I confess that the conclusions of some of his novels, and the lectures he sticks in, leave me feeling that he regards his genius as the means to an end. I happen to be a preacher's son, but that heredity does not preclude—in me—a liking for sermons unmixed with other material. No, that sentence doesn't mean anything, does it? I mean that I like my art straight.

> —from Thomas Beer's "Introduction" to Volume 7 of
> *The Work of Stephen Crane*, edited by Wilson Follett (1925–1926)

THOMAS BEER

He came to believe that *The Red Badge of Courage* was too long, and as this distaste for length—emblematically—included his own life he is to remain a halved portrait, an artist of amazing talent and of developing scope who died too soon for our curiosity. . . . A man so brilliantly impatient of shams had surely something amusing to say, and the legitimate pity of the case is that he did not live to say more.

> —from his "Introduction" to Volume 7 of
> *The Work of Stephen Crane*,
> edited by Wilson Follett (1925–1926)

WILLA CATHER

Perhaps it was because Stephen Crane had read so little, was so slightly acquainted with the masterpieces of fiction, that he felt no responsibility to be accurate or painstaking in accounting for things and people. He is rather the best of our writers in what is called "description" because he is the least describing.

> —from her "Introduction" to Volume 9 of
> *The Work of Stephen Crane*

JOSEPH CONRAD

Recalling now those earnestly fantastic discussions it occurs to me that Crane and I must have been unconsciously penetrated by a prophetic sense of the technique and of the very spirit of film-plays of which even the name was unknown then to the world.

> —from Conrad's "Introduction" to
> *Stephen Crane: A Study in American Letters* (1927), by Thomas Beer

Questions

1. What is it about Crane's style that distressed the critic who wrote in *The Nation*? Are there elements of literature today that are "allowable" and others that are not?

2. Wyndham and Wells, both reading from the British perspective, found in Crane a new literature. What about Crane's style is original? What are we to make of Wells's comments about the "American," and how does *The Red Badge of Courage* forge and define this concept?

3. Crane's style is often described as "impressionistic." What does this term express to you? It might be interesting to find a passage that seems "impressionistic" and analyze the concrete uses of words that give it its special flavor.

4. Crane thought of himself as a "realist." How do you understand this form? Fidelity to material actuality? A lot of descriptions? An absence of idealization or fantasy? A tough-mindedness about human emotions and motives? If Crane is realistic, in what sense?

5. Do you take the tall soldier to be an oddball or a representative type? Which of his characteristics make him either a special case or an everyman, subspecies *Americanus*?

FOR FURTHER READING

Biographies and Related Materials

The Correspondence of Stephen Crane. Edited by Stanley Wertheim. New York: Columbia University Press, 1999.

Davis, Linda H. *Badge of Courage: The Life of Stephen Crane.* Boston: Houghton Mifflin, 1998.

Stallman, R. W. *Stephen Crane: A Biography.* New York: George Braziller, Inc., 1968.

Wertheim, Stanley, and Paul M. Sorrentino. *The Crane Log: A Documentary Life of Stephen Crane, 1871–1900.* New York: G. K. Hall, 1994.

Historical Resources

Battles and Leaders of the Civil War. 4 vols. New York: Thomas Yoseloff, Inc., 1956. Since *The Century* magazine series was first collected in book form in 1887, this primary historical resource for Crane has been reprinted several times by several publishers. The 1956 edition is available in many American libraries. The essays involving the Battle of Chancellorsville are in volume 3.

Sears, Stephen W. *Chancellorsville.* Boston: Houghton Mifflin, 1996. A well-researched and balanced modern account of the battle.

Selected Critical Studies

Bergon, Frank. *Stephen Crane's Artistry.* New York: Columbia University Press, 1975.

Berryman, John. *Stephen Crane.* New York: Sloane, 1950.

Cady, Edwin H. *Stephen Crane.* Revised edition. Boston: Twayne Publishers, 1980.

Campbell, Donna M. *Resisting Regionalism: Gender and Naturalism in American Fiction, 1885–1915.* Athens: Ohio University Press, 1997.

Dooley, Patrick K. *The Pluralistic Philosophy of Stephen Crane*. Urbana: University of Illinois Press, 1993.

LaFrance, Marston. *A Reading of Stephen Crane*. Oxford: Clarendon Press, 1971.

Nagel, James. *Stephen Crane and Literary Impressionism*. University Park: Pennsylvania State University Press, 1980.

Pizer, Donald, ed. *Critical Essays on Stephen Crane's* The Red Badge of Courage. Boston: G. K. Hall, 1990.

Solomon, Eric. *Stephen Crane: From Parody to Realism*. Cambridge, MA: Harvard University Press, 1966.

Jude the Obscure	Thomas Hardy	1-59308-035-2	$8.95
The Jungle	Upton Sinclair	1-59308-118-9	$9.95
The Last of the Mohicans	James Fenimore Cooper	1-59308-137-5	$9.95
Les Liaisons Dangereuses	Pierre Choderlos de Laclos	1-59308-240-1	$9.95
Little Women	Louisa May Alcott	1-59308-108-1	$7.95
Lost Illusions	Honoré de Balzac	1-59308-315-7	$11.95
Main Street	Sinclair Lewis	1-59308-386-6	$10.95
Mansfield Park	Jane Austen	1-59308-154-5	$6.95
The Metamorphosis and Other Stories	Franz Kafka	1-59308-029-8	$9.95
Moby-Dick	Herman Melville	1-59308-018-2	$11.95
My Ántonia	Willa Cather	1-59308-202-9	$6.95
Narrative of Sojourner Truth		1-59308-293-2	$7.95
The Odyssey	Homer	1-59308-009-3	$9.95
Oliver Twist	Charles Dickens	1-59308-206-1	$6.95
The Origin of Species	Charles Darwin	1-59308-077-8	$10.95
Paradise Lost	John Milton	1-59308-095-6	$9.95
Persuasion	Jane Austen	1-59308-130-8	$5.95
The Picture of Dorian Gray	Oscar Wilde	1-59308-025-5	$6.95
A Portrait of the Artist as a Young Man and Dubliners	James Joyce	1-59308-031-X	$8.95
Pride and Prejudice	Jane Austen	1-59308-201-0	$6.95
The Prince and Other Writings	Niccolò Machiavelli	1-59308-060-3	$5.95
The Red Badge of Courage and Selected Short Fiction	Stephen Crane	1-59308-119-7	$6.95
Republic	Plato	1-59308-097-2	$8.95
Robinson Crusoe	Daniel Defoe	1-59308-360-2	$6.95
The Scarlet Letter	Nathaniel Hawthorne	1-59308-207-X	$6.95
The Secret Agent	Joseph Conrad	1-59308-305-X	$8.95
Selected Stories of O. Henry		1-59308-042-5	$9.95
Sense and Sensibility	Jane Austen	1-59308-125-1	$5.95
Siddhartha	Hermann Hesse	1-59308-379-3	$8.95
The Souls of Black Folk	W. E. B. Du Bois	1-59308-014-X	$8.95
The Strange Case of Dr. Jekyll and Mr. Hyde and Other Stories	Robert Louis Stevenson	1-59308-131-6	$6.95
A Tale of Two Cities	Charles Dickens	1-59308-138-3	$6.95
Three Theban Plays	Sophocles	1-59308-235-5	$8.95
Thus Spoke Zarathustra	Friedrich Nietzsche	1-59308-278-9	$9.95
The Time Machine and The Invisible Man	H. G. Wells	1-59308-388-2	$7.95
Treasure Island	Robert Louis Stevenson	1-59308-247-9	$6.95
The Turn of the Screw, The Aspern Papers and Two Stories	Henry James	1-59308-043-3	$5.95
Uncle Tom's Cabin	Harriet Beecher Stowe	1-59308-121-9	$7.95
Vanity Fair	William Makepeace Thackeray	1-59308-071-9	$8.95
Walden and Civil Disobedience	Henry David Thoreau	1-59308-208-8	$8.95
The War of the Worlds	H. G. Wells	1-59308-362-9	$6.95
Ward No. 6 and Other Stories	Anton Chekhov	1-59308-003-4	$8.95
Wuthering Heights	Emily Brontë	1-59308-128-6	$5.95

ℬ

BARNES & NOBLE CLASSICS